# THE RAVEN'S CRY

# THE RAVEN'S CRY

A Wynter Island Mystery

KIM HERDMAN SHAPIRO

*For my boys, with all my love*

# Praise for The Raven's Cry

"A fun mystery with an independent heroine, eccentric characters, a chilling murder, and one lovable canine."—Lorraine Sharma Nelson, President, Sisters in Crime New England

"Nice debut mystery with quirky characters and buried secrets."—Dale T. Phillips, author of the Zack Taylor mystery series

"*The Raven's Cry* pulls the reader in from the beginning with its atmospheric Pacific Northwest island setting, the disturbing dynamic among the people living on the island, and a shocking turn of events.  Kate Thomas, a young journalist whose life was upended by her experience in war-torn Afghanistan, hoped to build a new life on this island but her connection to a mysterious death propels her into grave danger. Tight, compelling page turner from start to finish."—Cheryl Marceau, crime fiction short story writer, published in numerous anthologies

"Kim is a marvelous Canadian ambassador to the world and a fantastic recorder of its places."—Chapters-Indigo, Canada's National Bookstore.

# Wynter Island, B.C.

*Population 2,342.*

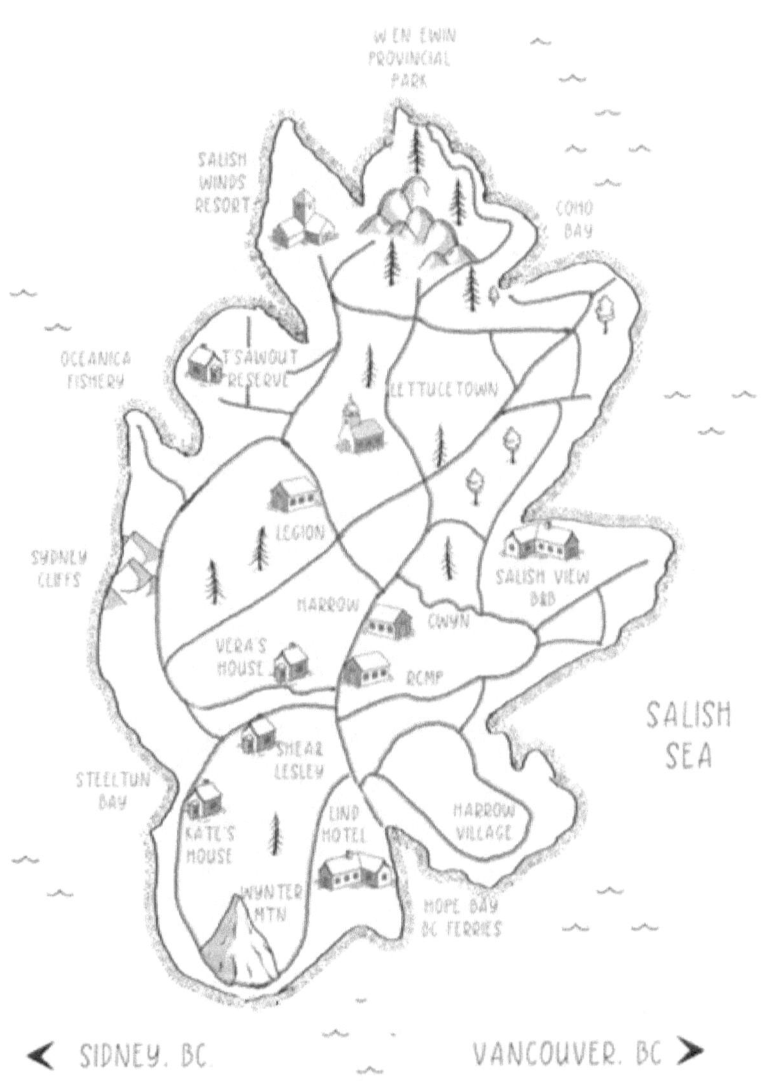

# Prologue

## May 24th

The water slapped against the side of the boat, playing a staccato counter-point to my racing heartbeat: beat, beat, beat, slap. Beat, beat, beat, slap.

I gripped the side of the motorboat and stifled the mixture of panic and rage that was trying to burst free from my mouth. *Stay calm. I've got to stay calm. That's the only way to survive this. Be calm.*

A warm body pressed against my leg, and I placed one hand down to rest on the silver-grey fur. I glanced up. Was this my opportunity?

Yes, it was. I took a deep breath.

*At least I'm not alone. I won't die alone.*

# Chapter One



Five weeks previously

The Spirit of Saanich pulled slowly into the dock at Wynter Island, its substantial white bulk inching past the timber guards like a hefty man trying to squeeze his way through a subway turnstile. The ferry maneuvered its way inch by inch into the small cove and settled, bobbing, to a clunking stop. A crowd of tourists pushed toward the bow, excited to finally see Wynter Island, British Columbia.

"Hey! You in the Red Sox cap!"

I spun around. A dark-haired female police officer seated in an RCMP squad car pointed towards the ferry.

"Don't stand in the middle of the road. The ferry is going to let out any minute, and this road is going to go from empty to Indy 500 in about 30 seconds flat."

"Sorry." I hurried across to the sidewalk. The last thing I needed right now was a jaywalking ticket. My cell phone buzzed, and I glanced down at it.

"No worries. Keep your eyes open, okay?"

As the sound of starting car engines grew to a cacophony, I headed towards the hotel perched beside the dock. It was a nineteenth-century grande dame, one of the old-school turn-of-the-century summer resorts. A white monolith with Victorian gingerbread trim, pinnacles, and dormers, it oozed authenticity right down to its fading evergreen shutters and doors.

A burst of crisp sea air swept in off the bay and smacked me right in the face. I pulled my Red Sox cap tighter down onto my chestnut-hued hair, making sure my ears were fully covered, and tugged my fleece jacket tighter around me. I didn't have that much extra fat on my body, but I was going to need every bit of it to try and retain some warmth.

*Isn't the West Coast supposed to be warm? This fifty-degrees is a hell of a lot colder than Boston was when I left.*

I pulled open the glass door of the General Store, which was nestled in the hotel's lower floor, and stopped in my tracks. Stretched in front of me, across the width of the store, were row after row of teetering shelves filled with everything from oatmeal to engine oil. Tampons, mousetraps, and lifejackets had been thrown in for good measure.

Kraft slices were two for one this week.

"Heeeellllllooooo!" a voice singsonged out from the bowels of the store.

I peered over a large floor display of Old Dutch potato chips, but saw no one.

"I'm over here. Far-left corner. No, no, that's my left. It would be your right, so yes, your far-right corner." She was tucked away in a back corner of the store, bent over some open boxes of fishing tackle.

"Hi. I'm looking for the post office?"

"You found it. Right over there between the nightcrawlers and the sunscreen. Give me a sec, and I'll be right over." The woman slowly inched her way up from the floor, grabbing her lower back as she did so. "You know, they say your body gets used to repetitive work. Well, I don't know about you, but mine bloody doesn't. What can I do you for?"

"I need a post office box. I heard you don't have home delivery here."

The woman entered a small cubby of a room in the corner of the store and rummaged beneath the counter. "No, never enough people to make it profitable for Canada Post." She pulled a pen out of her pocket and handed it to me along with a form that I quickly filled out.

"Here you go. Box 403. Post usually gets here around ten."

"Thanks." I pocketed the key, stepping quickly to one side as a carton of red wrigglers cracked open beside me. Several were attempting a last-ditch escape.

"I see you're staying at Michael and Anna's rental cottage. The one over by Steeltun Bay."

"Yes."

My stomach muscles clenched. I tried to relax, struggling to remember my meditation breathing. What had that psychiatrist said to me? Oh yes, meditative breathing is like praying the rosary without involving God. Of course, she assumed I knew what praying the rosary was. It was Boston, after all.

*In one, two, three. Hold. Out one, two, three. Hold.*

Could it really be starting already? The questions. The endless, inquiring questions. How are you feeling today, Kate? Tell me, are your panic attacks getting any better? Any nightmares last night?

On Wynter Island, they would be different questions, if no less difficult to answer. Who are you? Why did you agree to take this job way out here in the boonies? And why are your hands shaking like that?

"And your name?" The woman glanced down at the completed form in front of her. "Kate Zoë Thomas. I don't know any Thomases around here. It's a little too early for summer residents." A pause, a gasp of recognition, and she pointed her finger at me. "I know who you are!"

My stomach reclenched with a spasm. *Shit! How could she know already?*

"You're the girl who is going to run our new TV station!"

I slowly exhaled. *She doesn't know anything. Nobody knows anything. Yet.*

"You got it in one, Doreen," a husky female voice said from behind me.

I turned around to see two women, both in their sixties. One wore a loose green blouse, her gray hair waving back off her face to expose silver bumblebees dangling from each ear. On her legs were what appeared to be batik harem pants. Did I hear a faint accent?

"Is that an accent?"

The woman's laugh rasped sensually against the damp air. "Yes, German, but that was a long time ago. I guess I still haven't lost it." She gestured toward the woman standing beside her. "This is Gwen, and I am Vera. Vera Schmidt, a longtime resident of Wynter Island."

"Very long time," Gwen added. "Vera opened the first and only pharmacy on the island, still running today."

"It is, me not so much. I'm retired. Or at least that's what I tell myself."

"Gwen? Gwen Wynter?" I focused my attention on the second woman. "You're the person I'm supposed to be meeting this morning."

"Yes, I'm the one who started CWYN, Wynter Island Television."

Gwen looked a bit younger than Vera, with her shoulder-length gray hair pulled back into a ponytail. Her eyes were green, the pale skin along her jawline sagging slightly with age. A typical countrywoman, her faded jeans didn't quite cover the toes of her well-worn boots. She grasped a vintage Ford truck keychain loosely in one hand.

Gwen turned back to Doreen and Vera. "I'm afraid I'm going to have to steal my new station manager away from the two of you. As her arrival is the most exciting news on Wynter right now, I'm sure you two will be busy firing up the island telegraph."

Gwen turned, and I followed her to the door.

"Island telegraph," Doreen shouted in mock anger as we walked outside. "As if Vera and I would stoop as low as gossiping!"

* * *

Gwen led me across the two-lane road that had quietened now that the cars had been offloaded. "Let's find a seat at Annie's Bakery. We can chat there, and you can try the best cinnamon rolls in the province."

The bakery's outside patio was rapidly filling up, so Gwen led me inside into the wood-toned seating area. "It's pretty busy for a Thursday morning. You find us a table. I'll go and get the cinnamon rolls."

She quickly returned with two sprawling pastries, the maple icing oozing down their sides, and two earthenware mugs of coffee. I took a quick bite. The cinnamon roll dough, gooey and sweet, was tinged with a hint of wild blueberries.

"Delicious!" I took another bite and chewed for a moment.

In the bright sunlight of the bakery, I could see the wrinkles, like tiny lifelines, fanning out from her eyes to travel across her cheeks. Was she really in her sixties? Maybe mid-fifties?

"I'm glad to finally get a chance to meet you, Gwen," I said. "I was surprised when you didn't want a face-to-face interview."

She laughed, a raucous, throaty sound. "I didn't need one. Once I saw your resumé, I knew I had the right person for the job."

"Thanks."

"Canadian. Thirty-two-years-old. Video producer. Top of her class, Ryerson University. An intern at CBC Toronto; worked her way up to an associate producer on CBC Newsworld; picked up by WGBH in Boston; based in Kabul, producing news segments for PBS. Known for her love of Italian wines and The Office."

"Okay, you did your homework." *But how much homework, and how well?*

"Social media is the bane of our modern existence." Gwen took another sip of her coffee before taking a bite out of her cinnamon roll and chewing meditatively for a moment. "But it is a great way to find out details about your new station manager."

I placed my mug back down onto the tabletop with a sharp click, before glancing up, straight into her eyes. I could see, dotted throughout the green irises, tiny flecks of gold and hazel.

"If you're wondering if I know why you're here, Kate, I might as well put you out of your misery. Yes, I know why you left PBS and, presumably, was willing to take this job out here in the middle of nowhere."

I coughed. *Damnit! She knows!*

"I knew there had to be some reason a young woman as talented as yourself was willing to move from Boston to the other side of the continent. Hell, to another country! We have our pluses,"—Gwen gestured toward the bakery case packed with luscious pastries—"but not enough to draw people away from a great job in the big city."

"How much do you know?"

"Most of it, I think."

"Does everyone on the island know?"

Gwen hesitated. "No, I don't think so. Certainly not from me. Does it matter to you whether they know or not?"

I met her gaze with an unblinking stare that said very clearly how I felt. Yes, it mattered. It mattered a great deal. I tried to steady my trembling hand, but I was unable to stop the small ripples travelling across the surface of my coffee. She watched them lap up against the far rim of my mug, her smile slowly tipping downward.

"Okay, I guess it does matter to you. It will come out, you know. It's far too easy to find out anything about anyone on the internet these days."

I nodded. "I know, but I'd like some time to get my feet under me first."

"Well, they won't hear about it from me."

I took a long sip of my coffee, my fingers gripping the mug as the last tremors subsided. I looked out the window at the tourists, older couples enjoying a cup of tea, young kids running madly around the wrought iron tables, before returning my gaze to Gwen. "I have a few questions, if that's okay?"

"Go for it."

"With the last name of Wynter, I'm guessing you have some family history with the island?"

"Yes. My great-grandfather bought Wynter Island in the late 1800s and created a successful market garden business here. Our homestead is on the mountain—well, largeish hill—right behind you."

I swiveled in my seat to look out the window. I couldn't see the house itself, only the blur of apple blossoms cascading down the hillside in a white cloud.

"That's Wynter Mountain. For a long time, it was just my family and the Tsawout people here."

"Tsawout people?"

"Yes, they are the Indigenous people on the island. They have a reserve of about 300 or so acres over by the new Salish Winds Resort. Herbert was smart enough to befriend them. With no ferry service until the 1960s, this was an isolated chunk of British Columbia. He realized the only way to survive out here was with the help of your neighbors."

"And now?"

Gwen smiled and licked the tinted icing off her spoon. "You still survive with the help of your neighbors."

"I hope I have some good neighbors then."

Gwen tilted her head to one side. "Not many neighbors out near Steeltun Bay – Shea and Lesley, Vera—but the island itself is not that big. About fourteen miles long and eight miles wide. You've got Harrow Town, the main business center, Lettucetown, the agricultural area, and Harrow Village, where we are right now."

She gestured a hand out the window towards the bay in front of us. Nestled beside the ferry dock, a smaller marina was filled with a mixture of expensive-looking sailboats and beaten-up fishing trawlers. The contrast between the sleekness of the sailboats and the squat, utilitarian stoutness of the fishing vessels was difficult to miss.

"We're not large enough to have a traditional local government. Instead, we have a representative on the two councils that oversee the islands: the Capital Regional District and the Islands Trust. Michael Rossino, our island's lawyer, is Wynter's representative on both of them." She took the last sip of her coffee and pushed back her chair with a squeaking finality.

A loud whoop whoop whoop blared from outside the bakery.

"What's that?" I asked.

A red fire truck pulled up beside us, its lights flashing and siren sliding up and down the register like an angry hornet, before it turned onto the main highway and headed north.

"Huh, I wonder what that's about?" Gwen murmured. "They don't usually call out the Harrow Village truck. I hope it's not a bad fire. Anyway, let's get going. I have someone I'd like you to meet."

# Chapter Two

The cement patio, which had only been partially full when we arrived, was now packed with tourists.

"Hey, Gwen!" a woman's voice called out.

"Shea!" Gwen waved a hand in the air. "We're over here."

A young woman, perhaps late twenties, walked up the hill toward us. Her thin blond hair was pulled out of her eyes by a tortoiseshell clip, some strands breaking free to straggle loosely near her cornflower blue eyes. Her physique was slim, somewhat angular, mirrored by her strong, lunging gait. Her waterproof jacket had a scar of dirt, or perhaps something worse, running from her elbow to her wrist. Under one arm, she held a duck.

"I'm sorry I'm late, Gwen. When I got your text, I was over on the north shore picking up this injured mallard. Luckily, he's more stunned than anything else." She stopped in front of us. "Is this her?"

"Yes, this is Kate," Gwen gestured towards the young woman. "And Kate, this is Shea Porter, the island's part-time librarian, and full-time animal rescuer. We don't have an SPCA on the island, so Shea is our substitute."

"Animal rescuer. Sounds like a pretty important job."

The young woman's smile was joyous and honest, her demeanor almost childlike in its sincerity.

*She couldn't tell a lie if her life depended on it.*

Shea waggled the emerald-hued duck under her arm. "Yes, but the pay stinks. And there aren't any benefits. Did you guys see the fire trucks head out?"

"Yes," Gwen agreed. "It must be something big if they've called out the auxiliary stations."

"Auxiliary stations?" I asked.

"Yes, one for each of the three small settlements on the island: Harrow Village, Harrow Town, and Lettucetown."

"The settlers weren't terribly creative when it came to naming things on the island," Shea added.

"Did you see anything on your way here, Shea?"

"Yeah, it looks like there's a fire. That new house being built off Rte. 97. Lots of smoke."

"Damnit. I guess I'll have to go the back way to get to Sam's."

"Sam's?" I asked in surprise.

Gwen smiled, her cheeks reddening. "I have to dash to an appointment out on the Reserve. That's why I texted Shea. She's going to give you a ride home today. No need for you to walk back to the cottage." Gwen rummaged in the pocket of her jeans and pulled out her keys. "Kate, how about you take some time to unpack and settle in. In a couple of days, we can go over and check out the station." Gwen started across the street towards an old red Ford 150, turning to shout back over her shoulder, "I know you're going to do great things for Wynter Island!"

"Your cottage is in the opposite direction from the fire," Shea said as we turned towards the parking lot, "so we won't have to fight our way past the rubberneckers. Believe me, everyone is going to be over there trying to see what's going on. C'mon, you get to hold the duck while I drive."

She led me over to a blue Toyota Highlander. As I stepped up into the passenger seat, I noticed a stack of library books spread across the back seat as well as a half-opened first aid kit. A long strand of the same gauze that was knotted around the mallard's leg stretched from the kit to the back passenger door.

"Here." She clambered up into the driver's seat, key chain clenched between her teeth, and unceremoniously plopped the duck into my lap.

"Okay." I gently wrapped my hands around the feathered breasts. The duck looked up, wondering whether death was imminent, before preening his feathers and settling down on my lap. "Nice duck. Don't bite me. I'm a good guy."

She laughed and put her foot down hard on the gas pedal. The SUV squealed onto the main road, a good ten miles over the speed limit. "Don't worry, ducks don't bite. They nip."

I examined the mallard in my lap. "Nipping doesn't sound that much better."

"Well, he's in shock right now. He's not thinking about nipping you."

"What happened to him?"

"Not sure exactly. Someone saw him lying on the side of the road by the Reserve. Turns out it's only an injured leg. That gets him a bit of R&R at the Porter-Akiyama homestead."

"Is that your husband's name, Akiyama?"

She smiled. "No, not husband. Partner now. Wife someday soon, I hope."

I winced. "I'm sorry. I shouldn't have assumed."

"No worries. My mom thought for the longest time I was living with a male RCMP officer who happened to have a feminine-sounding first name."

"What's her name?"

"Lesley, so you see, it can be interpreted both ways."

I drew one hand over the duck's head. The bright green feathers slid, rainbow-hued, like a shimmering oil slick beneath my fingers.

"Is that how you ended up here on Wynter Island? Because of Lesley?"

"Oh no, I met her after I moved here. How about you? Are you on your own?"

A sudden thud plummeted into the pit of my stomach, like a coin dropping into an empty well. On my own. Yes, I am very much on my own.

"I broke up with my boyfriend, Daniel, before coming here."

Shea looked over, surprised. "Not because of this job?"

"Oh no." I shook my head. "Something else. I met him in Afghanistan while I was working as a producer for PBS's Dispatches. He's an AP reporter based in Kabul."

I closed my eyes and could see it all again.

*The Kabul River, like so much of Afghanistan at night, was cloaked in total darkness. Shouting and pleading scratched against the all-encompassing blackness, the sound carrying to where I lay huddled on the dirt. Someone's voice -was it my own? - screamed.*

I opened my eyes and tried to focus on what I was saying.

"I left WGBH in Boston about ten months ago, and we ended up going our separate ways. I decided I wanted to come back home to Canada. I grew up in Mississauga. And so here I am. *Sans* boyfriend."

"I'm sorry. I was hoping for a great love story."

"No, no great love story. Just the hackneyed tale of a woman finding out her boyfriend was cheating on her."

Great love story. At times it had felt like that. Until I decided to get that last-minute ticket on the Acela to surprise Daniel with a homemade dinner after his trip to Geneva.

*I turned the key in the lock of his apartment. The door swung open. The lights were on. Why did he leave the lights on? What was that sound? Music? Why had he left the radio on as well?*

*I took one step forward, my eyes taking in the rest of the room. The woman's jacket draped over Daniel's elliptical machine. The cloying, sweet floral scent of Flowerbomb by Viktor & Rolf wafting in the air. Two people sitting on Daniel's couch. One, a woman, mid-twenties, dark hair, dressed in a cheap, knock-off designer top. She looked over at me with surprise and irritation as Daniel's head began to slowly turn in my direction*

*The grocery bag slipped from my hand, the marinara jar shattering in an explosion of blood-red sauce.*

"I'm sorry. That really sucks." Shea turned the steering wheel, and the SUV skidded onto a dirt side road, her speed dropping only a hair. "That's Vera Schmidt's place," she said, pointing to a butter-yellow cottage surrounded on both sides by a large garden enclosed in deer netting. "Did Gwen tell you about her? She makes herbal teas and medicines. She used to run the pharmacy here."

"Yes. I met her this morning."

"Oh good. You'll have to come to the Legion tomorrow for Friday night dinner. It's roast beef this week, I think. There's a veggie option if you want it. Everyone comes."

The SUV slammed to a stop at the end of Vera's drive, causing me and the mallard to fall forward. A red cooler sat perched on a ramshackle wooden cupboard beside us. A small metal lunch box sat next to it with a sign reading *$4 a doz./ Please leave money here/ Make your own change if you need to/ Thank you* printed on it in waterproof black marker. Shea jumped out of the car and opened the top of the beer cooler. I rolled down the truck window, tightening my hold on the duck to make sure he didn't make a break for it.

"Can you hold both the eggs and the duck? It won't be for long."

"Sure." I juggled the duck with one hand and took the eggs with the other.

"Vera has the best eggs on the island," Shea said as she dropped two twoonies, the Canadian equivalent of a two-dollar bill in coin form, into the metal lunch box. They landed with a low clank. "But you don't have to buy from her if you don't want to. The only thing is, keep your empty egg boxes. Vera recycles them for her egg sales."

She climbed back into the SUV, and we shot off back down the dirt road as if the very hounds of hell were chasing us.

"Ahh, Shea, do you have some appointment you've got to get to?"

A wide grin cut across her face. "You mean, my driving? No, I've always had a lead foot. My mom says I've always been fast. Even came out of the womb too quickly." A small wink. "It also doesn't hurt that I live with one of the two people that write up the speeding tickets on the island. You're welcome to come over to my place if you ever want some company. I'm only about half a mile from your cottage."

"Thanks. That's very kind of you."

She slowed for a stop sign. Well, screeched to a halt might be a more accurate term. As the gravel dust cleared around us, I could see a red pickup truck pulled off quite a way down the side road. Someone—was it Gwen?—was walking down the middle of the road, dragging something large behind her.

"Isn't that Gwen's truck?"

Shea craned forward to look out my side window. "Yeah. She's doing something with the Sydney Cliffs sign. Must have blown over again." She put her foot down on the gas, and we shot through the intersection again, leaving Gwen behind us in another cloud of dust. "Speaking of Gwen, she's really got you hooked up with everything you need, hasn't she? There's a station vehicle coming, right?"

"Yes, someone from the garage is supposed to drop it off later today."

"And then there's the stuff at the cottage. Did you see the kayak? Michael and Anna leave it there for their summer rentals."

"Yes, I saw it. I don't think I'll be using it."

"Why not? You're almost across the street from Steeltun Bay. It's gorgeous kayaking around here."

"No." I cut her off more sharply than I had wanted to. "Sorry, it's just that I'm not that keen on water."

"Well, you're going to have to get over that," she said as we slowed down to turn into my driveway. "Why on earth did you move to an island if you don't like water?"

How could I answer that? That it was the right move at the right time? A perfect way to escape New England and restart my life somewhere far away? Perhaps the oldie but a goodie, I needed a change?

But there had been one drawback. The same drawback that had reared its ugly head in my life so many times before: water. Or, more specifically, my fear of it.

"I wanted the job and had to accept the fact that being on an island came with it."

"Well, water is a part of our everyday lives here on Wynter. We get around on it. We make our livings off of it. Can't escape it, even if you want to." She slammed on the brakes at the sight of a car parked ahead of us in the driveway. "Looks like you've got some company."

A middle-aged couple emerged from the car as we pulled to a stop behind them. I climbed out.

"Hi, Michael, Hi, Anna," Shea called out her open window. "I'm just dropping Kate off. See you tomorrow night at the Legion, Kate. Dinner's at six. Tickets are twenty bucks a head at the door."

She waved good by and then shot back out the driveway. I walked over to the couple, extending my hand as I did so. The man grasped it, his skin soft and warm, his handshake firm. I like a firm handshake. A sign of a strong sense of self, my father used to say.

"Hi, Kate. Nice to meet you. Michael Rossino."

Early forties, perhaps, wrinkles just beginning to carve their way in between his bushy brows and in the olive-skinned laugh lines bracketing his mouth. His hair, short, dark, interspersed salt and pepper, matched the trim beard encasing the lower half of his face. But it was his eyes that struck me. The humor and compassion I saw in their hazel depths. My pulse fluttered erratically like a butterfly brushing against my wrist. How long had it been since I felt like this?

*Since Daniel, of course.*

"And this is my wife, Anna." He gestured to the woman standing beside him, her mahogany hair swinging in a shiny bob above a French boat-neck sweater. She was petite and fine-boned, her hand, as she extended it to me, looking like a delicate piece of china. The blue-green veins showing through her pale skin made her seem even more fragile.

"Pleasure to meet you," she said in a soft, subtle burr.

Another accent? "Ahh, you're Scottish."

Anna nodded. "Yes, Edinburgh. Michael and I met when we were both attending Law School at UBC. I hope you don't mind us stopping by. We wanted to make sure everything was alright."

"Oh no, that's fine. Everything's great so far. It's a lovely place."

"Yes, it is, isn't it?" Anna's eyes traveled over the cottage. "This was our first home on the island, so it brings back a lot of happy memories for me. Is there anything you need?"

"No, I've got everything I can think of."

"Good. Well, if you do need anything, just let us know. Our home number and Michael's law office number are written on the chalkboard in the kitchen."

"Yes," Michael laughed as they climbed back into their car. "If you can't reach anyone at the house, you can usually get me at the office. And who knows? You might need a lawyer while you're here!"

I laughed. Like I'd need a lawyer on Wynter Island! This was the last place

I would get into any sort of legal trouble. "Thank you, but I'm pretty sure I'm not going to need your services."

"Well, what is it the boy scouts say?" Michael called out the car window as they backed up the drive. "Always best to be prepared!"

# Chapter Three

"That'll be twenty, please. Do you want the veggie meal? We've only got"—the young woman glanced at a paper on the table beside her covered with crossed-out numbers—"five left."

"The meat's okay. Is it roast beef? That's what I heard," I asked.

"Yes, roast beef with all the trimmings. Mashed potatoes, gravy, Yorkshire pudding. Apple pie for dessert." The woman put my twenty-dollar bill into the till and handed me a paper stub. "Go on in. I think Molsons are on special tonight. A buck off."

I shoved the ticket into the pocket of my jeans and headed inside.

The Legion bar oozed 1964, with its glossy wood paneling and ship's wheel clock stuck in pride of place in the center of the wall. It was standing-room-only, making it hard for me to move towards the bar. I could see two men serving drinks, Shea sitting on a bar stool in front of them. One of the men appeared to have a port-wine birthmark dotted along the left side of his face.

"Kate!" Shea pushed through the crowd to grab my arm and pull me forward. "Come here! I'll introduce you to our hosts." She deposited me on her empty stool. "Kate, this is Kurt and Harald. Kurt runs the Legion here, and his husband, Harald, runs the Salish View B&B."

Kurt was a bear of a man, in all senses of the word. Big and burly with a wide wingspan, taut biceps, and a short brown beard. "Nice to meet you, Kate. What can I get you?"

"Ahh, a Molson Canadian? I hear they're on special tonight."

Harald extended a hand across the bar to me. I took it, determined to keep direct eye contact rather than allow my gaze to travel around the bluish-purple stain covering the edge of one cheek and a bit of his forehead. He was a hair taller than Kurt, with a slimmer physique. He had shaggy, shoulder-length hair, his bangs attempting to conceal some of the mark.

I stared into his ice-blue eyes. His expression shifted from curiosity to concern and then, finally, to understanding.

*Shit. He knows what I'm doing.*

His mouth turned up into a sweet smile as he held my hand for a moment longer than necessary. It's okay, his gentle gaze seemed to say, thank you, but it's okay.

"Welcome to Wynter Island, Kate. It's nice to meet you." His voice was soft and sibilant with Scandinavian vowels.

"Harald is from Denmark," Shea added as Harald headed into the back room. "Copenhagen. They have quite the love story. Remind me to tell you one day."

I took another sip from my beer as Gwen rushed through the front door and headed straight for a table near the back.

"Gwen's arrived. If you don't mind, I'm going to go over and say hi."

"Sure. I'll be sitting with Stewart." She pointed to a man in his late thirties with a neatly trimmed moustache and beard. A pint of dark ale topped with creamy white foam sat on the table in front of him. He had the air of a man who could handle both his booze and a bar fight, at the same time if necessary. "He's the RCMP Sergeant on the island. It's only him and Lesley. She drew the short straw and is on duty this evening."

I picked up my beer and slowly made my way through the crowd. It was a mixed bag of people. Most were over fifty, some looking pretty rough in their dirty jeans and work boots, while others were crisply turned out in their Patagonia windbreakers and North Face trekking boots. One group had the slick look of an ad for a retirement community, while the other appeared to have just left an offshore fishing trawler. The demarcation line of Wynter Island, between those who work for a living and those who don't have to, couldn't have been clearer.

Music blared out from the speakers on the wall. Some oldies from the sixties, along with some Canadian bands I remembered, like Trooper and Tom Cochrane.

Gwen looked up from her drink. "Kate! I'm so glad you could make it. Here"—She scooted her bum down the bench and patted the spot next to her—"have a seat. You've met Vera already, but this is Shelley. Shelley Douglass. She works for BC Ferries."

Gwen gestured towards a woman sitting on the opposite side of the table. Her blonde bangs, badly in need of a trim, fell into blue eyes that were sinking into the folds of skin surrounding them. She wore a red sweatshirt with a ferry and union logo printed across it.

"And I do a bit of housekeeping over at the Lind." Her tentative smile lifted her upper lip just enough to expose smoke-stained teeth. I noticed a packet of Players Light cigarettes stuck out of the top of her purse. "I live in the Northern part of the island with my son, Greg."

I clasped the other woman's fingers. "Hi, Shelley. Nice to meet you."

"We were just talking about the fire that happened yesterday." Gwen took a small sip of her drink. "Do they know what happened yet, Shelley?"

"Greg said the house itself is okay, but all of the unused lumber went up, like, boom!" Her fingers exploded from her lap in a mime of a sudden explosion.

"Greg was working there?" Vera asked.

"Yeah, he and Dougie were framing up that new house that's being built. Luckily, no one was hurt." Shelley examined my face for a moment before taking a swig from her bottle. "You must have thought you were back in the city with all those sirens going off, eh?"

I laughed. "There were a lot of fire trucks, but there's no way you could ever confuse Wynter Island with Boston. I don't believe anything could disturb the peace and quiet around here."

Vera snorted. "Wait till the next time B.C. Ferries goes on strike! There won't be any calm on Wynter Island then!"

We all laughed as Kurt stepped into the bar. "Dinner is served!" he shouted, waving everyone to leave their seats. "Will those with the vegetarian meal please place your colored card on your placemat so our servers can find you? Thank you and enjoy!"

* * *

The cool evening air washed over my face. It felt lovely after the big meal in the crowded room. I, like most everyone else there, had consumed enough roast beef and Yorkshire pud to keep me fed for a week. And that didn't include the two beers I'd drunk. My jeans strained worryingly across my belly as I sat down in the driver's seat.

*Damn, I can't eat like this every Friday.*

I rolled the driver's-side window down and turned the station pickup truck onto the dirt road.

The darkness was all-encompassing, thick, dense, as if it were its own separate being. Without the headlights on, I couldn't see more than a foot in front of my face. I turned on my high beams, just to make sure I didn't hit any deer on the road.

*This is what life without streetlights is like, girl. You'd better get used to it.*

I slowed down and turned into my driveway. As I jumped out of the truck, the moon broke through the clouds behind me to spill a brilliant white light onto the road.

*Maybe a walk over to Steeltun Bay? It's not that far, and the moon reflecting off the water must be gorgeous.*

I grabbed a flashlight from the truck and headed back down the drive, pausing at each different rustle and squeak. An invisible nocturnal world surrounded me. No, not invisible. A small animal ran out in front of me, its big fluffy tail flicking in the moonlight. I stopped and held my breath. The animal stopped, too, a pair of golden eyes staring from across the road. A fox. We studied each other for a moment before he turned and raced into the woods.

"Good night, Mr. Fox. Watch out for the coyotes."

Shea was right, I realized, as I headed down the road. The cottage was in a fantastic location. Close enough to the small bay for someone to haul a kayak there, yet not exposed enough to be seen by everyone.

As I turned the corner, Steeltun Bay stretched out before me. The surface of the water lay still, so shimmering and mirror-like that I felt I could walk upon it, my silver carpet under the stars.

"It's beautiful," I murmured and made my way down to the pebbled beach.

There was no breeze, only the gentle hiss of the waves pushing onto the beach and then pulling away, like the the ocean's lullaby. It felt like it was rocking me back and forth to sleep. I sat down on a mossy log and dimmed the flashlight. Across the narrow channel I could just make out Pender Island, the moonlight threaded like a silver ribbon along its coastline.

*If someone is over there looking this way, I wouldn't know. They couldn't see me, and I couldn't see them.*

I stood up and walked to the water's edge. The sea flowed like liquid mercury, back and forth against the rocks. I stopped and pulled one of my sneakers off before dipping a toe into the surf. The icy cold shot through my foot with a force I hadn't expected. Like Afghanistan, the climate here could trick you into believing things were warmer than they actually were.

It reminded me of an early date in Kabul with Daniel, my pretty jacket—light and useless—being covered by Daniel's heavier coat.

*"You're going to freeze to death," I said.*

*"No, I won't. I am made of stronger stuff than that. Anyway, I've got enough cabernet in my system to keep me warm until we get you home."*

*He kissed me in front of my hotel, sneaking his lips closer as he unwrapped his coat from my shoulders.*

*"That isn't fair," I teased.*

*"All's fair in love and war."*

*He smelled like lemon and cedar. He always did.*

*His face came close to mine again, and I breathed in his scent as his lips touched my own.*

I closed my eyes tighter together as I tried to recall each and every detail.

*His hot breath against the side of my cheek. The scar along his jawbone from that teenage skateboarding accident. The crisp cotton of his shirt as my hand brushed against it.*

*"I think you might need some more cabernet."*

*He pulled back to look into my eyes. "I do?"*

*"Yes," I whispered." Luckily, I have a bottle in my room."*

*His lips curled up into a mischievous smile. He took my hand and led me into the hotel lobby. "Well, isn't that lucky?"*

I let my entire foot sink under the surf, slicing through the silver surface to vanish in the darkness below. Something brushed against my toes, and I yanked my foot back out, losing my balance and tumbling down onto the beach. My butt landed on the mossy rocks, splashing freezing seawater onto my jeans. The flashlight dropped with a clunk onto the stones beside me.

*Damn, it's cold.*

I stood up slowly, my head spinning, and rubbed my cold, wet hands over my face to try and reorient myself. I reached down for the flashlight and switched it on, its pale-yellow beam illuminating the water right in front of me.

A dark shape moved in the water at the far edge of the light's beam. What was it? A seal? I leaned forward and swept the area again with the light. Something was bobbing in the water. It couldn't be.

*My God, is there someone in the ocean!*

"Hello? Hello? Are you alright?" I shouted and ran straight into the surf. The water splashed against my calves, soaking my jeans and the one shoe I still had on. "Can you hear me? Are you okay?"

I pushed through the deepening seawater, wincing as the water splashed higher and higher, trying my best to ignore the voices screaming in my head: *Get out of the water! You're going to drown!* I could no longer feel my legs, the cold numbing my body from the waist down.

Was there really anything or anyone there? Or was I just imagining it?

"Hello! Hello!"

I came level with the dark shape.

"Oh my God, it's a body. Help! Someone! Anyone! Help!" I screamed and, without thinking, grabbed a lifeless arm and pulled to get the head out of the water. The shape flipped, like a kayak righting itself after a spill. I looked down at the dead face, its sightless eyes staring up at the moon.

*Daniel.*

# Chapter Four

"Kate! Kate! Come here!"

The night sky throbbed in a crimson haze. Why had it changed color? It had been so dark, and now it burned red, pulsing red.

"Kate!"

Hands grabbed at me and pulled me in from the water's edge. How did I get there? I'd been in the ocean, and it was so cold, and there had been a body...

*Daniel.*

A thick, musty-smelling blanket was thrown over my shoulders and wrapped tightly around my body.

*Daniel.*

"Kate, c'mon. We've got to get you warmed up."

A woman's voice. Who was it? My eyes finally focused on Shea standing in front of me.

"Shea! How?"

Shea rubbed the rough blanket against my wet skin. "I came with Lesley. She got the call from 911. You're lucky someone was heading home from the Legion, heard you screaming, and stopped."

Bodies pushed by me. Who were all these people? Where did they come from?

More people pushed past, most still in the clothes they'd worn to the Legion that evening. A group of people stood waist-deep in the ocean. I could hear someone calling out directions.

"Okay, on three, everybody lift."

Lift? Lift what? Lift who?

*Daniel.*

"One, two, three, lift!"

"Kate, let's get you out of the way."

It was a different voice now. A tall man stood beside Shea, his shoulder-length chestnut hair brushed back off his face. He took my arm and urged me back toward the log. Was that the same log I had been sitting on earlier? When I'd looked over at Pender Island?

"Who are you?"

"I'm Ben. Ben Navaerez, the island vet."

"We don't need a vet. We need a doctor."

He smiled and, with Shea's assistance, guided me down onto the log. "Well, like a lot of things on Wynter, we also double up with the emergency positions. I'm a volunteer EMT."

A rush of bodies carried something, someone, out of the water.

"Kate, don't look over there," Shea waved a hand in front of my face. "Look at me. Okay? Look at me."

With difficulty, I focused on Shea's face. Mascara had smudged beneath her eyes, and a faint stain of lipstick still clung to her lips.

"Daniel," I whispered.

"Okay, everyone, we don't know what happened yet," a male voice announced from behind me, "but we have to try and preserve any evidence we can. Put the body down on the tarp and then step back. Lesley, tape off the entire area."

I tried to turn to see who was giving instructions, but Ben blocked my view.

"Daniel," I whispered again.

"What is she saying?" Shea turned to Ben. "Ben, can you hear what she's saying?"

He leaned closer. "Are you trying to tell us something, Kate? Are you hurt?"

I shook my head.

"Okay, did you see something?"

I nodded slowly, as if my head might somehow fall off.

Ben and Shea exchanged worried glances.

"What did you see?"

"Ben, we shouldn't be asking her these questions. We've got to leave it to Lesley and Stewart to talk to her."

Ignoring Shea, Ben leaned closer, clearly concerned. "You know something, don't you?"

I nodded again, as the tears flooded into my eyes.

"Yes, I do. I know who's dead. Daniel."

* * *

The police interview room at the Wynter Island RCMP detachment doubled as the coffee room. So besides a table, chairs, and video recording equipment, there was a fridge, a Keurig coffeemaker, and half a package of maple cream cookies.

"Kate, you need to eat something." Stewart pushed a plate of cookies across the table toward me. "Lesley, can you get her something hot and sweet to drink, like hot chocolate or something?"

"Sure." Lesley, in full RCMP uniform, stood up and busied herself with filling the coffee reservoir with water from the tap.

In her mid to late thirties, Lesley was physically fit, her well-toned body accentuated by her fitted uniform. The only hint of femininity lay in a lick of mascara and a bit of gel taming her short black hair. Yup, Lesley was the same police officer who had spoken to me by the Lind hotel two days ago. Was it only two days ago?

"Are you sure you want to go ahead with this now, Kate? We can wait till tomorrow morning."

"No, I want to do it now. The sooner I talk to you, the sooner you can get out there and find out what happened."

Stewart considered this for a few moments before starting again.

"Okay, if you're sure."

"Yes, you have my consent to do this, to do whatever you need to do, to find out what happened to Daniel. ”

"Even though this is just a preliminary interview, we are recording this." He gestured to the tiny camera in the corner of the ceiling. "Anything you say can be taken down and used as evidence against you in court. You have the right to retain and instruct counsel of your choice."

"Yes, I understand."

"Good. Do you wish to have a lawyer present?"

I accepted the steaming mug of cocoa from Lesley. The heavy beige earthenware mug proclaimed: 'Life is better on Wynter Island.'

*Yup, that's what I had been hoping for.*

I took a sip of hot cocoa and placed the mug down on the table.

"No." My voice strengthened as the hot cocoa warmed my raspy throat. "I don't want to have a lawyer present. I don't really understand why I would need one."

My unspoken question hung tantalizingly in mid-air.

"Good, okay." Stewart flipped open a notebook and proceeded as if I had said nothing. "It is 23:47 on April 14th. Sergeant McLeod and Constable Akiyama present. Can you state your name for the recording, Kate?"

"Yes. My name is Kate Zoë Thomas."

"Alright, can you tell us what happened this evening?"

I closed my eyes and let the images float behind my eyelids. The moonlight. The silver sheen of the ocean. The icy cold water. The shape bobbing in the sea....

My eyes snapped open. "I drove home from the Legion. I don't know when it was, maybe nine o'clock? Lots of people saw me leave."

Stewart made a note and gestured for me to continue.

"I drove home to the cottage and decided to head down to Steeltun Bay."

"Why?"

"I don't know."

*Of all the places to go, why had I gone to Steeltun Bay? Why did I have to go there tonight, of all nights?*

I refocused and continued. "The moon came out. I thought it would look pretty reflecting off the water."

"Okay. You got home and headed to Steeltun Bay at around nine o'clock. Did you walk there?"

I nodded. "When I reached the water, I took one of my running shoes off so that I could stick my toe in the water."

"Why?"

"I know it sounds stupid, but I wanted to see how cold the water was."

"And then what?"

"My foot slipped. I fell and dropped my flashlight. When I picked it up, the beam shone on something floating in the water."

"What did you think it was?"

"The longer I looked at it, the more I thought it might be someone."

"So, what did you do?"

"I ran into the ocean. When I got closer, I realized it was a person. I," My voice caught and hesitated on the next word. "I don't know what I thought I was doing. Maybe seeing if the person was still alive? I don't know. I pulled on an arm to try and get the face out of the water. And I, I saw who it was." I stuttered to a stop.

"Did you recognize the deceased?"

I bit my lip to stop the tears from starting up again. "Yes. He is," I hesitated, "he was my boyfriend. Daniel. Daniel Apollinar."

"Age?"

"Thirty-seven."

"Were you still seeing each other?"

"No."

"When did your relationship end?"

"A few months ago. In New York City."

"And did you have any idea he was coming out to the West Coast? In particular, to Wynter Island?"

I shook my head. "I never told him that I was moving out here."

"So, how did he find out you were here?"

My mind traveled over all of our joint friends in the news business. Someone would have told someone else who told someone else, and it must have inevitably gotten back to him.

"I'm guessing from someone we both knew who heard I had taken this job."

"Any idea who that might have been?"

"No."

"Okay. So, you had no idea Daniel was coming here?"

I paused, weighing up my choice of words, before answering. "No."

"That's a long way to travel to see someone without letting them know you're coming."

I swallowed a bite of maple cookie. It crumbled into a thick and sandy blob in my mouth. "He probably didn't let me know because I would have told him not to come."

"But he wanted to come anyway? Even though he knew you would be unhappy to see him."

I shrugged my shoulders. "I guess. I don't know."

"Did your relationship end amicably?"

I thought back to the jar of marinara I had dropped, shattering in Daniel's front hallway.

*He had leapt up, pushing the other woman out of his way, as I turned and ran for the door. I made it to the elevator, stabbing at the door-close button as he dashed out into the hallway.*

*"Kate!" he pleaded as the doors closed. "Let me explain."*

*"NO!" I shouted, the elevator plummeting downward.*

I had never seen him again. Until tonight.

Stewart finally spoke. "It sounds like he might have wanted the relationship to continue even though you wanted it to end. Is that correct?"

"He wanted to apologize, and I wasn't interested," I gripped the mug of cocoa even tighter, noticing as I did so that my hands weren't shaking. That was unusual. My hands had been shaking since, well, since everything had happened in Afghanistan. Had I finally pushed my body to the point where my previous trauma was irrelevant? Were things that bad?

*Yeah, things are that bad.*

"You were pretty angry with him?"

"Yes, wouldn't most women be? I caught him cheating on me. He lied to me about being out of town on business and was instead in his apartment with another woman. God knows how many other times he'd been there when I believed he was away for work."

"Yes, I see." Stewart let his statement hang in the air for a moment before continuing. "Is there any reason why Daniel would come to Wynter Island other than to see you? Any other connections to this area? Work-related or perhaps friends or family?"

"Well, he lived in Seattle for several years."

"Did he know anyone here on Wynter?"

"Not that I know of. But he certainly knew his way around the area. He covered the Seattle to Portland region for Associated Press for several years before he was transferred to Afghanistan. He loved to sail around here."

"Do you know if he sailed to Wynter Island in particular?"

"No. I know he liked to head up to Tofino, so he must have passed Wynter on the way there."

"And did he ever stop off on Wynter Island?'

"I think so, but I'm not really sure."

"You weren't with him?"

A hint of iciness crept into my voice. "No, I don't sail."

"Okay, so, as far as you know, the only person on Wynter Island who knew Daniel Apollinar was yourself."

"Stewart, or should I call you Sergeant McLeod?"

One side of his mouth lifted in a half smile. "Stewart is fine."

"Okay, Stewart, are you trying to insinuate that I had something to do with Daniel's death? Is that why you asked me if I wanted to speak with a lawyer?"

He scrawled something quickly on a piece of paper and handed it to Lesley, who left the interview room.

"I asked if you wanted to speak with a lawyer because that is your right under the law, Kate. And I'm not here to insinuate anything. I don't need to. My job is pretty straightforward: figure out why a young, healthy man flies two thousand miles to an isolated island off the British Columbia coast and winds up dead."

Hysteria began to bubble its way into the back of my throat. "Why should I know anything about it? Couldn't it just be a coincidence?"

Stewart raised one eyebrow. "A coincidence? To die here? The place you moved to? That's a helluva coincidence, Kate."

I flailed around for ideas, anything that might make sense of this senseless situation. "Maybe he committed suicide?"

"Here? On Wynter Island? Why not do that in New York?"

"I don't know. Perhaps to make some kind of dramatic gesture?"

"A dramatic gesture?"

"Yes, like, I don't know, a cry for help. Look at what you made me do, Kate!"

His eyebrows inched even higher. "Without telling you he was coming, or leaving a note of some kind? He had no idea you would find his body, Kate. In fact, the odds are that if you hadn't spotted him, he probably wouldn't have been found. Within a few days to a week, scavengers would have started to feed on his corpse. You would have known nothing about it."

*Scavengers feeding. On Daniel. Oh my God, no! No!*

I pressed my fingertips into my eye sockets, hard enough that a jumble of kaleidoscopic colors swam before me as I slipped from the numbness of shock into a chaotic jumble of panic and confusion. What the hell was going on? How did I end up here?

"What does the coroner say?" I finally asked.

"The coroner will be coming over tomorrow morning, and the body will be transported by ferry to Victoria for the autopsy tomorrow afternoon."

Lesley returned and whispered something in Stewart's ear. He nodded, and she joined us at the table.

"Okay, Stewart. Enough questions for me. What do you think happened to Daniel?" I leaned forward to try and make eye contact with Lesley, but she avoided my gaze. "Lesley?"

Lesley said nothing and kept her gaze trained on an envelope she had placed on the table.

"Kate," Stewart said, "are you sure Daniel never tried to reconnect with you?"

"What are you trying to say?"

"I asked if Daniel ever tried to reconnect with you?"

"I blocked his number."

"That's not what I asked. I asked if he ever tried to reconnect with you again. Recently."

I glanced down at my lap, covered by the musty blanket Shea had draped around my shoulders earlier. My soaked jeans lay in a heap on the station bathroom floor where I had left them.

"Where's my phone? Who has my phone?"

Lesley reached into the manila envelope and pulled out my cell phone.

Stewart took the phone and held it up in front of me. "You mean this phone, Kate?"

"How did you get that!"

"It was in the pocket of the jeans you left in our bathroom. Luckily, it seems to have survived your trip into the ocean."

"You don't have the right to unlock my phone!" I shouted, half rising out of my seat in fury. "I didn't give you permission to do that!"

"We don't need your permission to search your phone if we believe the contents may be relevant to an arrest."

"Arrest?" My voice squeaked an octave higher, the sound holding for a moment in the quiet room.

Stewart nodded. "Yes, an arrest. And perhaps you've also forgotten that you gave us consent to do whatever we feel is necessary. Luckily for us, your smart lock feature was a bit laggy this evening."

Stewart tapped on the phone's surface. He pulled an image up on the screen and turned it to face me. My messages app showed the last text I had received. Yesterday morning. From a phone number I hadn't recognized and wasn't in my contacts.

*I miss you. I promise I'm going to fix everything. D. xxx*

I stared at it for a long time before looking up.

"I would like to speak to a lawyer."

# Chapter Five

I opened my eyes and stared up at the rough-hewn log beams above my bed. I could hear voices in another room. Where was I?

The memories suddenly flooded back, filling every crack and crevice of my conscious mind. How could I, even momentarily, have forgotten what had happened?

Daniel was dead. Daniel was dead, and I had found him. Daniel was dead, and I was the main suspect.

I sat up in bed and swung my legs over the side. The T-shirt and baggy sweatpants I was wearing didn't belong to me either. Oh yeah, they were Shea's. I was at Shea and Lesley's house.

I glanced around the bedroom at the aged white seams cracking in between the logs in the old farmhouse wall, the dark, antique Victorian dresser with a curved mirror placed against it. The floor was thick pine, perhaps the original flooring, complete with knots and bumps. Bright sunlight shone in through the only window.

*It must be late.*

I looked for my phone on the small table beside the bed, but it wasn't there.

*Oh, yeah, the RCMP kept it.*

The clock on the bureau said ten. It was already ten? What time had Shea brought me here? Around two? I remembered the hurried, hissed discussion between Lesley and Shea in the police station.

"What do you mean, you're taking her to the farm?" Lesley had whispered.

"What do you expect me to do, Les? She's a mess. I can't dump her at the cottage and leave her alone like this."

"For Christ's sake, Shea. She is the prime suspect in a murder investigation. We are still considering arresting her. How can you take her to our home, the home of a police officer investigating this case?"

Shea's voice had deepened into fury. "Because she has nowhere else to go."

"What about Gwen?"

"You want me to drive her over to Gwen's at two o'clock in the morning, wake Gwen up, and say: Here's your station manager, Gwen. You need to let her stay with you because Lesley won't let me take her to the farm?"

Lesley paused and thought about this for a moment. "Well, yes, that's exactly what I would like you to do."

"For Christ's sake, Lesley. You're being ridiculous. She's coming home with me. I'll make sure to keep her out of your way until you leave in the morning."

Shea had turned on her heel, pulled me from the interview room, and taken me outside to her SUV. The drive to the farm had been short and silent.

Finally, alone in the shower, hot water beating onto my face, I sobbed and sobbed. For Daniel. For myself. For what might have been.

Clean clothes and a towel were laid out on the bathroom counter when I stepped out of the shower. I mechanically pulled them on.

Shea led me to the guest room and the turned-down bed. My feet felt like they were encased in cement blocks as I dragged them down the hallway. How could I sleep after all of this? How could I close my eyes and not see Daniel's face? I fell on top of the handmade quilt, too tired to even cry again. Mercifully, my eyes closed, and I fell into an exhausted, dreamless sleep.

* * *

"Gwen called me first thing this morning. I need to talk to her, Shea. I know she's exhausted, but you've got to wake her up," Michael's voice said from the other room.

I opened the guest room door. "It's okay. I'm already up."

Shea was sitting with Michael and Anna in the living room, which seemed larger in the daylight than it had the night before. It was a mishmash of styles and periods, part log homestead, part cozy farmhouse. True to the age of the house, electrified gas lamps hung from the massive cedar beams. I ducked to avoid a low-hanging light fixture and walked into the living room.

*This is definitely not a home for tall people.*

"Hi, Kate." Michael stood up and extended his hand. "Gwen called me first thing this morning and asked me to come and talk to you."

I took his hand, his palm surprisingly warm against my own. Even in the haze of grief, the emotional pull was strong. I fought the desire to hold on to it for a moment longer than necessary.

"Well, I guess you were right, Michael. I am going to need a lawyer on Wynter Island, after all." I laughed at my little joke and thunked into an empty chair, all of the energy that had pulled me out of bed suddenly evaporating.

"Michael asked if I could join him this morning for another legal opinion on this." Anna said from her position on the sofa. She was dwarfed by the overstuffed furniture, her small bottom balancing carefully on the edge of a cushion. "I'm no longer practicing, but two legal minds are usually better than one."

I nodded and tried to push the image of Daniel's face out of my mind's eye. The bloodless skin, almost waxy in appearance, and the puckered wrinkling of his features.

*No! I have to do this! This isn't the time to fall apart!*

Michael pulled an iPad and stylus pencil from his bag. "Alright, Kate, how about you fill us in on some of the details of what happened."

I straightened my shoulders and swallowed a sizable lump of panic. "Sure. Shoot."

"Obviously, you knew the man who died?"

"Yes, his name is Daniel Apollinar. He's thirty-seven years old." I hesitated. "He was thirty-seven years old. He lived in Seattle for several years before recently relocating to New York. He grew up in Los Angeles. His parents and two sisters still live out there. Oh my God," I gasped, "I've got to call and tell them about Daniel."

Michael extended a palm. "No, the police have already done that. Since you identified the body, they don't need to fly up here. They have requested that the body be flown to Los Angeles once the police have released it."

It. Not him. I gritted my teeth. "Okay. Do they know anything? What was he doing out here?"

Michael and Anna quickly exchanged glances. What did that mean? What did they know that I didn't?

"I wasn't given much info from Stewart," Michael said, "But he did tell me that Daniel's family knew he was coming out here."

"They did? Why? Why was he coming?"

Michael paused for a moment. "Apparently he told them he had found a way to get you back, to prove to you that he hadn't been cheating on you."

I gripped the arms of the chair hard enough to cause the whites of my knuckles to show through my freckled skin. "I don't know anything about that. His last text to me was the same as all the others."

"Why didn't you tell the police about the text, Kate?" Anna asked.

"I panicked and thought it might look bad. From the text, it looked like we were communicating. Like I might have known he was coming, when I really didn't."

"To make things more complicated," Michael continued, "his family was under the impression that you knew he was coming."

"What! I didn't!"

"When you match that up with the text, Kate, the optics are not great."

"But—" I bit my lip and inhaled before enunciating each word slowly. "I didn't know Daniel was coming to Wynter Island."

Michael, Shea, and Anna watched me in silence.

"I got the text. What day is it today? Saturday? It was two days ago. It came from a number I didn't recognize."

"But you knew it was Daniel?" Anna asked.

"Yes, I knew it was him. He's tried all kinds of different ways to contact me. When I blocked all the texts and calls from his phone, he started borrowing other people's phones. I blocked theirs, too. That's what I thought he'd done again. Borrowed someone's phone."

"But this number had a local area code."

"I didn't pay any attention to the area code. Daniel could be anywhere in the world, borrowing God knows whose cell phone. I put my phone away and ignored it like I ignored all the others."

"Okay. That is something I can check out. It might come in handy to show that he had a history of texting you from other people's phones." Michael stopped to glance through the notes on his iPad. "We don't yet know who the number belongs to, but I'm sure Stewart and Lesley will have that answered in no time. So, you were completely unaware that Daniel was coming out here to B.C. to see you?"

"Yes."

"I take it you two broke up after you caught him with another woman."

"Yes."

"Did you threaten Daniel, or make statements about him that could be interpreted as threatening? You must have been pretty angry when you caught them."

"Are you trying to ask me if I did it, Michael?" I didn't try to stop my voice's steady rise in volume. Anger was beginning to seep through the cracks in my shock. "Just come right out and ask me then. Did I kill Daniel? After all, that's what you and the police must be thinking."

"We don't know what the police are thinking," Anna replied, her ivory features as smooth and composed as marble. "We don't know who the police believe did it, or if they even have any suspects yet. And that's not Michael's job to figure that out."

"It is my job," Michael continued, "to defend you against any criminal charges."

"Are there going to be criminal charges?"

Michael opened his mouth but hesitated for a second before speaking. "I don't know, Kate. Right now, it's just a lot of circumstantial details."

"Yes, but they always suspect the wife, the husband, or the lover, don't they?"

"Usually."

"It all comes back to me, doesn't it? Did I do it?"

"Did you?"

In the shocked silence, my eyes met Michael's. "No!"

"Then that is what I have to make sure the police understand. This is still early days, Kate. We don't even know the cause of death yet."

Corpse. Daniel. Dead. None of it made any sense. It felt as if I was trapped on some horrible carnival ride, whipping me round and round, faster and faster, unable to get off. Tears began to well up in my eyes. Again.

"Michael, can we move this along?" Shea asked as she scooted closer and put her arm around my shoulders.

"Sure. We still don't know the time of death, so it's pointless to see if you have an alibi. Do you know of anyone who might want to hurt Daniel?"

I considered the international press in Kabul, the army officers and soldiers, our friends in New York, Boston, London. And the Afghani people, always there, calmly accepting their destiny of being caught in a war between two different worlds.

"No, I don't.  There were people he angered, but that's part of the job. Three sides to every story: yours, mine, and the truth. Noses would get out of joint occasionally, but nothing that would lead to murder."

The front door opened, and Gwen hurried in, her gray hair hanging loosely around her face. With the morning sunlight pouring through the open door, she appeared lit from within, enrobed in a golden halo.

"Morning, Shea, Michael. Oh, hi, Anna. Wasn't expecting to see you here this morning. Kate, how're you doing?"

She plopped down beside me and enveloped me in a hug. Tears trickled down my cheeks as I buried my head in her shoulder. At times like this, I missed having a mom.

"C'mon, no crying now." Gwen held my shoulders at arm's length. "You've got to be strong. That is the only way to survive when horrible things happen to us."

*That's easy for you to say, Gwen. Whatever horrible things you've had to overcome in your life, being accused of murder is probably not one of them.*

"It's best to get it all out. Lay all your cards on the table." Gwen looked searchingly into my eyes. "You've got to tell Michael everything."

"Everything?"

Gwen stared at me a few seconds before speaking. "Yes, everything."

# Chapter Six

I pulled out of Gwen's arms, breathing deeply. How was I going to explain this to them? There were times when I barely believed it myself.

"You know why I left Daniel, but you don't know why I left my job. Why I was willing to fly all the way across the continent to come here to work." I stopped as my hands began to shake. Of course, that unpleasant side effect had to return. I gripped them together in a tight ball. "When I started working in Afghanistan, it felt like an adventure, exciting. It's where I met Daniel. That made it even more special to me."

My voice cracked, and I stopped for a moment.

"I started out in Afghanistan producing mainly political pieces for CBC, and then Dispatches when I got the WGBH job in Boston. I was always either embedded with a military unit or had private security. And an interpreter. We always had an interpreter." I paused. "You know, you're always aware of the fact that Afghanistan is a dangerous place. But you forget it's also a country where people work, have fun, and go about their daily lives. Sometimes, when things have been quiet for a while, you can trick yourself into believing you are safer than you really are."

*The weather had been lovely and dry that spring day. Sunny skies and warming temperatures across all of Afghanistan, even though the mountaintops were still crowned with snow. Flowers bloomed everywhere. The poppy fields, red with circular cups of blossoms, looked as if a giant had dripped blood from a finger-tip over the countryside.*

*A last-minute agreement for an interview unexpectedly came through, not far outside of Kabul. No security was available, but I knew we were alright. Our interpreter, Aziz, always carried an M4 rifle with him. Mark, our reporter, would handle the interview with an elderly Afghani politician while I shot it. We'd be done in a couple of hours. Easy-peasy.*

"We were headed back from a shoot with an Afghani politician when we were stopped by the Taliban."

Shea gasped in horror. Michael remained silent, but the creases deepened between his eyes.

"They thought we had information on U.S. battalion movements. But we didn't. We honestly didn't. But they didn't believe us."

*The initial blow of the gun butt against my back was a sudden, searing pain. How long did it last? Minutes? Hours? They finally left me in a heap on the dirt in a secluded ell of the Kabul River. I tried to block out Mark's screams while they interrogated him. And then it was Aziz's turn.*

I sat silent for a moment, choosing my words carefully. "We were all beaten in an attempt to get us to talk, but our interpreter, Aziz, got the worst. of it."

Was it the fact they could speak the same language that infuriated them? Was that why they had more barbarically abused Aziz? Or was it the fact that he was working for the *Englisi* that angered them so much?

"I went in and out of consciousness, so there are bits I don't remember. But I know they dragged Aziz down to the river. And they tortured him to get him to talk."

I squeezed my eyes shut.

*Splashing water. Shouts in Dari. Somebody screaming. I raised my head from the dirt and looked toward the river. I could just make out Aziz being dragged into the water and repeatedly held under. Each time longer than the time before. More shouting in Dari and the raspy sound of Aziz gasping for air as his head was hauled out of the river.*

*Aziz!*

Did I scream it out loud? Perhaps. A gun butt slammed into the side of my head, and I lost consciousness until I was awoken by a dribble of liquid from a US soldier's water bottle.

"They knocked me out. Luckily, some U.S. soldiers drove by. The Taliban fighters got away. Mark and I were okay. Hurt, but okay. Unfortunately," I hesitated, "Aziz didn't make it."

"So you quit your job and returned to the States," Anna asked.

"Yes." I nodded in agreement. "WBGH was great. They were willing to give me a leave of absence, but I had to quit. I knew I could never go back to Afghanistan again."

"What did you do next?"

"I puttered around the Back Bay in Boston. Daniel and I spent some weekends out on the Vineyard. He was still working in Kabul, but he made an effort to come back to the States more frequently to be with me."

"Did you get help?"

I stared at the floor. "Yes, I did."

"A diagnosis?"

I looked up to make eye contact with Michael. "PTSD."

Michael scribbled a note on his iPad. "Did they put you on any medications?"

"Yes. Ambien for sleep."

"Are you still taking Ambien?"

"When I can't sleep."

"Have you taken Ambien since you've been on Wynter Island?"

I hesitated. "Yes."

"Did you take any Ambien the night before last?"

"Yes. Yes, I did. Is that a problem?"

Michael looked at his notes for a moment before glancing up at me. "I don't know. Ambien has a history of causing people to blackout, sleepwalk, hallucinate. I'm not saying that's what happened here, but it's important to be prepared for anything the police may throw at us."

"For Christ's sake, Michael!" Gwen huffed. "Whose side are you on?"

Michael put down his iPad and leaned toward Gwen. "Gwen, try and see it from the RCMP's point of view."

Gwen rolled her eyes but nodded for him to continue.

"A young, healthy man travels across North America for one reason: to see Kate. Things ended badly between them. There are hard feelings. He wants to see her, but she doesn't want to see him. We have a family member who says Daniel told her he was coming out here to see her."

"But he didn't!"

"Hold on a sec, Kate. We also have a text that supports this from the victim to Kate. A text she did not tell the RCMP about."

Silence.

"To the best of our knowledge, no one else on this island has any connection with Daniel. Hopefully, we'll be able to get some info soon on how and when he got here. That may tell us something." Another pause. "The reality is that the RCMP have the basis of a criminal case here: motive, knowledge, and opportunity."

"But no evidence," said Anna.

"Yes, no evidence. Only the comment from the family and the text, which are both circumstantial."

"But with no other suspects, all attention is going to be focused on me," I said. "The angry ex-girlfriend who lured him here to murder him." I paused as a thought occurred to me. "How do they think I abducted him without a vehicle?" And why would I find the body and tell them about it? Wouldn't I just have kept my mouth shut and left him floating in the bay? Why would I have dragged the police into it?"

Michael shrugged. "Who knows? You did have access to the station truck during the window of time he went missing. And as far as finding the body: if you try hard enough, you can come up with an explanation for anything."

"Yeah. Maybe it was some kind of complicated double bluff: I told the police about the body because that is exactly what the murderer would never do."

"Kate," Gwen said, one eyebrow raised, "this is getting a little creepy. You're better off keeping these ideas to yourself."

"But don't you see, Gwen?" I raised my hands from my lap to rest on top of hers. "This is what I do. I tell stories. Real stories that have complicated plots. Real stories where it's my job to get all the facts, all the pieces of the puzzle, and then put them together so I can present a coherent whole to the audience."

"But this is not a television news program."

"No, you're right. It isn't." I returned my hands to my own lap. "It's more important than that. It's my freedom."

The panic that had settled in my gut began to slowly evaporate, like thin whisps of smoke escaping from a watered-down campfire. But a new emotion surged in its place, feeding a fire of its own through my body: anger. Anger at whoever did this to Daniel. Anger at whoever had upended my life when I thought I had finally found some peace.

"And it's justice. Finding whoever killed Daniel and making sure they pay for it."

# Chapter Seven

Finished with questions for the day, Michael and Anna said their goodbyes and left with Gwen on their heels. With a mixture of relief and exhaustion, I headed towards the door. So much had happened since I'd driven myself home from the Legion the night before. So much still for me to process. I needed to go home.

As soon as I closed the door behind me, I stopped in my tracks. Standing directly in front of me, a medium-sized gray dog blocked my path. Actually, he wasn't exactly grey, more a brindle of grey, white, black, and brown. In the morning light, he almost looked silver. Part Australian Shepherd?

I bent down and extended my hand. "Hey, pup."

The dog remained still, watching me intently with his one blue eye and one hazel eye, almost like he was judging me.

"C'mon, I'm not gonna hurt you. Come here."

The dog angled his head sharply to the left as if trying to understand what I was saying but still didn't budge.

"Really. I'm nice. I promise."

The dog flipped his head to the other side. Still, he didn't budge.

"Okay, if you're going to be anti-social, I will leave you alone."

I stood up and glanced back for Shea.

Lick, lick, lick.

I felt his wet, warm tongue brushing against my fingertips. I looked down. Silent as a ghost, the dog had moved to sit directly in front of me. His white muzzle came forward, a small tongue darting out to lick my fingers again. Lick, lick, lick.

"Oh, so you do want to be friends, huh?" I squatted back down, his mismatched eyes continuing to assess me. I patted the top of his silvery gray head, feeling oddly privileged as I did so.

"You're a strange pup, aren't you?" The dog tipped his head to the side once again and then leaned forward to give me the tiniest lick along the side of one cheek.

"Jupiter!"

Startled at the sound of Shea's voice, I stood up. "Sorry, Shea. I was just petting your dog."

Shea closed the front door behind her and twisted the knob to make sure it was locked. "Oh, Jupiter isn't my dog."

I looked back at the brindle-colored dog. "Really? Does he belong to one of your neighbors?"

"Nope. Jupiter doesn't really belong to anyone that I know of. Jupiter is most definitely his own man. He lives mainly in the barn, although he does occasionally grace us with his presence in the house."

"Huh?"

"Jupiter is one of my strays. The RCMP picked him up a year or so ago running loose; no collar, no tags."

I looked back down at the dog, who was unmoved by his own sad story. "That's too bad. Were his owners here on vacation or something?"

Shea shook her head no. "Not that we know of. Nobody reported him missing to the RCMP here or to any of the animal shelters in Victoria or Vancouver."

"I wonder what happened."

"It's not as unusual as you may think. Lots of unwanted cats and dogs get dumped here by day trippers. The owners think their unwanted pet can somehow survive out here in the country. Ridiculous, of course. If the pet's lucky, somebody finds it and brings it to me. If not, the poor thing starves to death or gets eaten by foxes or a cougar."

I slowly patted the silver-gray head, his eyes watching me with unblinking fascination. "Well, maybe he'll be lucky and find a new home somewhere."

Again, Shea shook her head no. "Nope, won't let anyone touch him. The only person who can get close to him is me, and that's mainly because I'm the one who feeds him. He's also totally silent. No barks, no whining, nothing. You wonder what his home must have been like for him to end up like this."

I didn't understand. "But he just let me pet him. And he licked my fingers and cheek."

"I know. That's why I shouted out his name. I couldn't believe it when I saw it."

I thought back to my childhood cocker spaniel, Goldie. I had loved him dearly, and he loved me, but … I couldn't help but grin.  Goldie loved everybody.  There wasn't any supernatural type of bond between us. But this dog, it was unnerving the way he stared at me.

"C'mon, you've had a helluva twenty-four hours, Kate. Let me get you home," Shea said and climbed into her SUV.

I clambered up into the passenger seat, pulling my seat belt across my chest and buckling in.  When I looked up, Jupiter was still sitting in the middle of the driveway, watching me.

# Chapter Eight

Gwen's old red pickup rattled down Rte. 97, the main north-south route on the island, in the direction of downtown Harrow. A lush green border of wild flowering bushes encroached along the side of the road as if trying to reclaim it for the wild. Behind the bushes, tall firs and fruit trees separated the patches of lime-green pasture from the denser forest.

"How are you doing, Kate?"

I considered my options. Grief-stricken? Traumatized? In shock? Was there a box to check for all of the above?

"I'm okay, I guess. Just trying to keep putting one foot in front of the other."

"Are you sure you're ready to check out the station? You don't have to, you know. If you need more time…."

I shook my head back and forth with more force than was necessary. The last thing I needed right now was more time: time to remember the curve of Daniel's lips, the hazel depths of his eyes, and then the horrifying mockery of what his face had become in death.

"Three days is enough. I need something to do. Something to keep me busy. Like finding out about Wynter Island. Can you give me the Grand Tour?"

"I don't know about the Grand Tour, but I can certainly hit the high points." Gwen pointed to a flock of alpacas in a field, their eyes wide and bulbous with long fringed lashes, like a Japanese manga character. "That's the Browns' alpaca farm. Apparently, petting cute alpacas and buying knitwear is more profitable on Wynter Island than beef farming."

"So, how do most people on Wynter Island make a living?"

"Well, it used to be pretty much all farmers and fishermen. But that's changed over the last few decades. Lots of retirees and summer people. Some islanders, though not many, work off-island. Like Ria Corker. She works for CBC Radio in Victoria, but they allow her to do some work from home. Her parents own the Lind hotel. You met her mother the other day, Doreen."

"Then how does everyone else make ends meet?"

"By supplying the tourist trade."

"But that's seasonal work, isn't it?"

"Unfortunately, yes. November through April are our slow months. The resort shuts down, as do most of the campgrounds and outdoor recreation companies. Bed and breakfasts try to hang on over the winter, but it's hard. Not enough permanent residents to keep an active job market going."

We rounded a sharp bend, and Gwen slammed on the brakes. A white goose waddled slowly down the center of the road, headed straight for us.

Gwen rolled down her window. "Crackers! One of these days, I'm going to hit you!"

The goose paused as if mortally offended. He swiveled his head in the truck's direction, his beady black eyes examining us with irritation.

"Crackers, get out of the road! You heard me! Move!"

Crackers stood immobile.

I smiled to myself. *Is this going to be a game of chicken, but with a goose?*

"I swear to God, Crackers!"

Gwen took her foot off the brake, and the truck started to roll forward. Crackers watched the rolling truck for a moment as if considering his chances. He then waddled hastily to the gravel roadside, turning to hiss at Gwen as he did so.

"Yeah, same to you, buddy. Go home to Guinevere, where you belong."

"Guinevere?"

"Yes, Guinevere. They're a bonded pair, Crackers and Guinevere. But Crackers goes off in search of wild goose love with those sexy Canada Geese that winter on the island."

I smiled. "You mean, he's a goose with a roving eye? A randy gander?"

"Yes, and he ends up all over the island. One of these days, he's going to get hit, and it's going to break Vera and Guinevere's hearts."

"Is that the same Vera I met earlier?"

"Yes, she has the two geese as well as a pot-bellied pig. Another animal escapee. And then all of her chickens, of course."

The truck powered up a hill and slowed as we came level with an assortment of small cedar-sided buildings. I could see potted palm trees decorating the lawn, along with picnic tables and a few benches.

"This is Harrow. The economic and political epicenter of Wynter Island." Gwen pulled into the entrance and idled beside the gas station. "I'm sure you realize that I am using the term 'epicenter' loosely."

The gas station appeared unchanged from the 1980s, complete with full-service gas pumps and a sun-faded Players Light cigarette poster in the window. A big white placard lettered with ICE had been posted above a red fluorescent sign that blinked Open. It reminded me of the old gas stations I had seen on camping trips to Georgian Bay, Ontario as a child.

To the side of the pumps, a truck was up on a repair lift, two boots and a pair of greasy overalls sticking out from beneath it.

"That's the only gas station and automotive repair shop on the island. And this is Tru-Value, our grocery store."

It looked huge compared to the Lind General Store.

"Wynter Island Pharmacy, Vera's place, is down the side over there. It's your one-stop shop for prescriptions, Vera's herbal concoctions and teas, shampoo, etc. They are the only place on-island that sells stationery and electronic supplies. Not a lot, but it's usually enough to tide you over until you can get to Victoria to stock up again."

A stand of brightly colored umbrellas held the pharmacy door open.

"There's our bookstore and one of Wynter Island's handful of restaurants. The Provincial liquor store is tucked in beside the restaurant, and there's Cecily's, our ladies' dress shop, over there."

The front window displayed a gauzy sundress. The mannequin appeared ready to traverse the beach in layers of orange organza.

"I wouldn't have thought this was a fancy dress kind of island, Gwen."

"No, but the tourists like to browse. And she stocks the stuff we actually need, rain jackets, boots, and sweaters, in the back." Gwen waved her hand as if to encompass all of the shops. "Don't be fooled. This may look prosperous, but it isn't. We're just keeping up appearances for the tourists. We, like so many small islands, are merely hanging on by a thread."

"How long a thread?"

Gwen's face stiffened, all harsh lines and rough edges. "Not long enough. If Wynter Island is going to survive, we need year-round revenue."

"And if you don't get it?"

"Wynter Island will cease to be. Or at least the Wynter Island I grew up with. What few businesses we have will close. Full-timers will start to trickle away, their homes bought up by mainlanders looking to make some money with an Airbnb. Before you know it, you don't recognize any of the faces in the Tru-Value and the only things for sale will be sunscreen, cold beer, and sand buckets. Wynter Island would become just another holiday tourist trap."

"That's why you started the station, isn't it? To get publicity for the island."

"Yes. We need to attract both visitors and full-time residents. As long as we pay the upfront costs, BC Cable is willing to carry CWYN on their system throughout British Columbia. That is a lot of eyeballs checking out our island."

"But running a TV station is not an inexpensive proposition."

"I guess it would be asking too much," Gwen's lips tilted up in a questioning smile, "for you to believe that I'm independently wealthy?"

"Please don't take this the wrong way, Gwen, but yes." The jeans, the beaten-up boots, even the gray hair which had not seen the inside of a salon for quite a while: Gwen was obviously not a wealthy woman. "The kind of gear we're talking about costs tens of thousands of dollars."

"Yes, I know. Alright, we have a silent partner."

"And that would be?"

Gwen mulled this over for a few moments as we idled in the parking lot.

"I called in an old favor."

"An old favor? Dare I ask what kind of favor it was? I hope we're not talking about horse heads in beds."

"No," Gwen laughed. "My grandfather, Herbert, befriended several of the robber barons who bought up huge chunks of British Columbia in the 1800s. Always good to have friends in high places, he thought. Those men's grandchildren and great-grandchildren now run the logging and mining industries in British Columbia. So, I had a chat with one of them. Encouraged him to see that it might be a good idea to help Wynter Island."

"And he gave you, what?"

"Three hundred thousand dollars. A tax write-off, as we are now a registered non-profit. I assure you, I didn't blackmail him. He gave it out of the goodness of his …" she trailed off, considering her choice of words, before continuing. "He wants to stay anonymous for now."

Gwen swung the truck into a space in front of a small shop. A faded Wynter Island Insurance sign still hung over the glass door. A large piece of white paper had been taped to the door with CWYN written on it in thick black felt letters. Underneath, it read: *The voice of the people of Wynter Island. Wynter Island Insurance is now available online at www.wynterislandinsurance.ca.* The rest of the glass storefront had been covered with rectangles of poster board.

"And here we are! CWYN!"

"I'm guessing"—I gestured toward the blacked-out windows—"that's to stop ambient light getting in."

Gwen turned off the ignition. "Yup. Nate ordered some blackout curtains, too. He said indirect light was the death of any TV production. It's amazing what he's been able to teach himself on the internet."

I climbed out of the truck. *Yeah, nothing like a station staffed by people who learned their skills on YouTube!*

Gwen opened the station door and gestured me inside. A small foyer furnished with a few office chairs and a desk greeted us. The desk was covered with empty Coke tins and a half-eaten sandwich. I leaned forward. Yup. Bologna on white bread with a squirt of ballpark mustard.

A thick black curtain was suspended from floor to ceiling in front of us. It appeared to have been newly hung and, from the state of the walls, with incredible difficulty. Various holes and gashes zigzagged across the ceiling, accompanied by copious amounts of silver duct tape. Voices and scraping noises emanated from behind it.

"Nate? Are you back there? It's Gwen. I brought Kate with me."

The voices stopped, and a pair of feet scrabbled in our direction. The long blackout curtain jerked once, twice, before a loud thunk reverberated through the office.

"Damnit," a male voice said softly from behind the curtain.

The curtain held for a moment and then drifted downward, almost like a prize reveal on a Hollywood game show. The bars and hardware followed, smashing down onto the desk and scattering across the floor.

"Hi," a young man said, propping himself up with one hand, his lower half covered in curtain and bits of duct tape. "I'm Nate."

# Chapter Nine

The now unobstructed space looked nothing like a television studio. The ratty carpeted floors had patches worn through where decades of office chairs had rolled back and forth. Dusty piles of old mail decorated empty metal desks. An ancient Mister Coffee machine sat in one corner, waiting for a fresh brew.

I scratched my head. *This is crazy! What the hell am I doing here? I used to work for PBS!*

Gwen stepped forward. "Here, Nate, let me help you get this stuff picked up."

Nate unraveled himself from the curtain with the help of an older man. In his early sixties, the man's tucked-in flannel shirt created a stomach bulge that drooped over his belt like rising dough that has bubbled over the top of a bowl. He glanced at me, and our eyes met, the anger in his zinging me like an unexpected jolt of electricity.

*What the hell is his problem?*

Nate stood, shaking bits of plaster from his hair. A blue hoodie and jeans covered his tall, thin frame, and a slight five o'clock shadow stood out on his pale, lantern-jawed face.

"Are you okay?" I asked the wiry scarecrow of a young man.

Nate grimaced and brushed the remaining ceiling dust off his jeans. "Yeah, yeah, I'm fine."

He stuck out his hand towards me, and I reached forward to give it a shake. His palm stuck to mine, tiny beadlets of sweat clinging to my wrist. A small tick flicked, with the constant beat of a metronome, at one side of his mouth.

*Why is he so anxious?*

"Nate is one of our most enthusiastic volunteers. He's sixteen," Gwen said. "His parents are Michael and Anna, your landlords at the cottage."

"Yeah. Umm," he started out, "I just wanted to say …" He stuttered to a stop before trying again. "I'm sorry for your loss. We all heard about what happened on Friday night."

Tears welled up in my eyes, and I fought to keep them under control. "Thank you, Nate. That's very kind of you. The police don't have any idea what happened yet, so I think it's important that I try and push ahead with things at the station." I turned around to look at the room ."So, this is CWYN."

Even to my ears, my attempt at jovial excitement rang hollow.

"Yes, it is." Nate's nervousness had abated a bit, but the hesitation in his voice was still there. "I can't wait to get started."

"It's going to take a while before we can get started, Nate."

"We have cameras," He gestured to several large boxes pushed up against the wall. "They just haven't been opened up yet."

"Well, we may have cameras, but I can't just snap my fingers and create a TV station overnight." I turned to Gwen. "You never mentioned to me that there was no infrastructure set up for the station."

Gwen bent down to pick up a chunk of ceiling plaster. "I thought it was probably best for you to build the place from the ground up."

I kicked my way through some of the curtain mess. "Well, I agree that this is from the ground up." Gwen ignored my strained glance and smiled brightly in return. "You should have told me about the state of the station, Gwen. There's a lot of work to be done here."

"Yes, but I know you can do it!"

"I'm glad one of us does."

Could I do this? My eyes scanned the dimensions of the room, mentally blocking off space for a small studio and control room, an equipment room, and editing bays. Yes, it was doable. I could turn this ramshackle space into a small television station. Just not easily or quickly.

"Are you saying we're not going to open the station right away?" Nate asked, his voice rising in concern.

"Nate, even if I can get plans drawn, permits pulled, and construction ready, it's still going to take several months before this space is ready to go. "

"A few months! But we need to open in a couple of weeks!"

"Why? Why do we need to open so soon?" Gwen asked suspiciously. "What have you done, Nate?"

He turned to the man standing beside him for support, but only received a shrug in return. The older man was more focused on glaring at me. "Well, you know my idea for Fish Bingo?"

"Fish Bingo?" I asked.

Gwen waved a hand in my direction. "Yes, Nate, I remember Fish Bingo."

"Because Kate was arriving this week, I thought the station was going to open. You. know, start production. The bingo cards are already scheduled to go out in the newspaper."

"Go out in the newspaper?" Gwen repeated in surprise.

"I'm confused," I said. "Is Fish Bingo a TV show? How on earth do you play bingo with fish?"

"The same way everyone else plays bingo." Nate gave me a strange look. "The balls have numbers and letters on them. You spin them around, they drop out of the cage, and the first one to get five in a row...."

"Nate," Gwen said, "she understands the basics of how to play bingo."

"Yes," I agreed. "But what I don't understand is where the fish comes into it?"

"The prize, of course."

"Oh, Nate," Gwen murmured, "I love your excitement about the station. But there's being enthusiastic about something, and then there's just plain foolhardiness."

"I'm sorry. I should have checked with you first."

I patted him on the arm and tried to summon up some shred of positivity within myself. Okay, not only was the station a disaster, but I now had to pull together a live television show in just one week.

"Nate, don't worry. I'm not sure what, but I will figure something out. And who is this? " I nodded at the silent, simmering man standing next to him.

"This is," Gwen hesitated, as if unsure whether to continue, "this is Bob Corker. You met his wife, Doreen, at the Lind hotel. They run the hotel and general store there."

Bob was not tall, maybe five foot seven, with a short shock of steely gray hair peeking out beneath his navy baseball cap. Beaten-up work boots were on his feet, and a fleece jacket hung open over his sizeable belly.

I hesitated at the open fury in his eyes before extending a hand for him to shake. It hovered alone in midair for a few moments before I slowly returned it to my side.

"Bob, for God's sake," muttered Gwen. "Bob's a bit … irritated about something, Kate. Please excuse him."

"I haven't done anything, Gwen, that needs to be excused."

"Bob, you promised me you wouldn't make a scene."

Bob laughed. "I haven't made a scene, have I?" He turned toward me, his face alight with an anger that carved his features into light and dark, negative and positive. "I don't believe in playing games, Miss Thomas."

"Games?"

"Yes, games. On this island, we look after our own."

"Bob, for God's sake, not this again!" Gwen sputtered out.

He shifted his stare to Gwen. "As I said, we look after our own. At least until now. This job doesn't belong to you, Miss Thomas. It belongs to my daughter."

In the sudden silence of the room, the distinct ticking of an old wall clock echoed.

"This job belongs to your daughter." I mechanically repeated his words.

"Yes, my daughter. Ria Corker."

"I thought she worked for CBC Radio in Victoria?"

Bob glared over at Gwen. "Yes, she does. The journalist with a degree from Carleton University. The journalist who grew up on this island! The journalist who would have killed to get a full-time on-island job so she wouldn't have to keep commuting to Victoria."

"Bob," Gwen cut in, her face tight with barely contained anger, "you and I have already had a lengthy discussion about this. Well, a discussion might be a bit too tame a word for it. It was my decision, and I chose Kate."

"Yes." Bob's choleric cheeks flushed even brighter. "A decision your father or grandfather wouldn't have made."

Gwen paused, either to control her anger or decide if the assault charge was worth the pleasure of slapping him across the face. "I don't know what my father would have done, Bob, but I'm guessing he would have chosen the most qualified person for the job. And that person was not Ria. However much you may have wanted it to be."

"What's going on here?" a raspy voice asked from behind me.

I turned to see an elderly man standing in the open doorway of the office, his angular, hard-worked body clothed in oilskin overalls. He had a filthy baseball cap perched on the back of his gray-fringed head with *Betts Marine Towing* written across it. In his hands, he held a shimmering, freshly caught salmon.

"Bob, you look like you're about to have a goddamn heart attack."

"I. Am. Not. Going. To. Have. A. Heart. Attack, Phil." Bob's face became redder with each successive word.

The fisherman stepped into the room and dropped the salmon down on top of the desk. Bits of dust from the fallen plaster flew up into the air. "Well, I think you are, Bob. But don't listen to me if you don't want to. Nate, " His eyes connected with the teenager, "your dad ordered a salmon."

Nate's brows drew together in confusion. "Phil, I don't know what you're talking about."

"Well, if I tell you he ordered a salmon, that means he ordered a bloody salmon. I called his cell phone, and he says he's in Vancouver for some business today."

"Yeah, he's catching the seaplane back this afternoon."

Phil waved his filthy hand in the air as if shooing away pointless details. "Whatever. He ordered this from me last week. Something about your mother throwing a dinner party tonight."

"Yeah, so?"

"Well, here she is." Phil made a ta-da gesture with his hands as if he had conjured up the salmon from a magician's hat.

"But why are you bringing it here, to the station?" Gwen asked.

Phil turned to look at Gwen. "Cause his dad said Nate'd be here at the station, and he could take it home for him. You know"—he placed his hand on his chest—"it's not my job to ferry fish all over this damn island. I brought it here as a favor."

"Fine. Fine." Nate took a corner of the damaged curtain and ripped it free from the whole before wrapping it around the damp fish. "You know you could have wrapped it in some newspaper, Phil."

"Well, excuse me for upsetting your delicate sensibilities."

Gwen grabbed his arm as he headed back to the station door. "Phil, before you go, this is Kate, our new station manager. Kate, this is Phil Stittle, otherwise known as Fisherman Phil. His boat is the Wet Witch, docked down at Hope Bay. He's a native, like me. Born and raised on the island."

Phil stopped, gave me a silent up-and-down stare, and then pushed open the station door. "I heard about you coming. Another newcomer. Like we need any more of you. You buy up our waterfront, build your mansions, and then clog up the harbor with your fancy boats!" he said and stomped out the door. It slammed shut behind him, the bell tinkling like a friendly afterthought.

"Welcome to Wynter Island," Gwen muttered under her breath

"He doesn't sound like he is on board with the whole 'Let's bring new people to Wynter Island plan."

"No, he's part of the group who wants nothing around here to change. In fact, Phil is probably allergic to change. Breaks out in a rash any time he sees a new house being built."

"I can understand hating change, but it's certainly not practical in the long term. Not for Wynter Island."

"Exactly. Islanders need work to survive, and the island needs taxes to keep these roads paved and the school open. Don't let him bother you. He's like this with everyone." Gwen paused for a moment to gather her thoughts. "Okay, we need a plan. Kate, you start thinking about building ideas. I have an architect who can draw them up for you as soon as you're ready. The Capital Regional District has said they will green-light the permits as soon as possible. Nate, you see if there's any way you can cancel the bingo cards going out in the paper next week. And Bob," She shifted her body closer to him, her tone dipping lower, "if you want to volunteer for the station, you are more than welcome to do so. But not if you're going to be bringing this negative energy into the workplace." Gwen paused, hands-on-hips. "Agreed?"

"Agreed," Nate replied.

Bob stared at me for a moment before turning to Gwen with a shadow of a smile spread across his face. "Sure, Gwen. Agreed."

But there was something in his gaze as he headed out the door of the station, with Nate and his salmon following right behind him, that worried me. The anger still simmered in his green-eyed gaze, along with something else. Determination? Revenge? I wasn't sure.

*Agreed, my ass. I wouldn't trust you as far as I could throw you, Bob Corker.*

# Chapter Ten

"How are you holding up, Kate?"

I took another sip of my wine. After a couple of days of trying to numb my pain with a combination of hard work and copious amounts of tequila, I had texted Shea to see if it was all right for me to stop by.  Margaritas were only going to be a salty stop-gap measure for me.  I needed someone to talk to about everything that had happened.

"Okay, I guess. I met Bob Corker a few days ago."

Shea snorted and put her wineglass down. "And how was Bob? Pleasant as usual?"

"I don't think those are the words I'd use to describe him."

Shea hiccuped to a stop and raised her wineglass back to her lips. "Well, Bob is known on the island for his explosive temper."

"Is there such a thing as a 'non-explosive' temper?"

"It's an inside joke.  Bob was an explosives expert in the army before he retired, and he and Doreen bought the Lind."

"Why on earth did he retire? It sounds like he was in the perfect job for him. Destroy everything! Create havoc!!"

Shea smiled.  "Well, I'm not exactly sure why he retired early.  But one thing I do know is that his bark is definitely worse than his bite. It's just a shame he has such a huge blind spot when it comes to his daughter."

"And I took her job."

"No, you took a job that Bob felt was hers. That's a big difference."

"Either way, he has it in for me now. How is it possible that I created an enemy before I'd even set foot on the island?"

"Don't worry about Bob. Focus on the important stuff."

I took a long sip of my chardonnay. "That's true. I need to figure out where I need to start."

"Start what?"

"My investigation. Finding Daniel's murderer."

"Leave that to Lesley and Stewart. That's their job, not yours. You've got enough on your plate just getting the station up and running."

"No. I have to fix this. I have to find out who killed Daniel."

"No, you don't." Shea placed her glass on the coffee table and reached across to grab my hand. "Running that station and grieving his loss is enough for you to handle right now."

"No," I pulled my hand free with more force than was necessary. "I'm sorry, Shea, but this is what I do. I ask questions. I find answers."

"Well, a murder is a lot different than investigating a corrupt politician."

I shook my head. "I know it looks like it is, but it really isn't. The pieces may be different, but they go together in the same way. There must be a reason why Daniel was coming here to Wynter Island."

"To try and get you back."

"Yes, but it was more than that. He said he had proof he wasn't cheating on me. What changed? Why couldn't he show me that proof months ago? He must have had something new to tell me."

"Okay. Let's say that's true. Daniel's dead. How are you going to find out anything now?"

"I don't know. But that's question number one."

"Question number one?" she laughed. "How many questions are there?'

"Five," I answered without pausing to think.

"Five?"

"Yes. Who. What. Why. Where. When. Who killed Daniel? What changed to make him decide to come out here now? Why would someone on Wynter Island have a reason to murder him?"

"We don't know it was someone from Wynter Island."

"That's true. It could be a tourist, but why would someone intentionally choose to murder Daniel out here on this small island? It would make much more sense to kill him in New York or even Vancouver. It would have offered the murderer far more cover."

Shea weighed this thought for a moment. "Okay. I find it hard to believe one of my neighbors killed anyone, but go on."

"Where and when was he killed?"

"Hopefully, the coroner will be able to answer those."

"Yes."

"You know, Kate, all these questions point to just one suspect."

"I know. Me. I'm the only person who knew Daniel, supposedly knew he was coming, and had a motive for killing him."

"It's a good thing for you that I get suspicious when things fit together too neatly."

I laughed. "I suppose I should say thank you? I'm not sure whether that was a compliment or an insult."

Shea took another sip of her chardonnay. "I'm not really sure either."

A clunking sound came from outside the farmhouse. I looked over to see a white panel van pulling into Shea's driveway with Royal Canadian Legion #492 written across its side. Harald retrieved a cardboard box placed from the passenger seat. Holding the box, he ran up the steps and knocked lightly on the front door.

"What is Harald doing?" I asked. "Delivering a package?"

"I've no idea. Come on in, Harald," Shea shouted. "It's not locked."

The front door opened, and Harald stepped forward into the foyer.

"Sorry to bother you, ladies," he said, his words lilting with his musical Danish accent. "I have something for you, Shea. Well, that is, if you're willing to take him."

"Him?" she repeated.

Harald tilted the cardboard box toward us. Inside, curled up in an old blanket, lay an orange cat. A tiger cat, or at least that's what I called them when I was a child. Thick orange fur with darker orange stripes, a bright white muzzle, and large golden eyes.

Shea stood up and placed one hand into the box to gently scratch his ear. "Where did you come from, Cat?"

"I've been calling him Oskar," Harald supplied and then blushed. "But you don't have to call him that if you don't want to."

Shea smiled into Harald's face. "Oskar sounds like a perfect name to me. How did you end up with him, Harald?"

"He's been hanging around the dumpster at the Legion. He showed up about a week ago, no collar, quite tame, so I assumed he was a local cat. But he keeps coming back, and I can tell he's getting thinner."

I moved closer to the box and put one hand inside to run over the smooth fur of his back. He lazily glanced up at me, his golden eyes huge in his furry face. My fingers massaged the area of his ribs, but there was still enough fat there to know he hadn't been starving.

"Not too thin yet," I said.

"Well, I may have been feeding him a bit," Harald mumbled and reached in to run a hand over the cat's head. Oskar leaned his head into Harald's hand and squeezed his eyes shut with an expression of drowsy bliss.

"You do know, Harald, that's the best way to ensure an animal returns," Shea said. "By giving them food?"

Harald flushed a deeper shade of pink, the color clashing against his birthmark. "I know, but he looked so hungry." Harald looked at us, his grey-blue eyes pleading. "Kurt has allergies, so I can't keep him. Can you take him?"

Shea reached in and pulled Oskar out of the box, his body elongating like an accordion before her. There was no fear in his eyes, only a quizzical gaze that seemed to ask whether she, too, was willing to feed him.

"Well, Oskar, you've found yourself a temporary new home."

Harald blew out a sigh of relief. "Thanks, Shea."

Shea cradled Oskar in her arms like a limp rag doll. "What's one more animal when you've already got too many."

I reached over to scratch underneath Oskar's chin. "It's been nice meeting you, Oskar, but I've got to get going."

"More questions to answer?"

I smiled and nodded my head yes.

"Sure you don't want a cat?" Shea laughingly offered as she and Harald followed me out onto the front porch.

"No, I do not need a cat," I said firmly.

At that moment, I caught a glimpse of Jupiter sitting in the middle of the driveway and extended my hand to him. "Hey, Jupiter!"

He ran over, licked my fingers, and then sat. I patted his head for a few moments before trying to step past him. He stood up, moved a few feet away, and sat down again, effectively blocking my way.

Shea laughed from the front porch. "You know, I am up one animal. If you take Jupiter, I'll be back to where I was."

"I don't think so." I stepped over and around him before running towards the station pickup. "I'm getting out of here before he gets any other ideas."

His hot breath panted against the back of my legs as I pulled open the driver's side door and jumped in.

"Okay, I'm going to get going," I called through the open window.

Shea pointed in the direction of the truck bed. "Not until you get rid of stowaways."

I twisted around in my seat to face Jupiter. He sat in the middle of the truck bed, staring through the cab's back window at me.

"Are you kidding me?" I got out and walked around to the back of the trunk, Shea and Harald joining me.

"Jupiter, c'mon, get outta there," Shea commanded.

Jupiter looked at her briefly before returning his attention to me. She handed Oskar to Harald and reached to grab Jupiter, but he darted to one side, avoiding any attempts to restrain him. I dashed around to the other side of the truck and made a lunge for his collar. He skittishly darted away and danced around the edge of the truck bed.

Shea stopped and slapped her hands on her hips. "He is part Australian shepherd, you know, Kate. He can herd the crap out of us if he wants to."

"What are you saying? That I just leave him there?"

Shea leaned against the side of the truck and examined Jupiter. "I mean, I guess we could both climb in and try and pin him in a corner, but...I don't know. For some crazy reason, he has decided he belongs to you." She looked over at me. "Is it so hard for you to take him home?"

I stood there, my mouth open in shock. "You want me…to take this dog…now? Because I don't have enough other things on my plate at the moment?"

She reached out a hand to Jupiter, but he refused to move. "Yes, I do. Would it be so terrible for you to have something in your life right now that loves you?"

"It wouldn't be terrible, no, but it's the responsibility. Who's going to look after him when I work?"

"Just take him with you. He will most likely ignore everyone. And he won't make any noise. He doesn't bark."

I pinched my lips together into a stubborn line. "What about food and supplies and, and, everything? I'm not prepared to have a dog. I don't even know if I *want* to have a dog."

"I can give you some food and one of our spare leashes. Also, some poop bags. You must have bowls at the cottage you can use for food and water. You don't need anything else."

"Kate," Harald added, "he needs you."

I turned in consternation to look at Jupiter. His gaze, once again, was trained on my face, almost as if I was some kind of messiah.

*Are you looking for a savior, Jupiter? Because right now, I'm on God's shit list.*

Would it truly be so terrible to take this dog? I couldn't believe I was even considering this. It was odd, but the thought made me feel almost…happy. Comforted. Maybe there was a part of me that needed a savior as much as Jupiter did.

"Get the food and leash, Shea. I'll take the damn dog."

# Chapter Eleven

I spotted Michael's Subaru Forester as soon as it turned onto the road that led to the Sydney Cliffs. With a small skid of gravel, he pulled into the small parking lot that had been carved out of the rainforest. I leaned across and pushed open the passenger door of my truck, allowing Jupiter to leap out and sniff the rocky loam.

Michael had messaged me first thing that morning to meet him at the Sydney Cliffs, of all places, to discuss some news on Daniel's case. It was my first visit there, although I had driven by it numerous times. The sizable park had always been closed, a large No Entry sign blocking the entrance.

Jupiter ran right back to my side as soon as I clambered out of the truck and stood expectantly, his gaze focused on me with laser-like intensity.

"Are you excited, Jupiter?" I squatted down and scratched him behind one ear. "I think you're happy to be going for a walk. Finally, a normal dog reaction from you. If you keep this up, you're going to be begging for food scraps in no time."

"Don't encourage him."

Michael had joined me, his tall body looming behind me like a basketball player blocking out the sun. His naturally olive skin held a faint hint of winter color, probably from skiing at Whistler. His body, fit but not overly so, seemed comfortable in his jeans and navy-blue fleece, the denim cuffs beginning to fray slightly along the edges.

"Is this where you usually meet your clients, Michael? In the rainforest?"

His low laugh bubbled up from behind me. "No. I have an office in Harrow Town. But why sit inside on a beautiful day like this, when I can show you the Sydney Cliffs?"

"Do I need a coat? I've got a windbreaker in the back."

Michael glanced up at the steep path of ferns and evergreens in front of us. I followed his gaze to the top of the canopy of trees. There was a small flash of blue sky.

"I think you'll be okay.  C'mon, Jupiter"—he clapped his hands together—"let's go for a walk!"

Jupiter's head tilted and gave Michael a hefty serving of side-eye.

I laughed. "He's not a social dog, Michael. For some strange reason, he and I have bonded.  That's about as far as he's willing to go for human companionship."

"Okay, well, you can ignore me if you want to, Jupiter. But either way, we're going for a hike!" Michael waved me ahead of him.

The trail was steep and slippery, the soil underfoot dangerously moist and fragile. Thick profusions of lime-green ferns grew abundantly beside emerald moss-covered tree trunks, many of them half-fallen over and decaying against the hillside. The firs still standing grew a vertical forty-five degrees against the hillside.

"We're lucky to be able to hike up here today. It's been closed to visitors for the past few months." Michael said, pointing to the No Entry sign leaning against a tree.

"Yeah, I saw Gwen moving the sign into place the other day. Is the ground unstable?"

He nodded. "Yes. If we've had a particularly wet spring, the path here becomes too dangerous to use. Luckily, it's dried enough to get us up to the top."

"*If* we get up to the top," I mumbled under my breath.

"I heard that, Kate. Don't worry. It's safe. But still, be careful. It's steep in places."

Jupiter ran up ahead of us, snuffling his nose noisily in the surrounding underbrush.

"How long have you lived on Wynter Island, Michael?"

"Quite a while. Since Nate was in elementary school. We lived in your cottage while we had our home built."

I looked ahead, the path slicing a milk chocolate scar into the hillside. Half-split logs had been placed into the earth to be used as steps at the points where it was too steep to climb.

"Anna is no longer practicing law?"

"Yes. She's more interested in politics. The Green Party. She has a part-time position at the party headquarters in Victoria." He paused again, and when he finally spoke, I could hear a forced lightness in his tone. "It's great for her. She misses Vancouver, so it's nice for her to get off the island."

I turned to look back at him. The tall firs cast a purplish shadow across his features even though I could see the blue sky high above us.

"She didn't want to move to Wynter Island?"

"No," he paused, one foot balanced on a log, "we both wanted Nathan to have a safe, healthy environment to grow up in."

"But?"

"But," he hesitated, "it's proven harder for Anna. Nathan and I are perfectly happy with the ocean and the trees, but Anna likes a bit more cosmopolitan flair." He pointed towards the top of the hill. "We're never going to get to the top at this pace."

"Sorry," I started back up the path again. "What's the news you needed to tell me?"

"Stewart called me this morning."

"Umm-hmm?"

"The coroner in Victoria has the results of Daniel's autopsy."

Daniel's autopsy. It sounded insane, an impossible blending of words, like dog's rainbow saxophone. It might sound nonsensical, but it was real. Very real.

"Okay."

"The closest time of death they can come up with is sometime between noon and six on Thursday."

"Last week?"

"Yes. It gets tricky when the body is kept cold by the ocean, but the coroner believes it's a fairly accurate guess."

"Right." I focused on Jupiter's tail swaying on the path ahead of me, as if that could somehow block out Michael's words. "Silver, gray, and black," I repeated under my breath. "Silver, gray, and black."

"The coroner is pretty sure it wasn't suicide or an accident."

Blinded by the news, I stumbled over a tree root. Michael grabbed my elbow from behind. I started at the shock of his warm fingers on my bare skin, the pressure of his hand gripping me from behind.

"I'm fine. Go on."

"Alright. If you're sure?"

I nodded and returned my attention to Jupiter ahead of me.

"If he had drowned himself, either accidentally or on purpose, his lungs would have filled up with water. That's why there are so many diving recoveries of drowning victims. The water in the lungs makes the body sink to the bottom."

"But his body didn't sink to the bottom. He floated."

"Yes, which means he was dead when he went into the ocean. Drowned bodies do float, but only once they've decayed enough for gases to raise them to the surface."

"But what about the contusions to his face?"

"He appears to have been hit several times. The coroner thinks it may have been more than one person as the abrasions are on different parts of his head and appear to have been made with different weapons."

"Weapons. Meaning this was premeditated."

Silence stretched into a few moments. "Watch out up ahead, Kate. One step can get a bit loose from time to time."

I jumped over the loose piece of wood, sending a rock tumbling down the hillside. I watched its bouncing path downwards. My truck and Michael's car looked significantly smaller from up here.

"We're almost at the top," Michael said.

Jupiter disappeared over the top of the hill.

"It was premeditated, wasn't it, Michael?"

Another silence. "Yes, it was."

"And the only person on this island who would have any reason to kill

Daniel is me."

"That we know of."

But was I really the only one? There had to be some reason for Daniel's murder. If it was premeditated, then that meant someone on Wynter Island had planned his murder.

*Someone planned his murder!*

The fury whipped through my veins, like an infection spreading out from its host.

*Why? Why did someone do this?*

Could there be someone else on Wynter Island who knew Daniel? Had something happened here during one of his many sailing trips? Something so terrible that it made someone angry enough to kill him?

I took the last big step up to the grassy top of the hill. Stretched out in front of me were granite slabs, heading to the cliff edge before dropping into oblivion.

*Just like my life.*

We sat down on the sun-warmed shelf of stone. Clumps of moss had been gouged from it, almost as if animals had been hunting or digging. Below us, the rest of the Gulf Islands chain loomed like strange bristling sea creatures surfacing out of the ocean.

"That island is Pender," Michael said, pointing directly in front of us, "and the long, low one behind it to the right is Saturna. Mayne is the one peeking out behind Pender on the left, and there's Galliano, stretching north over there. If you lean out, you can see the edge of Saltspring to our far left. It's pretty much level with Wynter."

"Beautiful. It's beautiful."

Free of the forest behind us, the full force of the wind swept in off the water. The sharp saltiness of the air filled my lungs. Luckily, the sun's warmth neutralized the cold.

"Yes, it is. You know, I've always said this is the prettiest spot on Wynter."

"I can see why. What else did Stewart learn about Daniel?"

"Well, they tracked down the cell number he used to text you. It belongs to a woman who lives in Vancouver. She was on the nine-thirty ferry from

Tsawwassen last Thursday. Daniel asked her if he could borrow her phone to send a quick text as his cell was dead."

I could see it. The wide-open eyes, the gentle smile: of course, she had given him her phone. Who wouldn't trust Daniel Apollinar?

"That means…"

"He arrived on Wynter Island about eleven fifteen or so on Thursday morning."

"But I was down there on Thursday morning. Harrow Village. The Hope Bay ferry dock. I stopped at the Lind General Store to get my P.O. Box and then had coffee at the bakery with Gwen."

"You didn't see him, right?"

I shook my head, my mind tripping over a single image: the white and blue ferry docking in Hope Bay with all those passengers standing at the bow. Had one of them been Daniel? Had he been looking towards me, neither of us realizing the other was right there?

"Stewart is still waiting for the CCTV footage from the Tsawwassen terminal and Hope Bay dock, as well as all the onboard footage from the ferry. Hopefully, we will spot Daniel on it."

"We know when he arrived. What else?"

"Lesley has been checking with the local B&B owners to see if anyone had a reservation for him."

"And?"

"Harald had one. At the B&B he owns with Kurt."

"Harald from the Legion. With the—" I gestured to the left side of my face.

"Yes, that's him. Daniel booked it online last week. For three nights."

"Enough time to find me and force me into listening to him."

"Yes."

"But he never made it to the B&B?"

"No. When Daniel didn't show up by nine on Thursday evening, Harald called his cell phone, and it went directly to voice mail."

"Because Daniel was most likely dead by that time."

"Yes. Probably already in the ocean."

"With his phone."

"We think."

"Damn!" I grabbed a loose stone and threw it with all my might over the cliff edge.

Jupiter skittered back to me, tail drooping, afraid the stone had been meant for him.

"No, Jupiter, it's all right." I buried my face in his long, fine-haired coat. "I'm not angry with you. I'm just…angry. Michael, is the Salish Views the only B&B on the island?"

He shook his head. "No, there are several."

"Why do you think Daniel chose that one?"

He shrugged. "Probably just picked one randomly off the internet. Why?"

"I don't know. Just hunting. Hunting for something, some clue, to explain why all of this happened."

I stood and approached the cliff edge, Jupiter hovering beside me.

"What are you doing, Kate?"

I leaned over the edge and gazed down at the hillocks of grass growing into the vertical side of the cliff.

"Kate?"

"It's okay. I'm okay." I could see the white fringe of waves smashing the cliff face beneath me. "You know, I've always been afraid of the water. Even as a little kid. Even before what happened to Aziz." A seal popped up out of the ocean and then slipped effortlessly back underwater. "When I was a kid, my family, my dad, my sister, and I, would spend part of our summers up at Georgian Bay in Ontario. We rented the same cottage every year. And every day we would go to the beach. That's what you do on a summer holiday at the lake, isn't it? You put on your swimsuit and some sunscreen, pack up your plastic bucket and shovel, and trek down to the lake. My older sister, Lizzie, knew I was scared of the water and teased me mercilessly about it."

"Older siblings have a tendency to do that."

"Yeah, well, Lizzie was a master at it. She would pretend she was going to throw me off the dock or pull me out into deeper water, knowing I couldn't swim very well. A back float and a poor dog paddle was all I could manage. Sometimes she would swim underwater and pinch at my legs, pretending to be a trout. I would scream and run out of the water."

"Didn't your dad do anything to stop it?"

I shook my head. "He thought it was just kids roughhousing. At least until the day she pushed me off the dock and into water that was deeper than she thought." I glanced back at Michael. "You know, people say you learn to swim if you're thrown in the deep end. Well, they're wrong. You panic, flail around, take in water, and start to drown."

"Oh my God! What happened?"

"Lizzie realized what she had done and jumped in to save me. Dad dove in off the dock to help. The two of them dragged me out of the water."

"Were you okay?"

"Physically, yes, but I never went in the water again."

I pushed the sudden image of the lapping waters of the Kabul River lit only by the moon's glow away from my mind.

"What happened to Lizzie?"

"She was grounded for the rest of the summer. And just to twist the knife a little bit more, I scratched up her favorite Backstreet Boys CD."

"Oooh, brutal."

I grinned. "It was. She cried herself to sleep for a week over it."

"C'mon." Michael stood up, gesturing me back from the cliff edge. "Enough revisiting the past. You've got a whole new life on Wynter Island to look forward to." He brushed some of the loose moss off his jeans. "Let's get headed back down."

"Okay. Jupiter! Let's go!" I called out.

Jupiter ran back from the cliff edge and skittered ahead of us down the narrow trail.

"Be careful, Kate. It's not as easy as it looks to get back down. The loose soil can suddenly shift under your feet. You wouldn't be the first person to slide down this hill on your ass."

"What a lovely image."

I jumped over the loose log at the top of the path and landed off-balance, the dirt skidding out from beneath my sneakers. Before I could even make a sound, two strong arms encircled my waist from behind and pulled me back.

"Whoa. What did I tell you?"

The tautness of his chest behind me contrasted with the soft fabric of his navy fleece against my bare arms. I breathed in his scent: clean, fresh, like soap and seawater. For a moment, I relaxed into his arms. Who had last held me like this?

*Daniel. Of course, it was Daniel.*

"Kate. Earth to Kate. You're okay. You can start walking again."

Jupiter, who had run down the hill ahead of us, raced back up the path. He lowered his head, his hackles raised.

"Jupiter! What are you doing!" I called out.

Jupiter raised his upper lip slightly, vibrating with menace, and let out a long, low growl at Michael.

He quickly released me, and I felt a pang of loss at the sense of separation. "I wasn't trying to hurt her, Jupiter. I was just saving your mistress from falling down the hillside, that's all." He took a few steps back up the path.

I knelt down and gingerly held out my hand to Jupiter. Was this another side of him that I hadn't yet seen? But after giving one final suspicious glance at Michael, he trotted up to me, his hackles subsiding. "It's okay, boy. I'm okay." His head darted forward, and his small tongue popped out to give me one quick kiss on the nose.

"Let's get going, Kate. I don't want to give that dog another chance to come at me."

I stood up, relieved that Jupiter's moment of protective anger was over. "He wouldn't do that!"

Michael stepped past me and continued down the hillside, talking back over his shoulder. "Yeah, well, you also thought he was silent, didn't you?"

# Chapter Twelve

"Dougie, could you move your camera a little bit to the left?"

I pointed towards the brightly colored sailboats bobbing in Hope Bay harbor. Dougie swiveled the camera on its tripod to focus on one of the larger boats.

"Like this?'

"Yeah. Everyone else, can you put the equipment away in the truck? Now that I've finished my little spiel about how wonderful CWYN is going to be, we just have to let Dougie get some b-roll."

Dougie and Greg had arrived at the station for the first time that morning, two more to add to my small stable of volunteers. Dougie looked to be about thirty, with an early receding hairline and a ginger beard. "I'm from Newfoundland originally. Came out west for the oil fields," he informed me in his thick accent as we packed up the truck with equipment at the station, "but I couldn't make it stick. So, I ended up here. Now I do a little bit of everything. My main business is trees: cutting 'em down, pruning 'em, carting 'em away."

"And you are?" I turned towards the other young man. He was maybe twenty-five or twenty-six. His face matched his body, long and thin, with slightly sunken cheekbones and a general air of unhealthiness. When he moved nearer to me, a particularly pungent mixture of Axe cologne and marijuana wafted over.

"I'm Greg." His voice was sibilant and soft. "Greg Douglass."

"Greg grew up on the island," Bob said. "Lives with his mom, Shelley, up near Coho Bay."

"Oh yes, I met her at the Legion dinner."

Greg nodded his head, his smile slow and deliberate. Was he high? I wasn't sure. But what could I do about it anyway? Make him pee in a cup? He was a volunteer. His private life was his own business.

"So, what do you do, Greg?"

Before he could answer, Bob spoke, his tone as brusque and aggressive as it had been on the first day I met him. "Nothing, that's what he does. A whole lotta nothing."

Greg turned to look at Bob, a wave of anger rippling over his placid face. "You don't have to be a dick about it, Bob."

"I'm not being a dick. I'm just telling the truth. When was the last time you had a forty-hour-a-week job? Well, I guess other than when you were," Bob bit down on his final words, leaving the remainder of his sentence hanging in mid-air. Everyone waited for him to continue, but he said nothing.

Dougie stepped in to break the awkward silence. "Greg and I are kinda jack of all trades, Kate."

"Yeah, we do all the odd jobs that need doing around the island." Greg glared at Bob as he returned to his packing. "The shit other people don't want to do."

The tension, luckily, lessened as we drove to Hope Bay to shoot the short promotional video for the station. Bob's negative energy, however, still hovered like a malevolent presence over the group.

"The ferry is just coming in. Do you want me to get some shots, Kate?"

I turned to look as the large white ferry turned in a wide berth and lumbered into the bay. "Yes, Dougie. That would be great."

How many days had it been since I stood here and watched Daniel's ferry enter the harbor? Ten, maybe? It felt like forever. What would have happened if I had stayed out on that sidewalk for a few minutes longer? Continued to watch as the ferry pulled into the dock, the workers connecting the ramp to the dock. Would Daniel's long-legged frame have come walking off the ferry and up the hill towards me? And then what? What would I have done?

Been shocked, angry, most likely. Maybe attempted to duck into the general store? But he would have followed me in regardless, grabbing me by the arm and insisting that I listen to him. And he would not have continued up the hill and into the arms of a murderer.

A cough behind me roused me from my thoughts. I turned around to see Phil standing there, dressed in his filthy overalls, his grey hair askew under his oil-stained baseball cap.

"Hi, Phil. How are you doing?"

He stared me straight in the eye, his lips clamped in an unforgiving line. "Whose dog?" He nodded towards where Jupiter had curled up on a spot of grass.

Apparently, the art of small talk was not one of Phil's strengths.

"Mine."

"Looks like one of Shea's."

"He was. Is there something I can help you with, Phil?"

"When do you want your fish?"

"My fish? I didn't know I wanted any fish."

He waved one oil-stained hand toward me, wafting the smell of diesel fuel and fish bait with it. "You know, for your TV thing. Nate was saying you'd want a big salmon this week."

"Oh, you mean for Fish Bingo."

"Yeah, whatever. I don't care what you call it. I just need to know when you want 'em and how much you're gonna pay me for 'em."

"Well, we're not going to be starting any productions until the studio construction is finished. Fish Bingo won't be starting for a couple of months."

"But the bingo cards just went out in the Wynter Island Times!"

I turned to where Nate was working, breaking down equipment with Bob. "Nate? You weren't able to stop the bingo cards from going out in the newspaper?"

A wash of crimson spread across his cheeks. "No, I'm sorry, Kate. I couldn't. I was going to talk to you about it today."

Phil waved his hand in front of my face to draw my attention back to him. "Are you saying you aren't going to be doing Fish Bingo this coming Thursday? I made a point of keeping my card out of the newspaper and everything."

"You were going to play, Phil? But it's your fish that's the main prize."

He snorted. "So? My salmon will taste as good in my belly as it will in anyone else's."

"But there are rules about participating in contests that you are working for."

Phil rolled his eyes and continued. "What about all the other folks? A lot of people on the island kept their bingo cards from the paper. They're all going to be expecting to play Fish Bingo on Thursday night. And they're not going to be happy if there's no damn show or salmon."

I sighed. How could I put out a live broadcast without a studio or even a properly trained crew? I didn't want to disappoint my audience before I had even begun, and yet ...

"Perhaps I could set up a livestream on YouTube. Most people on the island seem to have some sort of access to the internet. But where could I shoot it?"

"The library? The Community Centre?" Nate suggested. "Maybe Bob would let you shoot it in the restaurant at the hotel?"

All eyes turned to Bob. His face had gone rigid, emotionless, and yet I could sense his inner battle. Should he do the right thing and help the new station manager? Or surrender to bitterness and revenge and allow me to fail?

*Well, I know what that answer is going to be.*

"I think we have something on at the hotel that evening," he finally replied.

"No, you don't," Nate said, turning to look at Bob with a mixture of confusion and irritation. "The Lind isn't even open until the Victoria Day weekend. You must have your dates mixed up, Bob. I'll run across and check with Doreen."

Nate put down the camera and had started across the street when Bob's irritated voice halted him in his steps.

"Fine. You can use the restaurant," he glared at me, supplying the most ungracious offer I have ever received. "But you're going to have to clean up after yourselves!"

I smiled. "Sure, I can do that. But I still don't know how we get the news out to everyone on the island? You know, about where they can watch the broadcast."

"Well, um, I can tell people," Phil said.

"I was hoping for something a bit more expansive than that, Phil."

Phil bristled. "I know lots of people on this island, you know."

"Of course you do, Phil. But how do we let everyone, like *everyone*, know?"

"Once you get people talking, believe me, it'll spread faster than shit through a goose."

"Shit through a what?"

"Shit through a goose. Don't tell me you haven't heard that one before."

"How about the island Facebook page?" Greg suggested. "That's the best place to get out any news on the island."

Dougie laughed. "Or complain about politics."

"Or people's dogs barking," Greg added.

"Yeah, they're right. Post it on the Facebook page, Kate, and word will get around pretty quickly," Nate agreed.

"Yeah, just like shit through a…"

My cold stare caused Phil to stutter to a stop. "I get the picture, Phil. I'll write something up and post it on the Facebook page."

Dougie pushed the power button on his camera. "Alright, I got a nice shot of the ferry coming in, so I think I'm done."

Phil, pleased that he was going to be selling his salmon, stomped off in the direction of his cottage. We piled the remaining gear into the truck and headed back to the studio. Nate was unusually quiet on the return trip. Was he still upset by the mess he had made of Fish Bingo? Perhaps I needed to have another talk with him. Bob's mood, on the other hand, had brightened considerably. *He must be feeling better about the station*, I foolishly thought.

When I pulled the camera out the next morning to review the previous day's footage, there were a few seconds of my introduction before the screen went suddenly black. Nothing more. I fast forwarded and then reversed. Nothing. Somebody had accidentally turned off the camera in mid-shoot.

"Damn it," I muttered and placed the camera back down onto the desk.

Okay, I absolutely had to have a talk with Nate.  First, the mess of Fish Bingo, and then he accidentally stops recording in the middle of the promotional video! I paused. Whose face had stared back at me as I talked to the camera yesterday? No, it wasn't Nate. It was…Bob.

Had Bob stopped shooting on purpose in order to ruin my attempt to promote the station?

"That bastard!"

# Chapter Thirteen

"Hello? Hello?"

Still mostly asleep, I picked up my cell phone and held it to my ear. It kept on playing my ringtone, Alanis Morissette's *Ironic*.

"Damn!" I removed it from my ear and stabbed blindly at the screen with a finger. "Hello?"

"Kate?"

"Yes."

"It's Gwen. Have you had a chance to go on your phone or laptop this morning?"

"Gwen, I don't even know what time it is. I was dead to the world up until about thirty seconds ago."

"Oh, yes, sorry."

"That's okay. Why are you calling?"

Beep. Beep. Beep. Beep. Another call signal buzzed into my ear.

"Sorry, Gwen, someone's calling on the other line. I'll be back in a sec." I stabbed at the phone, and the line cut away to a new caller. "Hello?"

"Kate? It's me, Shea."

"Shea, why are you calling me at this time in the morning? By the way, what time is it?"

"Six-thirty."

"Six-thirty! Are you kidding me?"

"Sorry for waking you up, but—"

Beep. Beep. Beep. Beep.

"It's Gwen. She's on the other line."

Another frantic stabbing at the phone. "Hello? Gwen?"

"No, it's Michael."

"Michael? What the hell is going on? Shea and Gwen are on the other lines."

"Okay, ask Gwen if we can meet at her place at eight-thirty. We can talk then. Bye." Michael hung up with an abrupt click.

Using my fingertip, I tapped the phone button. "Hello? Who is this?"

"It's me. Gwen."

"Hold on, Gwen. Shea's still on the other line. Oh, Michael wants to know if it's okay to meet at your house at eight-thirty? I have no idea why."

"Yes, that sounds good. See you here at eight-thirty."

"But, Gwen, why are we meeting at your house?"

Silence. Gwen had already hung up.

I hit the screen again. "Shea?"

"Yes?"

"I have no idea what's going on, but Michael and Gwen were on the other lines, and now we're all supposed to meet at Gwen's house in two hours."

"Oh, I can't come. I'm working at the library today."

I blew out a gust of air. "Shea, what is going on?"

"It's the Wynter Island Facebook page."

"So?"

"Well, it's better if you look at it yourself than have me try and describe it to you over the phone."

* * *

With Jupiter as my faithful sidekick, I followed the winding gravel driveway up to the top of Wynter Mountain. The drive was quite steep, dangerously so. The view from the top, however, was breathtaking, especially on a spring day, with the ocean glimmering with crystals of sunlight.

*I'd hate to do this drive in bad weather, but this view might make it worthwhile.*

The drive wound to a stop beside a white clapboard heritage homestead. Hydrangeas and rhododendrons bloomed in planted beds around the front porch, big blousy blossoms of white and teal trailing over the railings. Behind the house, a row of three long greenhouses sat along with an assortment of farm equipment.

The acreage around the farmhouse teemed with fruit trees. In one area, gnarled apple trees blossomed while cherry trees just started to come into bud. The fluffy white-pink blossoms of the pear trees floated in a miasma down the mountainside.

"C'mon, Jupe."

I climbed out of the truck with Jupiter following right behind me. I headed up onto the wide covered porch which encircled the farmhouse and knocked on the front door. Nothing.

"Over here," a woman's voice called out to my right.

I sidestepped a few feet over to see Gwen's head poking out from a side door.

"No one uses the front door unless they're being married or buried. Everyone comes in through the kitchen here."

Jupiter and I followed Gwen into a side wing of the house. It was really a single large room—part family room, part kitchen—with an ancient black cast-iron wood stove sitting against the far wall. The black and white cracked tiles in front of it had seen better days, as had the rest of the room. The furniture looked as if it hadn't been changed in decades.

"This is where I live, except for maybe the porch in the summer." Gwen stepped over to a yellowing linoleum counter and poured out a mug of coffee for me. "The parlor and dining room are all for show."

"Hi, Michael." I nodded to where Michael sat, nursing a cup of coffee at the pine kitchen table. His tousled salt and pepper hair and general air of having just rolled out of bed made him look quite handsome.

*No. No. No. I'm not thinking about that!*

"Gwen, that's a lot of house to have just for show." I sat down at the table and took my mug of coffee.

"Well, you had to have somewhere nice to entertain the minister and have all your family gatherings." Gwen waved her arm around the kitchen, with its soot-stained walls and beadboard paneling, the air rich with the traces of old wood fires and musty antiques. "But this is where everyone really lived. It has the two things you truly need: heat and food."

Gwen joined us at the table after attempting and failing to give Jupiter a friendly pat. "That is one weird dog you've got there, Kate. Anyway, I'm guessing you had a chance to look at this?" Gwen pulled her open laptop across the kitchen table and placed it where we could all see it.

"Yes, I did."

I hesitated for a moment before looking at the computer, remembering the horror I had felt when I had opened mine after Shea's call. Why couldn't I simply pretend that none of this had happened? Sit here and have a nice cup of coffee with Gwen and Michael? Just chat like normal people and somehow make this all go away?

I allowed myself a mental snort of disgust. *Like Daniel's murder might go away? Like being a suspect might go away? Just grit your teeth and get through it, girl.*

I finally pulled the laptop closer to me. It was open to the webpage for the Wynter Island Facebook group. "For those who live here, or wish they did" was the tagline across the top of the page with a photograph of the Lind Hotel at Hope Bay.

The first of many posts flashed in bright colors at the top of the screen. "Do you know the whole truth about Kate Zoë Thomas, CWYN's station manager?" The next lurid post, blue text on a white background, said: "There's a reason why we don't know much about her past. She has been hiding it from us! And she has a good reason to keep it secret!" The next one was a crimson background with large black letters: "If you don't believe me, check these links out."

And cascading down the post were links to news stories about my capture and Aziz's death: TV producer and reporter kidnapped by Taliban; Murder of Afghani interpreter working for WGBH's Dispatches; Lucky break for PBS TV crew based in Afghanistan, etc., etc. The list went on and on. The final post was the most damning.

"So, her interpreter was murdered in Afghanistan, and then her ex-boyfriend is murdered here on Wynter Island. Everywhere she goes, people seem to end up dead. But that's just a coincidence, right? Or is it? Perhaps we should be worried about another murder occurring here on our island? Is this someone we really want living in our community?"

And there was a photo of me with a black line drawn diagonally across my face.

"Well, that didn't take long to come out," I steadied my shaking hand to close the lid of the laptop with an audible snick. "So much for getting a fresh start."

"It's slanderous," Michael said, "and wildly inflammatory."

Gwen took a long meditative sip of coffee. "And it smells of a kind of vigilantism that hasn't been seen on Wynter Island since the Second World War."

"Someone called the Truth Warrior posted it. Does anyone know who that is?"

Gwen and Michael both shook their heads.

"No idea. I've never heard that screen name before," Michael said. "I'm not even sure who the administrator is for the island Facebook page."

"Doreen Corker," Gwen said and raised her hand to stop both of us before we could say anything. "Doreen didn't have anything to do with this. She may have married Bob, but she isn't stupid. She created the Facebook page so that everyone would have somewhere online to discuss stuff."

*But what about Bob? Does he have access to her computer?*

"I used the Facebook page last night to let everyone know about Fish Bingo," I replied.

"See," Gwen said. "It's useful. In fact, I'm guessing she'll delete these posts as soon as she sees them."

"It doesn't really matter now anyway."

"Why?" Michael asked. "You want this stuff to stay online, Kate?"

"No, but whether it stays or goes, it doesn't really matter. Everyone on the island will know about it. Probably already do."

"Unfortunately, she's right," Gwen said.

"Who did it, though?" I asked, half to myself. "And why? Would Bob really be stupid enough to do something so blatant? On his wife's Facebook page?

Surely, he would have chosen another way to try and get back at me for taking the job away from Ria."

*Maybe like sabotaging my video shoot?*

"And who on Wynter has the training to do something like this? To create a fake user profile, hack into the private Wynter Facebook page, and then post this crap?"

Gwen and Michael mulled this over for a few moments before Gwen finally spoke.

"Will. Will Sixto out on the Reserve."

*　*　*

The road was empty when I headed out from Wynter Mountain to Tsawout Reserve No. 9, save for a doe with her three fawns eating grass along the side of the road. Gwen had informed me that the entire Sixto family was off-island: the two sons at the WSANEC Tribal school in Saanich, their mom, Selesia, looking after a sick aunt over there.

"Go talk to Sam," Gwen had said. "He has a wealth of knowledge about everything, especially what's going on at the Reserve. Who knows, he might be able to tell you something. He is, after all, Selesia's brother and the boy's uncle."

I turned on to Rte. 97 and headed north from Harrow Town. I continued north, passing the small store/pizza place in Lettucetown. It was surrounded by, not surprisingly, lettuce, acres of it, growing in vinyl-wrapped greenhouses. Next was St. Andrews Anglican Church, perfect for an English village mystery with its fieldstone steeple and rose garden.

Why would the kid do this? I mean, what was his motivation? Was it because I was new to the island? Was that why I had been targeted? Or was it because I took the job at CWYN? If Ria had gotten the job and I had never arrived, would any of this have happened?

The highway angled sharply left toward the western side of the island.

Was it Ria then, not Bob, who was the key to all of this? But why Daniel? What connection could Ria possibly have with Daniel?

A large sign loomed on the road up ahead of me. Left for Oceanica Salmon Fishery, Tsawout Reserve No. 9, and Crimson Bay. Straight ahead for Salish Winds Resort. Right for Coho Bay and W'en'ewin Provincial Park.

"Okay, so left it is."

I turned and followed the smaller road until another colorful sign stopped me.

"You are now entering the property of the Tsawout First Nation. Our members are exercising their Douglas Treaty rights as defined in the treaty between James Douglas and the Saanich tribes, signed on Feb. 11, 1852."

"Okay, that's quite the welcome sign," I informed Jupiter, who was riding shotgun with his nose stuck out the window.

I took my foot off the brake and allowed the truck's momentum to carry us forward. Deep fissures cut through the tarmac, making the road bumpy and uneven. A dog barked loudly from a front yard. With its plain stucco houses and tumbledown fences, you could feel the sense of loss. Loss of resources, loss of culture, loss of identity: those were the real problems here.

Sam Hanks' house, I had been told, was the rancher overlooking the ocean. It looked nicer than the others, but still, a far cry from the gorgeous waterfront mansion some weekender would have built on a similar plot of land outside of the Reserve.

I pulled into the gravel driveway and stopped for a moment to listen to the quiet. No people or cars, no tractors or farm noises. Only open fields and the distant sound of gulls squawking overhead.

Sam's front yard consisted of long beach grass interspersed with the granite slabs that rimmed the island's waterfront. A wooden sign had been placed at the driveway's edge with a thunderbird carved into the right corner: *Dr. Sam Hanks, Indigenous Consultation & Engagement.*

"That's pretty impressive," I murmured to Jupiter as we walked up to the front door. "I hope he likes dogs, Jupiter, or you're going to have to wait in the truck."

I knocked on the front door, which was followed immediately by the sound of a dog barking inside. Its nails skittered across the wood floor as it ran toward the door.

"Well, he's got a dog, Jupe, so you might be in luck."

The front door opened, and a young black lab bounced out onto the front step. Jupiter gave it the side-eye treatment, which accomplished absolutely nothing. He stood there balefully while the lab sniffed and pawed around him.

"Nice dog. Australian Shepherd?"

An older man stood in the doorway, dressed in an old T-shirt and jeans with slippers on his feet. His face was richly colored and seamed with age, his warm brown eyes busy assessing me. A silver earring engraved with a thunderbird hung from his left earlobe while his long, graying hair was pulled back off his broad face with an elastic band.

"Yes, a mix, I think."

"It looks like one of Shea's."

I bent over to pat the back of the wiggly black lab. "He is. Jupiter. Do you know him?"

The man smiled and stepped back from the front door, gesturing me inside. "Of course. I know all the animals on the island. And if that's Jupiter, then you must be Kate Zoë Thomas, our controversial new station manager. C'mon in. We've got things to discuss."

# Chapter Fourteen

"We do?"

I stepped into the front hall, Jupiter and the lab following right behind me. It was a comfortable, time-worn 1960s rancher. Not fancy or modern, but homey. From the front door, a small wood-paneled living room led off to the right with an overstuffed beige couch, and a La-Z-Boy recliner pointed toward the rectangular front window. The view was stunning: the Salish Sea lapping mere feet away while a white B.C. Ferries ship slowly sailed by.

"Yes, we do."

Sam continued through the living room and into the kitchen, which was at the back of the house. It was painted a bright yellow and had a pellet stove radiating heat from the corner. A small kitchen table sat against the back window. He gestured me toward a seat. "Iced tea?"

"Yes, please."

The black lab circled round and round Jupiter, so pleased to have a possible playmate. Jupiter, on the other hand, wanted a friend about as much as he wanted a bath. In other words, not at all.

"Your lab is looking for a friend."

Sam laughed. "Jojo is always looking for a friend. She embodies the saying: Every stranger is a friend I haven't met yet."

I sipped the sweet peach tea. "Well, Jupiter is the opposite of that. He doesn't want to get to know anyone, stranger or not."

"Except for you."

I smiled. "Yes, that's right. How did you know I had adopted him?

"Well, word around here travels faster than…."

"Shit through a goose. Yeah, I've heard."

"My sister, Selesia, is a good friend of Shea's. They're both big animal lovers. If Shea can't get out to do a rescue, she calls Selesia to do it. All I can say is, thank God they keep all the animals at Shea's farm. I don't mind Selesia collecting them, but I'd hate if this Reserve became Dr. Doolittle's menagerie." He sat down with a thump in the seat across from me. "Shea was chatting to Selesia about how Jupiter had taken a shine to you. I put two and two together."

"Well, two plus two has added up to me having this dog in my life."

"Jupiter knew what he needed. He just had to wait for the universe to bring it to him."

"Yeah, I guess so. You said you have something you need to discuss with me?"

He nodded, his long, graying ponytail bobbing against the shoulder of his faded grey Manfred Mann's Earth Band T-shirt. "I'm not much of a one for social media, but the drama on the island Facebook page this morning managed to penetrate even my existence. It looks like someone would like you hung, drawn, and quartered."

"Or at least off the island," I replied.

"Yes. That's unusual for Wynter. We have our bigots and our fools, but they usually aren't quite so public about it. Or at least they haven't been for the past eighty years."

"Well, someone here definitely wants me gone."

"That's what makes this interesting."

"Interesting?" I glanced out the window at the backyard. A fire pit and some lawn chairs rested in the middle of the lawn. An open field with two pastured horses in it lay behind. "I don't know if I'd call it interesting."

"I would. I don't know if Gwen told you, but I have a degree in First Nations & Indigenous Studies as well as Organizational Psychology."

"No, I didn't. But I did see the sign on your front lawn."

"Yes, Gwen and I went to UBC together. Class of '74. Got my degree there. Unfortunately," Sam paused, "Gwen didn't. She packed up and moved to

Toronto in her final year. Got her master's and stayed there to teach."

"Gwen taught at the University of Toronto?"

"Yup. English Lit."

"How did she end up back here?"

He took a long sip of his tea. "Well, she moved on to a teaching position in Portland after a few years. She never returned to the island until she flew back for her father's funeral."

"Which was?"

"About fifteen years ago. We all thought she would sell the farm, perhaps see if she could get the land on Wynter Mountain subdivided into lots. Make a nice amount of money and then fly back to her job in Portland."

"But she didn't. She stayed."

"Yup. Moved into the old farmhouse up there on the mountain that she grew up in. Took over the fruit business as if she'd never left Wynter. Picked up the family mantle and continued on as our much loved, benevolent leader."

"I had no idea. So, what is it that you do, Sam?"

"I help businesses work with First Nations bands."

"Is there a call for that?"

He smiled. "When there's a dollar in it for them. It's amazing how the possibility of profits can enlighten the worldview of a corporation. I work as a consultant for companies that would like to do business with First Nations bands. I walk them through the niceties of culture, tradition, and the unusual and complicated legal rules that apply to Indigenous communities."

"I see."

Jupiter, in desperation, squeezed up against the wall behind my legs in an attempt to escape Jojo.

"But that's not what you're here for, is it?"

"No." I stopped and took another sip of tea. "I came here to talk to you about the Facebook post."

"Yes, that's what I thought. I'm assuming you suspect Will?"

I gulped. I had hoped there might be a more subtle way of bringing Will into the conversation. "Yes. The Facebook page was hacked by someone.

We don't know who."

Sam paused to pet Jojo, who looked forlorn at the loss of Jupiter in her life. "Are the things they said true?"

"The things they said about me?"

"Yes."

"Some of it's true, and some of it's fantasy. Either way, I would prefer they hadn't made any of it public in the middle of Daniel's murder investigation. I'm guessing whoever did it realizes that."

"He was your boyfriend? The man who was found in Steeltun Bay?"

"Ex-boyfriend. Yes."

"Which is why you are here. Because someone told you Will is the computer whiz kid on the island."

"Yes."

"Will didn't do it." Sam stood up and opened the refrigerator to bring out the Tupperware container of iced tea. He gestured it toward my empty glass, but I shook my head no. "I texted him this morning as soon as I heard about all of this because I knew what everyone would think. He told me he didn't do it."

"And you believe him?"

He refilled his own glass and took a long sip. "Yes."

"With no proof other than his word?"

"Yes."

Silence.

"You didn't kill your boyfriend, did you?"

I sat silent, stunned, for a few moments. "No, I didn't."

"As soon as I saw you drive up here this morning, I knew you hadn't."

"How?"

"Because people rarely set traps for themselves."

"I don't know what you mean."

"Why would Will hack something like the island Facebook page, knowing he would be the obvious suspect?"

"But stupid people do things all the time and get caught."

"Yes, but Will isn't stupid. And neither are you."

I didn't know what to say to that.

"If you were the killer, the smartest thing you could do right now would be to lie low and pray they don't find any evidence. You would have a reasonably good chance of not being caught. God knows, how much evidence could there be left on a body that's being floating in the open water for days? But you're not doing that. You're trying to find the killer. That's why you need to know who the Truth Warrior is. Because the only reason someone posted all of that crap was to draw attention away from themselves and put it on to you. And why would someone want to do that?"

"Because they killed Daniel."

"Exactly."

"But who?"

Sam stretched his legs out in front of him and took a long sip of his tea. "That's the tricky part. If we take your name off the suspect list, who else might have a beef with him? It would have to be someone on the island."

"But that's the whole problem. I don't think he knew anyone on the island."

"So, neither of you had been here before?"

"Well, I hadn't. I think Daniel may have. He was a reporter based out of Seattle for a few years."

"So, he came to the island for a newspaper story?"

"Not that I know of."

"Oh," Sam hesitated, "I thought I had something there for a moment."

I leaned forward. "What? What did you think you had?"

"Well, quite a few years ago, a reporter from the States flew in to do a story."

"Why? What story?"

"If memory serves me, they were writing about the problems over at Oceanica."

"Oceanica?"

"Yeah, the salmon fishery just down-island from us. They farm salmon there, coho, sockeye, chum, in large net pens."

"Never seen them."

"No, you wouldn't unless you were in a boat. From above, it looks like a simple wood grid floating on the ocean surface."

"But underneath?"

"Underneath, you've got millions of dollars' worth of salmon just waiting to be harvested."

I glanced down at Jupiter. He was still curled up in a ball, warily watching JoJo. "So, no need for trawlers to go out and catch salmon anymore?"

"Fewer and fewer every year. I mean, a wild-caught salmon from Phil will be worth a lot more than a farm-raised salmon from Oceanica. But the wild population is dwindling rapidly."

"So, what was the problem at Oceanica?"

"It's not was. It still is. Theft. People stealing salmon from the pens."

"How could they tell that anything had been stolen?' I imagined a massive fisherman's net, but one that was 12 ft. across rather than 12 inches.

"Damage to the net. Man-made damage."

"Did they ever catch anyone?"

He shook his head. "No. They installed special gates and a security system, but nothing yet. It's still on a small scale, so it's not that big of a deal. But if it gets worse? Oceanica's looking at a significant financial loss."

"Perhaps it was Daniel who came to cover the story. I don't know. All I know for sure is that he used to sail through here."

"Did he ever moor here? In Hope Bay?"

I shrugged my shoulders. "I don't know. It's possible, I suppose."

"Who might he have met at Hope Bay?" Sam muttered to himself. "Graham Standard used to run the marina, but he and his wife left a couple of years ago. I mean, Phil would have been around. Also, Bob and Doreen at the Lind. But all of the kids who worked there during the summers have moved on to lives off the island. Well, everyone except Ria."

"Ria?" The name sent a surge of electricity through me. "Ria Corker?"

"Yeah, Ria Corker. She used to work summers at the hotel when she was home from college. The restaurant, I believe."

Ria. Why did her name keep turning up? Could she have met Daniel? Had he wandered up from the marina to order a meal at the hotel restaurant? Had she, a pretty, young college student, been his waitress?

Sam finished his glass of tea and patted Jojo methodically for a few moments. "Do you know anything about First Nations culture? About the Raven?"

"You mean, like in stories and myths?"

"Yes."

"Not really. I've seen him in carvings, but that's about it. The big black bird holding something in his beak, right?"

He settled back in his seat, still absentmindedly petting his dog. "In our culture, the Raven is the creator, the giver of all things. He is the one who brought our people out of the clamshell into this world and gave us food and sunlight. But he is also the trickster."

"A what?"

"A trickster. Although he is immortal, he embodies many human qualities: greed, lust, hunger. He is both admired and disliked, mainly because of the many tricks he played on our people. You see, his powers allowed him to change into anything he wanted."

"Like a shapeshifter?"

"Exactly. Although he was still a cunning raven, he could appear as an animal, a child, or whatever he wished."

"Almost like wearing a mask."

"Yes. So, no one ever suspected him. And you know why? Because he always presented himself as the one creature you would least expect to do something evil."

I silently digested this. Was Ria my Raven?

"Remember this while you hunt for your Raven. He can hide in the most unexpected of places."

# Chapter Fifteen

"Well, that was interesting, Jupiter, wasn't it?"

Jupiter, glad to be free of the cloying adoration of JoJo, stuck his head out the window of the truck and ignored me.

"Well, I found it interesting, even if you didn't."

Sam had helped me add a few more arrows to my quiver of information. And all of those arrows seemed to point at Ria, or at least in her general direction. I had taken her job at CWYN, giving her a reason to want me off of Wynter. She also had opportunity, as she lived on the island. Perhaps there was even a tenuous connection to Daniel through her summer job as a waitress. But why kill him? You can be pissed off with someone who took a job you wanted, but murder? And if revenge was the reason, why murder Daniel? Surely, I would be the intended victim?

I pulled the truck into a small gravel parking lot. The entrance into the park consisted of two tall lodge pole pines topped by a carved wooden sign which read, The Enchanted Forest.

"The Enchanted Forest, Jupiter. This was where Sam said I should take you. Do you want to go for a walk?"

Jupiter spun his head around, his white-and-gray face split by an undeniable grin of happiness.

"I would say that's a yes. C'mon, let's go and see how enchanted this forest is."

Jupiter bounded out of the truck and dashed ahead of me through the entrance. I noticed that his stride widened into a bounce when he ran, as if overcome with joy.

"Don't get too far ahead, Jupiter."

He stopped at the sound of his name, tilted his silky head to one side, and waited a moment for me to catch up before shooting off again.

The path wound through the lush trees ahead of us. Raised wooden planks had been placed over the sodden soil in an effort to keep hikers out of the muck.

I sniffed the air. It was rich with a moist fertility, an unusual mix of both new growth and old rot. Green, that was the word for this place. Green in the uncountable different hues of the leaves and trees, the ferns and lichen. Green in a shimmer of dampness that was almost permeable. If I closed my eyes, it was easy to believe I was walking through a humid, shaded room. Perhaps in an old abandoned house in the woods that had been long overtaken by dank growth.

*I wonder if they have the same problem here that they have at the Sydney Cliffs? Ground too saturated to walk on?*

I glanced behind me, but there was no closed sign to be seen. Jupiter stopped ahead of me, his body bracing and leaning forward, his tail ramrod straight behind him. Before I could even call out his name, he ran back to where I was standing.

*Oh no, not another incident like I had with Michael.*

"What's up, boy? I'm going to be fine. Just chill." I looked up to see a young woman jogging down the path toward us. "It's all right, Jupiter. It's just a runner, that's all."

Spotting us, the young woman slowed to a walk. She was quite petite, her loosely curled red hair held back from her face by a headband soaked with a slick of perspiration. She was more well-rounded than heavy. A Rubenesque woman, I thought, but one who carried her weight well. On her legs were black leggings, topped by a light gray zip-up jacket.

"Good morning," she greeted and stopped, bending over to catch her breath. Her round face was moonlike and freckled, her small eyes a deep blue. "Or should I say good afternoon?"

"Yes, I think it's around noon. Nice day for a run."

"Gotta take advantage of sunny days when we have them. Are you and your dog visiting Wynter Island?"

I pulled Jupiter a little closer, his body still stiff with protective concern, but not showing any of the aggression he had displayed towards Michael. "No, I'm a new transplant. Kate Thomas."

The woman's rosy cheeks flushed a brighter shade of pink. "Kate Thomas? The head of our new television station?"

"Yes, that's right. And this is Jupiter. I'm much friendlier than he is, though. I wouldn't try and pet him if I were you."

The woman laughed. "Well, welcome to Wynter Island. My name is Ria, Ria Corker."

"Corker. Like in Bob and Doreen Corker?"

"Yes, that's right."

"Ahhhhh."

I was tongue-tied. What do you say at a time like this? *Hi, nice to meet you. I hate your father, and I think you may have had something to do with my ex-boyfriend's murder.* There were no Emily Post responses appropriate for this situation.

"Look—" Ria started out.

"Well, it's—" I said at the exact same moment.

We both laughed. I gestured towards her. "You go first."

"I just want to apologize for my dad. I know he hasn't made things easy for you, and this morning we've got all this craziness on Facebook." She stumbled to a stop. I nodded for her to continue. "He can come across pretty strong, but he's not a bad guy." Ria laughed. "I mean, he's my Dad, so I'm probably a bit biased, but he does have some good qualities."

"I'm glad to hear it." I bit my tongue before I could say anymore.

"He's just, umm—"

"Blunt?"

"Yes, blunt and bad-tempered. And incredibly overprotective of his only child."

"Yes, I got a sense of that when I met him."

"I'm glad I ran into you today, Kate. I want you to know that I don't feel any ill will toward you. You got the job fair and square. Your CV is a lot more impressive than mine. My dad just can't, or won't, see that."

"I'm guessing he puts his only daughter on a bit of a pedestal."

"Yeah, which can be a pain in the ass sometimes."

"Especially if you fall from that height."

She grinned sheepishly. "Believe me, I know. But it's because he loves me so much." She hesitated, nervously picking at the hem of her jacket. "I heard about his blowup at the station. I'm sorry that he's made things hard for you. Especially after …."

"After Daniel," I finished for her.

"Yes. I'm so sorry for your loss."

"Thank you."

Ria's lower lip began to tremble, and her eyes filled with unshed tears, making her pupils glisten like watercolor irises.

"Are you okay?"

The other woman sniffled and rubbed a hand over her eyes. "Sorry, I'm just a really emotional person. It must be terrible to lose someone like that."

I recognized real distress, actual loss, in her eyes. Almost as if she was grieving for someone she actually knew. Had my guess out on the Reserve been correct? Did Ria actually know Daniel?

She reached down to pull her earbuds out of her pocket. "Well, I've got to get back to my run."

"No, no, wait for a second." I panicked and grabbed her wrist. Her eyebrows drew together in confusion, so I quickly released her hand. "I'm sorry. I shouldn't have grabbed your arm like that, but I wanted to ask you something."

"What?" Ria asked, her bluish-purple eyes studying me warily.

"It's," I quickly ran through all of the possible excuses I could use to meet her again. I needed something, anything, to gain some extra time to ask her questions about Daniel. "It's a real shame to have someone with your training on Wynter Island and not utilize them for the station. I was wondering if you might be interested in coming up with your own show for CWYN?"

"Show?" Her expression shifted from suspicion to curiosity. "What kind of show?"

I shrugged, making it up as I went along. "I don't know. That's up to you. I'll have the final say, but other than that, you can do whatever you want. Produce, shoot, edit. I don't know if you want to be in front of the camera as well. Just come up with some ideas, and we can get together to discuss them."

Ria's smile spread, splitting her full moon face into a crescent. "I'd love to. I'd have to fit it around my job at CBC, but it sounds like a lot of fun."

"Great. Text me or give me a call when you're ready. Bob," my voice caught momentarily on his name, "has all my contact info." Another thought came to me. "But don't leave it too long, okay? Our schedule is really filling up."

"Great. I'll get right on it." Ria slowly began to jog backward away from me. "Maybe we can talk in a couple of days?"

"Sounds great. Nice meeting you, Ria."

"Nice meeting you, too, Kate."

She turned around and ran off into the distance.

"Well, that was an interesting discussion, wasn't it, Jupiter?" His eyes stared up at me, confused. "But enough about that. Let's get back to the purpose of this excursion." He shivered in happiness. "The walk!"

* * *

"Nice dog you've got there."

I stood in the open doorway of the RCMP station, Jupiter beside me. Stewart waved us both inside from his position behind an old office desk.

"Thanks, Stewart. Is it okay if Jupiter comes in with me?"

"Sure, no problem. Billy is at home today, so there won't be any competition for the alpha dog in the station." He gestured toward a wooden chair positioned in front of his desk. "Have a seat. I thought it would be me trying to find you, not the other way around."

I sat down heavily in the seat, a sudden weariness setting in. Jupiter circled and circled beside me before settling in for a nap on the floor. "It's been an interesting morning, Stewart."

He leaned back in his chair, placing one boot on the edge of his desk to keep him from tipping over. "I'm assuming you're talking about the Facebook stuff?"

"Yeah, among other things. Do you know who might have done it?"

"Not my problem. Someone's going to have to reach out to Facebook about it. It's not illegal, you know. It just violates their terms of service."

"But somebody hacked the Wynter Island page so that they could paint me as a murderer!"

He nodded, his chair shifting underneath him as he momentarily lost his balance. "Yes, but they didn't say anything untrue, did they?"

I glared at him. "Saying that I am a serial murderer is untrue."

"Okay. Taking the name-calling out of it, all of the links they posted about you were valid. I must admit, it's not the kind of thing I expect to see on Wynter Island. There's only one person on the island that I can think of who has the skills to do something like that. You know, hack into Facebook."

"Will Sixto. I've already been out to see Sam Hanks."

"And what did Sam say?"

I exhaled a whoosh of pent-up breath. "That Will is innocent. He texted him this morning at his school in Saanich, and Will insists he didn't do it."

Stewart slowly lowered his seat back down to the floor. "And you don't agree with him?"

I threw my hands up in the air. "I don't know what I believe anymore, Stewart. What possible reason could there be for anyone on this island to have killed Daniel?"

"I don't know, but it's not like we, the RCMP, haven't been working on this. Lesley and I have been going around the island, checking on everyone's whereabouts on that Thursday."

"And?"

He glanced down at the pieces of paper on his desk, covered with scrawled notes. "Most have an alibi, but not everyone."

"Like who?"

"And why should I tell you that? You're a suspect in this case, in case you've forgotten."

I leaned forward. "What harm could it do, Stewart? Let's say I did it."

One of his bushy brows angled upward, but he said nothing. "This is just an example, okay? Don't take this as some kind of confession." He smiled. "So, if we say I did it, nothing you tell me will change the facts. If I didn't commit the murder, any information you give me could be really useful."

He considered. "Don't try and do our job for us, Kate."

"I'm not. I'm just trying to gather information. I'm a journalist. That's what I do. If I'm lucky, I might find something that can be useful to you and Lesley."

He paused to consider my offer. "It's not like any of this information isn't already common knowledge." He glanced down at the paperwork. "I know I'm going to regret doing this." He looked me straight in the eye. "Don't do anything stupid with this."

I crossed my heart and hoped to die.

"Harald was working all day at the B&B to get ready for Daniel."

"With no witnesses."

"None."

"Who else?"

"Ria was on the same ferry as Daniel, as was Shelley Douglass. Ria returned to the Lind, and nobody saw her until dinnertime."

"Okay, Harald and Ria."

"Shelley ran some errands. Vera can vouch for her there. Ben had no vet appointments, so he took his spaniel for a walk on the beach. Alone. Shea went home after dropping you off and has no alibi until Lesley got home from work. Phil was out fishing. Gwen visited Sam and then spent the rest of the afternoon working alone in her greenhouse. No witnesses."

"Is that it?"

"Pretty much." He scanned over the paper. "Only one more suspect."

My eyes connected with his. "Is that…?"

"You? Yes. No one saw you from noon on Thursday until you arrived at the Legion on Friday night. That's a long time to go unnoticed on a small island."

I glanced around the office. There was not much furniture other than the two metal office desks, a couple of filing cabinets, and a bookcase. Stewart's desk was covered with faded Edmonton Oiler stickers and a bobblehead Wayne Gretzky. Lesley's was neat and organized, with a small framed photo of Shea on a beach somewhere. Corkboards covered the walls, an assortment of pinned notices for various island activities vying for attention.

"Stewart?" a female voice called out from the hallway.

"In here."

Anna walked into the office, a handful of flyers held in one hand. She was dressed in a simple shirt and jeans, her sleek bob tucked behind one ear. The hairstyle showed off the rosy flush along her cheekbones. She must be a good ten years older than me, I realized, but I wouldn't look that good in a pair of jeans and a T-shirt.

"Oh, hi, Kate. I'm sorry if I'm interrupting something." She hesitated, her Scottish brogue softened by the wide vowels of her growing Canadian accent.

"Oh no, it's fine," I answered. "Come on in. I just stopped by to talk to Stewart about something."

Anna walked up to the desk. "Yes, I heard about what happened on Facebook. That kind of stuff doesn't usually happen around here." Her eyes settled sympathetically on my face. "Someone will figure out who the culprit is. No secrets on a small island, eh, Stewart?"

He nodded his head in agreement. "Yup. A mouse can't fart on this island without somebody noticing. What do you need, Anna?"

She handed one of the flyers to him. I leaned forward to read it. *Save the Orcas! Join our MLA on May 28th at the Wynter Island Community Centre to discuss how best to preserve our endangered Orca population.*

"Could you post one of these on the Upcoming Events board? I'm going to see if I can get some posted at the library and the Tru-Value as well."

"Sure, no problem. Since you're here, I actually have a question for you. I heard a rumor that June is considering retiring from politics."

Anna did a lousy job of appearing surprised. "Really?"

He chuckled. "Yes, really. I don't suppose you have any idea who the Green Party is going to pick to run as her replacement?" He leaned back in his seat again, a teasing grin spreading across his ruddy face.

Anna shrugged with a nonchalance that fooled neither of us. "No, I don't, Stewart. Thanks for your help with the poster. I've got to get over to the library and talk to Shea."

"Anna, you know you can always count on my vote!" Stewart shouted to her retreating back before breaking into laughter.

"Is it true? Is Anna going into politics?"

Stewart shrugged his shoulders. "Don't know. She's certainly well respected on the island. There's just one thing...."

"What?"

"Well, I don't know if Michael's going to be happy about it."

"Michael's not keen on her going into politics?"

He shrugged. "I don't think so. As it is, she's already pretty involved with the party. Spends a lot of time in Victoria. And one of the Green party bigwigs has been over here on the island visiting her several times."

"Grooming her for a possible run for office?"

"No idea." He straightened himself up and sat his chair leg back down on the floor. "But enough gossiping. You also have no alibi for Thursday afternoon."

I sighed. "I already told you, Stewart. I got my PO Box, did some laundry, watched stupid cat videos on YouTube, and then ate a Kraft dinner. That's it. And there's no way I can prove to you I'm telling the truth."

"I know," he said. "that's what makes all of this so difficult."

* * *

Difficult was the perfect word to describe all of this, I thought as Jupiter and I headed out to the truck. Nothing on Wynter Island was as it looked on the surface. It was an island paradise which, in reality, was only hanging on by its fingernails. The citizens seemed friendly, helpful, and yet there were outliers in their midst. One was trying to destroy my attempts at creating a successful TV station, another was posting horrible things about me online, and a third was, of course, the killer. Or maybe one person was all three? It was going to take someone outside the bubble of life on Wynter Island to be able to solve this, someone whose vision wasn't clouded by loyalty or friendship. Someone like me.

"We're going to have to solve this, Jupiter. Just you and me. On our own."

# Chapter Sixteen

"Kate, this is my mom, Shelley Douglass," Greg said as he walked up to where I was readying the table in the Lind Hotel restaurant for our first Fish Bingo broadcast.

The middle-aged woman I had met at the Legion stood in front of me. She smiled a cheery smile and said, "I've heard a lot about you from Greg."

"Not about her, Mom. About the station," Greg said, all but rolling his eyes at his mother.

Shelley laughed. "Sorry. I mean, I've heard a lot about the station. I asked Greg if he thought you'd mind if I tagged along with him tonight to see things in action."

I placed the golden bingo cage down and centered it before looking back up. "Of course, Shelley. That's fine. You're more than welcome to watch. Are you interested in volunteering as well?"

She shook her head. "No, my schedule is pretty packed, with the ferries and the hotel just about to reopen for the season."

"Oh, well. Can't say I didn't try. Greg, could you bring in the camera from the truck? It's the big black box."

"Sure, no problem," he said and headed out the door.

"Bob, can you move the main light a little bit to the left for me?"

"Here?" Bob moved one of the large stand lights so that it better lit the table.

"That's right. Thanks, Bob."

I had avoided mentioning anything about the filming mishap the other day to anyone. The last thing I wanted was to give Bob the satisfaction of knowing his little trick had upset me.

"How long have you worked on the ferries, Shelley?" I asked.

"Almost twenty-five years now. Started not long after my ex and I moved to Wynter Island."

"Do you enjoy it?"

Shelley waggled her head back and forth as if unsure of the answer. "It has its good points and bad points. But it's the only well-paying job that drops me off on Wynter Island at the end of my shift."

"I can see how that would be a big plus, living here."

"Yup. That's the hard thing about living on an island. Getting anywhere off-island is complicated. What do you think about Wynter? Do you like it?"

I hesitated. Did I like it? Yes, I guess I did. When people weren't conspiring against me or murdering people I loved.

"It hasn't been an easy few weeks, but I'm starting to get the hang of things."

"I heard about your boyfriend." Shelley paused. Her eyes, so similar in color to her son's, were profoundly sad. "I'm sorry."

"Thank you. The people on the island have been very kind."

"Are you planning on staying here?"

I spun around from the table in surprise. "On Wynter Island? Why wouldn't I?"

"Well," she stumbled over her words, "I just wondered if it might be too much for you. You know, the memories."

I said nothing for a few moments. I had pushed those memories to the furthest corner of my mind and busied myself instead with work. What was it Daniel had once said to me? Ahh, yes, denial is a river in Egypt.

"I don't know. We'll have to wait and see."

"Here you go," Greg said as he hauled the videocam box in through the door and plunked it down on the floor in front of me.

Doreen placed a small card on the edge of the table. It read: *Lind Hotel, Hope Bay Harbour, Wynter Island, B.C. Where beautiful memories are made! Season Opening on Victoria Day weekend.*

"A little bit of free publicity doesn't hurt, does it?" she said.

"No, it doesn't. Although, I'm afraid, most of the people watching tonight will be locals."

Doreen moved the card a little to the left and then to the right, humming as she did so. "That's okay. This is just the start. CWYN has big things to accomplish in the future!"

I nodded in agreement. "I hope so, Doreen."

"I'm sorry if what I said upset you," Shelley whispered to me once Doreen had left. "I should have just kept my mouth shut."

"It's fine. Don't worry about it," I replied briskly and walked over to make sure my laptop was connected to the hotel Wi-Fi. "Why don't you take a seat over there, Shelley? It'll give you a good view of what's going on. Okay, Nate. I'm going to do the announcing, and you are going to spin the balls and hand them to me."

Nate nodded. "Yeah. Greg will man the camera, and you will let us know when the winner's photo arrives."

"Exactly."

I glanced down at my cell phone. It had been the one problem I'd been unable to fix with the livestream. How were we going to figure out the winner of Fish Bingo if none of the players were present in the room? By using my cell phone, I had finally realized. A small card in the corner of the YouTube screen listed my cell phone number and advised the winning player to text a photo of their completed bingo card as soon as they had won. The first photo of a winning card to arrive would win the five-kilo sockeye sitting in the Lind's restaurant fridge.

"Nate, did you, by any chance, see the Wynter Island Facebook page? The one where all that stuff about me was posted?"

Nate stopped in the midst of threading his mic underneath his shirt, his already long face grimacing in surprise. "Yeah, I did. Everyone did."

"I don't suppose you know anything about it?"

A long pause. "No. Why should I know anything about it?" His skin had blanched even paler, if such a thing was possible. And why was he so jumpy about the Facebook stuff?

"I'm not accusing you of anything, Nate. Since social media is a young person's game, I just thought that you might have heard something. That's all."

"No. I don't know anything," he said brusquely and hurried over to take his seat behind the table.

Why was he so upset? Did he know something about the Facebook hack? Was he the Truth Warrior? But why? Why would he do that to me?

"Greg, set us up on a two-shot and lock off the camera, ok?" I directed as I sat down at the table.

"No problem."

"I can handle the computer," Bob said and grabbed for my laptop.

Just as his hand reached for it, I swept the computer off the table and into my lap. I looked him straight in the eye, my expression saying everything that needed to be said: Don't you dare put your hand anywhere near that device, Bob Corker.

His pleasant expression slipped to reveal the irritation lurking behind it. "Kate," he said, trying and failing to hide the anger in his voice, "you're being ridiculous. Give me the laptop. I can handle it."

"Thank you, Bob, but no," I said, my tone making it clear that I wasn't going to budge on this issue. "I can handle it myself."

He stood there for a moment, forcing me to consider my options if this turned into a Mexican stand-off before he grumbled and walked back to his seat.

I readied my MacBook to start the livestream and then signaled Greg to push the button and start filming.

"Good evening, Wynter Island," I said, smiling into the camera. "Welcome to our inaugural broadcast! My name is Kate Zoë Thomas. I am the new station manager for CWYN. Beside me is one of our volunteers, Nate Rossino. CWYN is your local TV station, bringing the good life on Wynter Island to people throughout British Columbia. For the next few months, we will be using this YouTube channel to connect with you while we work on getting our studio up and running. Soon, you will be able to find us on your digital TV dial at channel 201." I took a quick sip of water. "Tonight we are playing"—dramatic pause—"Fish Bingo! Isn't that right, Nate?"

"Yes, Kate, that's right. Bingo cards went out in last week's edition of the

Wynter Island Times and will go out again next week."

"Why is it called Fish Bingo, Nate?"

"Well, it is called Fish Bingo because our main prize is a beautiful, freshly caught salmon. Tonight's prize is a five-kilogram sockeye."

"Yum!"

"Yes. Our first winner of the evening gets our grand prize. Our second winner of the evening gets a lovely basket of homemade jams and pickles from Doreen Corker of the Lind Hotel and General Store."

Before he could say another word, Doreen ran in front of the camera, waving happily. "The Lind Hotel restaurant opens for the season on the Victoria Day weekend!" she declared and then ducked back out of the camera frame once again.

Nate glanced over at me, who was as stunned as he was, before continuing on gamely. "And our third prize is a gift certificate from Jake's bookstore and art gallery, where you can," he glanced down at a piece of paper in front of him, "enrich your mind and nurture your soul."

"What?" I mouthed silently.

Nate shrugged and continued on. "Okay, I'll start spinning the bingo cage and pass you the balls, Kate. Here we go!"

The handle cranked, and the colorful balls began to pick up speed in their golden birdcage. Nate reached inside and pulled out a green ball. He held it up so the camera could see the number.

"Alright, our first ball is...I-27. That is I-27. Okay, next one, Nate."

Another spin and a red ball came out. "N-36. N-36."

"Aren't you supposed to say A like an apple or something more descriptive?" Doreen called from off-camera. "You gotta make sure people understand what letter it is."

I fixed Doreen with a death stare. "Okay. Our next ball is G-39. G like golf, 39." Another spin. "B-3 is B like boy, 3. Our next ball is O-24. O like orange, 24. Well, we've got five balls out there, Nate. Maybe we'll have our first winner of the evening soon!"

"I hope so!" Nate cranked the handle again and handed me the next ball.

Suddenly music began to blare out from my cellphone.

"Oops, looks like we've got a phone call rather than a text." I picked up my phone. "Hi. This is CWYN's Fish Bingo! Do we have a winner?"

"You're damn right, you've got a winner! I told you I would win that salmon for my own belly!"

"Phil? Is that you?"

"Did you say Phil?" Nate leaned closer to ask. "Is he our winner?"

"Yes, it's me, and I won the fish!"

"Phil, you have to prove you are the winner by texting me a photo of your completed bingo card."

"I know. I know. Don't get all snarky on me. I'm just calling in to make sure I hold my place at the head of the line."

I gritted my teeth and attempted a smile. "Yes, Phil, you have your place at the head of the line. Text me the photo, please."

"So, is Phil the winner?" Nate asked. "Is he allowed to win? I mean, he supplies us with the—"

"Not now, Nate," I muttered.

A tweeting bird chirped from my phone to announce a photo of a grinning, unshaven Phil, holding a brown bottle of Molson XXX along with his crossed-out bingo card.

I sighed. "It looks like we have a winner. Fisherman Phil has won the first-ever Wynter Island Fish Bingo." I stared with a deadpan expression directly into the camera. "Congratulations, Phil. You can collect your prize at the Lind Hotel tomorrow."

"Okay! Our first winner is Fisherman Phil!" Nate called out. "Let me spin the balls and see who wins our preserves basket!"

* * *

"That old bastard."

I glanced up from where I was packing up the camera equipment. Greg and Shelley had left as soon as filming was finished. Bob, apparently still displeased that I had refused to allow him to handle my laptop, had made an excuse and headed off to their living quarters in the hotel.

"I'm guessing you're talking about Fisherman Phil?"

"Yes. Just because he's as old as dirt, he thinks he's above the rules. He gets to win the salmon, even though he shouldn't have even been playing the game in the first place."

I chuckled. "I'm guessing he believes he is above the rules."

"Do you know where he lives?"

"No."

"In the most rundown cottage in all of Harrow Village. The grass is as high as his windows. Cars go and die in his backyard. He thinks he can get away with anything, but he can't."

I placed the light stand on top of the other gearboxes. "What do you mean?"

"It's nothing." He brushed away my question and walked over to clear off the table we had been using.

"What is it, Nate?"

"It's nothing. Just some rumors."

"Rumors about Phil? What kind of rumors?"

"Just some people talking."

"About what?" I continued to push. However unlikely a murderer he might seem, Phil didn't have an alibi for the time of Daniel's death.

Nate sighed, clearly uncomfortable that he had started the subject. "About how Phil has been seen heading out late at night in the Wet Witch."

"To do what? Go fishing after dark?"

"No one fishes at night here. Only during daylight hours."

"Then what is he doing out there?"

Nate shrugged. "Some people think he may have found another way to catch his salmon."

"You mean, Oceanica?"

"You know about Oceanica?" Nate asked, surprised.

"Yes, Sam told me about it. He apparently knows a great deal about all the nefarious things going on in the waters off Wynter Island at night."

The glass vase full of carnations Nate was holding slipped through his fingers and crashed onto the parquet floor.

"What on earth is going on here?" Doreen scuttled into the room. "What happened to my vase?"

Nate said nothing, his eyes glued to me in fear. I walked over and placed my hand on his arm. "It was just an accident, Doreen. I'm sorry. The station will pay for any damage."

"Well, it's not like it was expensive or anything. I just hate to see things pointlessly broken," she grumbled to herself and went off in search of a broom and dustpan.

"Nate. What is going on with you?" I tightened my grip on his arm. His eyes widened to double their size in his pale, thin face. I could see both panic and fear in his frantic expression.

"You know, don't you?"

I stepped in front of him and put both hands on his shoulders. His weight shifted towards me, almost as if I was the only thing holding him upright. "I don't know what you're talking about, Nate."

"You know about the boat, don't you?"

Boat? What boat was he talking about? "Nate, you're not making any sense."

He leaned away from me, still staring at my face, confused. "You really don't know?" He sat down heavily on one of the restaurant chairs.

I squatted down in front of him. "I don't know how many different ways I can say this, Nate, but I don't know what you're talking about."

"I can't do this anymore," he whispered, more to himself than to me.

"Can't do what?"

"Pretend."

"Pretend what?"

Nate looked me straight in the eye and steeled himself before speaking. "Pretend that I didn't kill your boyfriend."

# Chapter Seventeen

"Okay, okay. One at a time. It's," Stewart glanced at the clock on the wall. "nine 'o clock, and I am missing the hockey game. It's the Oilers tonight, you know. This better be as important as you say it is."

"Kate, you start." Lesley moved her chair into the coffee/interview room to make space for the four of us to sit more comfortably.

I saw Jupiter through the open door having a staring contest with Billy, Stewart's French bulldog. Neither dog was willing to relinquish alpha status just yet.

"Okay. We had Fish Bingo tonight."

"Did Phil really win, that sneaky old codger?" Lesley asked, shaking her head and smiling. "That's what Shea said."

"Yes, he did, but the important point is what happened after the livestream event ended. Nate told me something. Something important."

Lesley and Stewart turned their attention to the teenager. His face had regained a bit of its color. His eyes, no longer terrified, seemed more at peace, as if resigned to what was happening. He had crossed the rubicon now and could never go back.

"I killed Daniel," he said simply.

In the silence following this announcement, they could hear the two dogs growling at each other in the office.

"Billy!" Stewart called, and the little Frenchie came scuttling in. "Sit. You stay here and leave Jupiter alone." He closed the interview room door. "Okay, Nate, are you trying to tell me that you killed Daniel Apollinar."

"Yes."

"How?"

"By running him over with my Dad's boat."

"What?"

"I ran him over with my Dad's boat."

"When did you run him over with your Dad's boat?"

"Thursday night."

Stewart made a note on a piece of paper. "Where were you?"

"Between Wynter Island and Pender Island."

"Okay," Lesley said. "You're talking about the boat your Dad docks over near Coho Bay, right? What were you doing with it?"

"I stole the keys and then told my parents I was going over to work on a school project with a friend," Nate answered.

"And then what happened?" Stewart asked.

"I was going to join some kids from the high school. They were having a party."

"Party?" I asked.

Stewart turned to me to explain. "Teens use boats to get to isolated spots on the island or maybe one of the little uninhabited islets. Once they are there, they light a campfire, get drunk or stoned, and party with their friends. No adults to spot them."

Nate nodded, his eyes briefly worried at the *omertá* he was about to break. "It was supposed to be on that little island between Wynter and Pender."

"Muggs Isle," said Stewart. "I'm guessing you also had some booze with you?"

"Yeah, but I hadn't drunk any of it. I was totally sober when I hit something. Er, someone."

"Daniel," Lesley finished for him.

Nate nodded yes. "I wasn't going very fast. I was trying to be quiet so that no one would spot me when I heard a thunk."

"About what time?" Stewart asked.

"Sevenish. It was still light out, so I went up to the bow to see what I'd hit. I thought it was going to be a log or something, but I could see right away that it was a body." He looked over at me with a mournful expression. "I could see that he'd been hit in the head."

"How did you know he was dead?" Lesley cut in.

"Well, I didn't jump overboard and examine the body, if that's what you're asking."

"No, Nate," Stewart continued, his tone deadly serious. "Lesley meant exactly what she said. How did you know he was dead?"

"Well, he was just floating, and I could see on the back of his head where the boat had hit him. Before that, he must have been swimming."

"Is it possible he was already dead when you hit him?" Stewart asked.

Nate shook his head with a definite no. "He must have been alive. He definitely didn't look like a dead body."

"And what," Lesley pushed, "does a dead body look like?"

"I don't know. Green. Disgusting. Gross."

"Not off Wynter Island, it doesn't," said Stewart.

"What do you mean?" Nate asked.

"What I mean is that the average ocean temperature off Wynter Island at this time of year is about eight to ten degrees Celsius."

"So?"

"Well, there is a reason why hospitals store bodies in a morgue and why morgues maintain bodies just above freezing."

"To stop decomposition," I inserted.

Lesley nodded. "Yup. The cold doesn't completely stop decomposition, but it does slow it down significantly when compared to a corpse left out in room temperature."

Nate leaned forward over the table towards Stewart. "What does that mean?"

"What it means, Nate, is that Daniel was most likely dead when you hit him."

"How can you be sure?"

Stewart leaned back in his chair and stared at the ceiling as if he was totting up his yearly bar tab. "Well, Daniel went missing sometime after walking up the hill from the ferry dock. The last footage we have of him is on the Hope Bay CCTV at eleven twenty-four Thursday morning."

"So?"

"So, if he was alive when you hit him, that would mean he had been wandering alone around Wynter for about seven or eight hours, before deciding to jump into the freezing ocean for a swim, fully clothed. Eight hours on this tiny island without a single person seeing him. Anywhere," Stewart finished.

"Okay? So, what does that mean?" I asked, confused.

"It means he most likely ended up in the water relatively soon after arriving on Wynter Island. Definitely soon enough so that the only person who had a chance to notice him was the murderer." Stewart bent over to briefly pet Billy. "But this does give us a couple of important clues."

"What clues?" I asked.

"Well, it gives us a second time and location for the body. The currents off Wynter," he got up and walked into the office, pulled a maritime chart off the wall, and brought it back to the coffee room, "were going northwest around the island. Which means if Daniel was here at nine p.m. on Friday," Stewart pointed at Steeltun Bay, "and here approximately twenty-four hours earlier." He drew a line with his finger right towards Muggs Isle. "That would mean he traveled approximately one and a half miles over a twenty-four-hour time period."

Lesley leaned over the map and looked closely at the distance between Stewart's two fingers. "If travelling that distance took him twenty-four hours, and he may have been dead for four to six hours when he was hit by the boat"—Lesley traced the line further right and came to a stop—"this is approximately where he went into the ocean."

"Where is it?" Nate asked.

I craned up on my tiptoes to see over Lesley's shoulder at the name printed underneath her finger: Sydney Cliffs.

My mind flashed back to my hike with Michael. The sight of Michael relaxed and stretched out on the rock face, the tufts of disturbed moss sticking to the bottom of his jeans.

"Oh my God!" The words slipped out, far louder than necessary.

Jupiter began scratching at the interview room door.

"Jupiter, it's okay. Nothing's wrong," I called out and placed my finger on the map. "I know where Daniel was killed."

"Where?" both Lesley and Stewart said at the same time.

"Here. At the top of the Sydney Cliffs."

"How do you know?" Lesley asked quickly.

I bent closer over the map. "Michael and I went for a walk, well, a hike really, up there. It was sunny at the top, so we sat down on that large shelf of granite."

Stewart nodded his encouragement.

"Well, the moss was ripped out of the rocks. Michael had to brush it off his jeans when he stood up. I thought it was animals. You know, digging or hunting. But it wasn't. It was ripped out in some kind of a fight. Like Daniel fighting for his life."

The front door slammed open as Michael and Anna rushed in. Michael, his hair askew, a Gore-Tex jacket half pulled on over an old t-shirt, resembled someone tossed from a tornado. Anna, clad in brightly colored LuLuLemon leggings and sneakers, hunted frantically around the room until her eyes locked on to Nate.

They opened the coffee room door, and Jupiter dashed to my side. He made one low growl at Billy. Stewart scooped the Frenchie up and into his arms.

"Michael, Anna, thanks for coming so quickly."

Michael's olive forehead had a sheen of perspiration across it, his expression strained. Anna rushed over to Nate, pausing first to do a quick check to see if he was injured, before wrapping her arms around him.

"What's going on, Stewart," Michael asked, fear making his voice deep and brusque.

"First off, Nate's okay."

"Thank God," Michael murmured, turning to look again at his son as if to reassure himself that Stewart was correct. "What the hell is he doing here then? We thought that he'd had some kind of accident after Fish Bingo."

"Nate told me something after the livestream ended," I started out.

"Told you what?" Anna asked, her arms still wrapped around Nate.

"That he hit Daniel Appolinar on the day he arrived on the island."

"What?" Michael's confusion rocketed quickly into indignation. "Are you saying he hit Daniel with the car?"

"No," Lesley said, "not the car. Your boat."

"Our boat?" Michael's brow furrowed in confusion. "I don't know what you're talking about."

"What they're trying to tell you, Dad, is that I took the boat out on the Thursday evening that Daniel was murdered."

Anna, startled, momentarily released her hold on him.

"You did what?" Michael shouted.

"Michael, calm down," Anna demanded. "Shouting is not going to help anything. Why, Nate? Why did you take the boat out without permission? You don't even have a license."

"That's just the first of the misdemeanors," Lesley said.

Anna looked over at Lesley, a trace of fear returning to her face. "What else did he do?'

"Well, we have the issue of underage possession of alcohol and illegally taking a maritime vessel. There is also the fact that he found a dead body and did not notify the police."

Anna looked to Michael for confirmation of this news, but his attention was focused solely on Stewart.

"Are you going to charge him, Stewart? Lesley?" he asked.

Stewart ran his tongue over his top lip, assessing the situation. "We don't have any proof that Nate had alcohol, only his confession that he did. I'm guessing you are not interested in laying charges concerning the theft of your boat?"

Both Michael and Anna nodded their heads quickly.

"As for finding a body and not reporting it to us, I'm willing to let that go under the circumstances. I will write it up as a minor who was unaware of the legal implications of finding a dead body."

Anna buried her face in Nate's hair, her shoulders relaxing, a small sigh of relief escaping from her lips.

"But I'm still going to have to go out and take a look at the boat. As well as confirm Nate's timing of events with the CCTV footage at the marina."

Anna's head snapped up. "What? Why, Stewart?"

Michael turned to look at her, confused at her sudden emotional shift. "They just need to confirm Nate's story. What's the problem with that, Anna?"

Anna's attempt to physically control her panic was painful to observe. What was she so upset about? Her reaction wasn't based on her son hitting a dead body while illegally operating their boat. No, her distress had ratcheted up at the mention of Stewart checking out the CCTV footage at the marina. What had happened at the marina that she didn't want Stewart to see?

"I'm just overwhelmed, that's all," she finally answered in a calmer voice. She may have smoothed out the furrows on her forehead, but I could see that her pupils still flickered like those of a trapped animal.

*What on earth is going on with her?*

"Can we take Nate home now?" Michael asked.

"Yes, you can," Lesley said. "We will get a signed statement from him tomorrow, as well as have him show us on which part of the boat he hit Daniel."

Michael and Anna stood up and hurried Nate out. Before exiting through the doorway, Anna turned, and her frightened gaze connected with Stewart's. I couldn't quite put my finger on the emotion I saw flickering between them, but it looked almost like Anna was begging for something from Stewart.

Like his help.

# Chapter Eighteen

I watched as Shea glanced around the chaotic mess of what had been the office foyer, her eyes assessing each new detail before speaking.

"Well, Kate, it looks like construction has started to move ahead." She squatted and extended her hand for Jupiter to sniff. He stood and walked over to her before condescending to allow her to pet him. "Remember me, Jupiter? The lady who saved your life and fed you for almost a year?"

"Yes, the builder had some free time in his schedule to start demolition work. It's still going to be a while before we have final drawings and the go-ahead to start construction." I pointed toward the far right-hand wall. "That's where the control room is going to be, and there"—I waved toward the back of the open room—"will be the enclosed studio."

"Very nice." Shea stood after petting Jupiter. He looked at her as if to say, 'is that all?' before returning to his bed. "This is going to look so professional when it's all done."

"I hope so. At least it will help us deal with the basic problems like—"

"Ambient light," we both said at the same time and broke into laughter.

Shea's laughter drifted to a stop. "How are you doing?"

"I'm okay, I guess. I have my moments, but Jupiter is great as a shoulder to cry on."

"Dogs are like that. Great furballs of love."

I smiled. Before I could say anything more, an RCMP squad car sped by outside. We both looked out in time to see the RCMP SUV following behind it, lights flashing.

"What's going on?"

"That's the whole detachment, both Lesley and Stewart," Shea answered. "Something big must have happened." She checked her watch. "It can't be an accident coming off the ferry. The ferry isn't in yet. I wonder if—"

"If it's something to do with Daniel?"

"Yeah," she said. "That's the only big police investigation going on right now. Do you want to follow them?"

"Like an ambulance chaser?"

"Well, it would technically be a police cruiser chaser. But, yeah. No rule says we can't drive down a public road if we want to."

I weighed my options. "Sure, let's go see what's going on. If not, my curiosity is going to drive me nuts." I grabbed my bag and keys, whistled for Jupiter, and followed her out to the Highlander.

"It sounds like they stayed on Rte. 97," she said as we pulled out of the parking lot. "I didn't hear them veer off on to the eastern side of the island."

"Me either. Let's stay on this road and see if we can spot them."

It wasn't long before we arrived at Harrow Village. The two RCMP vehicles had angled themselves in front of the Lind hotel.

"The Lind?' Shea said in surprise. "What the hell is going on there?" She pulled into a parking spot behind the vehicles.

"What are you doing?"

Shea had unbuckled her seat belt and ripped the keys from the ignition. "I'm going to find out what is going on."

"But we can't just walk into a police investigation!"

Shea frowned, saddened by my ignorance. "We aren't going to walk into a police investigation, Kate. We are going to ask Lesley an important question that can't wait until she gets home tonight."

"Which is?" I opened the passenger door, motioning Jupiter to stay inside.

"I haven't figured that out yet."

She started toward the front door like a ship under full sail, determined and with the wind at her back.

"Jesus Christ, Shea." I trailed behind her like a lemming preparing to fling myself over the cliff.

We snuck in through the open door to the lobby and followed the voices to the dining room. We inched our way along the wall and then peered in through the crack in the partially open doorway.

"Who the hell do you think you are, Stewart McLeod?" Bob thundered.

Stewart replied in a calm, conciliatory tone, "I am the Sergeant of the RCMP Detachment on Wynter Island. You already know that."

"Well, what right do you have to just barge into our place of business!"

Stewart pulled a piece of paper out of his notebook. He unfolded it and handed it over to Bob.

"What's this?"

"This is"—Stewart pointed toward the paper—"a search warrant."

"A what!"

I gripped the back of Shea's arm, fearful Bob would drop dead of a heart attack on the spot.

"You heard me. It's a search warrant to search your home for any evidence we can find regarding the death of Daniel Apollinar."

"Who?" Doreen asked, clearly confused.

Stewart turned to look at her, his voice softening. "Daniel Apollinar, Doreen. The young man who was found dead in Steeltun Bay."

"But—but what does that have to do with us?"

Stewart glanced around the tidy dining room. "Where did you say Ria was?"

"What does Ria have to do with this?" Doreen asked in a sudden panic.

"We need to talk with her, Doreen."

"Well, she's in Victoria. At work."

"That's what I thought," Stewart said. "Lesley and I have been trying to reach her all morning on her cell, but there's no answer. It just goes to voice mail. Is it possible her phone ran out of charge? Maybe she went somewhere without a cell signal?"

Doreen's face scrunched up into a puzzled frown. "Well, I don't know. I suppose her phone may be dead. The CBC Radio offices are right in downtown Victoria, so I don't see how they wouldn't have any cell signal at the station."

"I will call her manager at the station. See if she knows what's going on,"

Bob spat out and walked over towards the kitchen entrance to pick up a phone.

"Stewart, Ria hasn't done anything bad, has she?"

"I don't know right now, Doreen. We're just trying to gather information. That's why it is so important for us to talk with her. As soon as possible."

Doreen nodded robotically as if she hadn't understood a word Stewart had said.

"What do you mean, she left?" Bob's voice reached us from the kitchen.

"Holy crap," Shea whispered.

"Yes, I'm her father! I would know if she was planning to go away on a trip. She didn't even pack a suitcase!"

Silence ensued as we all eavesdropped on Bob's end of the conversation.

"Yes, yes, I know she's an adult, and it is not your job to keep track of her whereabouts. But she is also my daughter, and the police are here."

Another gap of silence.

"Yes, that's right, I said the police. They would like to speak to her immediately. You need to tell me where she has gone. Now."

Bob agreed with the person on the other end of the line before shouting at full force, "She's gone WHERE?"

"Oh my God," Shea whispered, "has she run away to Rio de Janeiro or something?"

I didn't make the immediate connection. "Why Rio de Janeiro?"

"Isn't that where all the murderers and bank robbers go to evade extradition?"

I paused and mulled this over. "I don't know. I never really thought about where I would go to escape extradition."

"Yes, yes, I heard you," Bob continued at a more moderate volume. "Please let me know if she contacts you. Thank you." He ended the conversation and stormed back into the dining room. "She's gone."

Doreen's hands flew up to her face. "Gone where? She didn't tell us anything!"

Bob strode over to Stewart, still gripping the phone with white-knuckled fingers. "She left for Haida Gwaii this morning."

"Haida Gwaii?" Stewart and Doreen said at the same time.

Bob nodded, his anger deflating into sadness. "She apparently asked a crew taking a floatplane up there if she could tag along."

"But why Haida Gwaii?" Stewart asked.

He shrugged his shoulders. "I have no idea. There's a radio crew recording a show on First Nations life. They're going to be up there for several days, out in the bush. No cell signal for any of them."

"What is her manager's name at CBC Radio?" Stewart asked. "I'll have Victoria police talk to her and see if we can come up with any more details."

Before Bob could answer, a shout echoed from the other side of the hotel.

"Lesley?" Stewart called out. "Is everything okay?"

After a short silence, Lesley's voice shouted back. "Yeah. I found something. I'll bring it out to you."

Shea and I exchanged a glance, like two Keystone cops determined to avoid running into each other as we attempted to escape detection. Before we could react, Lesley walked into the lobby.

"Shea? Kate? What are you doing here?"

"What? Someone else is here?"

Stewart, Bob, and Doreen walked into the lobby.

"What the hell are you two doing here?" Bob growled.

"I had an important question for Lesley. Couldn't wait till later."

"You do?" Lesley asked. "What is it?"

Shea took in a deep breath, most likely trying to buy herself some extra time. "It was umm, yes, what would you like for dinner tonight?"

Bob attempted to storm forward, but Stewart held out his arm to prevent his forward progress. "How dare you two just walk in here like you own the place? Haven't you done enough harm to this family already!"

"Okay, you two have got to stop acting like the Hardy Boys," said Stewart.

"The Hardy Boys were men, and like, last century," Shea muttered.

Stewart considered this. "Well, whatever the female version might be. Nancy Drew? No, that was my mom's generation, too. It doesn't matter. What does matter is that you are sticking your nose into police business."

"But it's about Daniel!" I burst out. "I need to know what's going on."

"No, you don't," Stewart replied before being shushed by Lesley.

"Actually, she might be helpful right now, Stewart," Lesley said as she brandished a long voile scarf folded around something small.

"How so? What did you find?" he asked.

She stepped closer toward us, carefully unfolding the layers of gauzy fabric from around the object. I gasped as I realized what lay in her palm.

"That's Daniel's," I said, stunned. "That's Daniel's cigarette lighter."

# Chapter Nineteen

"Daniel's lighter. Are you sure?"

I leaned closer to Lesley's hand and then reached forward to pick up the lighter. Lesley quickly moved it out of my way.

"No, you can't touch it, Kate. Just look at it."

I leaned closer. It was a rectangular silver Zippo lighter, heavily worn around the edges. I remembered the first time I had seen it.

*Daniel lit a cigarette in a Kabul street, and I spotted the unusual lighter in his hand.*

*"What's that?" I asked.*

*Daniel smiled that sweet smile of his. "It's a Zippo lighter from Operation Enduring Freedom."*

*I bent over to look at it.. On the scratched silver surface, there was an engraved shape of Afghanistan layered over with a camo print. Underneath, Baghram Air Field, Afghanistan, was inscribed. On the back was a name, C. RENNEDAY.*

*"Who is C. Renneday?"*

*"Someone I knew. I was embedded with his platoon." Daniel paused and rubbed his finger over the gouged surface of the lighter. "Sometimes, I'd have a drink or a smoke with him. You know, just shoot the breeze. Find out where he was from. What he wanted to do when he got back home. That kind of thing. He was a good guy. One night he left his lighter with me."*

*Daniel looked up into my eyes, and I knew I didn't need to ask what had happened to C. Renneday. "No next of kin?"*

*"The captain told me to keep it. Just to remember Chris any time I used it. Kind of a sentimental thought for a soldier, really. So that's what I do. I think of Chris*

*every time I use it." Daniel pocketed the lighter and reached for my hand. "Does that answer your question?"*

*I smiled and said, "About the lighter, yes. About whether you should stop smoking, no."*

I straightened up and looked at Lesley. "Yes, I'm sure."

"That makes no sense at all!" Bob blustered, his usual fury blunted by fear.

"Why on earth would Ria have it? She's never met this Daniel person," Doreen asked, her aging hands fluttering around her face.

Stewart gestured to Lesley to bag up the lighter. "I'm afraid she has."

"How?" Doreen asked. "We've never heard of him."

"Lesley went over the onboard footage from the ferry for the hundredth time yesterday. We know Daniel sat in the front observation lounge on the ferry and only went outside once to have a smoke. When he was out on the deck, Lesley thought she spotted a sliver of something on the footage. She zoomed in on that part of the frame, and she was right. There was someone there."

"Ria?" Shea seemed unbelieving.

"Yes, Ria. We didn't initially know who the person was. All we could see was a hand reaching out to take Daniel's lighter, apparently to light a cigarette. But the thing is, the person never returned it. Daniel threw his cigarette butt into the ocean when he was done and walked back inside. Without his lighter."

"How did you know Ria had the lighter?" I asked.

"We didn't. But there was something about the arm that bothered me," Lesley said. "I couldn't put my finger on it, but there was something familiar about it."

"What?" Shea asked.

"Ria's charm bracelet. It's hard to see clearly on the video, but it's a distinctive piece of jewelry, with large charms dangling from the silver chain."

"It was a graduation present from us." Doreen began to sniffle.

"When we magnified the footage, it became clear enough that we were able to obtain a warrant to search the hotel, in particular your living quarters. We were hoping Ria would be here so we could talk to her. But unfortunately," Stewart paused for effect, "she's gone."

"Bob! Oh my God, what has she done! What is going to happen to her?" Doreen threw herself into Bob's arms.

He wrapped one arm protectively around her. "It's going to be all right," he whispered in her ear, showing the first sign of humanity I had seen from him. "We just have to find her and bring her back. Then she'll be able to explain everything."

"I'm taking this back to the station, Stewart," Lesley said from the doorway, a taped-off evidence bag in one hand. "Shea?"

Shea sighed and turned to face Lesley. "Yes, Lesley, I know. You don't have to say anything. We need to talk about how I have invaded your professional life once again."

"You two! Get out!" Bob barked as soon as he realized we were both still in the lobby. "Now! Get out of here!"

He didn't have to say it twice. Shea and I ran past Lesley, down the steps, and into the Highlander. Jupiter was waiting in the passenger seat, looking worriedly out the window for us.

"Hi, Jupe," I said as he jumped on my lap and gave me darting little kisses on the cheek. "Sorry it took us so long."

Shea backed the Highlander onto the main road and pointed it toward the station.

"Trust me, Jupiter," she said as we picked up speed, "you wouldn't have wanted to be in there. It wasn't pretty."

# Chapter Twenty

I sat on the small deck at the back of the cottage, nursing an iced glass of raspberry seltzer. Jupiter had splayed himself out in front of me, soaking up the warmth in a spot of sunshine.

*Daniel's lighter. Why did Ria have his lighter?*

My mind jumped between the two images: Daniel holding the worn lighter in one hand and then the shock of seeing Lesley unwrap it from the scarf. Ria had purposely pocketed it, there was no doubt about that, but why? Because she liked the look of the lighter and wanted it? No, too easy. And why would someone run off to Haida Gwaii over something so simple? Had she wanted a memento that belonged to Daniel? If so, why? Was Sam right? Had Ria Corker served Daniel as a waitress on one of his sailing trips through the islands? Had she recognized him on the deck of the ferry? Was that why she spoke to him?

I took another sip of seltzer and let out a long, low sigh. Why would a waitress remember some random guy she served seven years ago? My breath caught in my chest. Unless he hadn't been some random guy. Perhaps he had been the guy who played her along? Perhaps he was the guy who whispered sweet nothings into her ear and then sailed off into the sunset?

*But Daniel wouldn't do that!* said one voice in my head.

*Why?* said another. *Like how he didn't cheat on you with that brunette you found him with in his apartment?*

Part of me felt guilty for even having such a thought. But another colder, more rational, part thought I might just have landed on the correct answer. Had Daniel broken Ria's heart? And had Ria gotten her revenge?

My cell phone rang, shocking me out of my musings.

"Hello?"

"Hi. Kate. It's Stewart. They found Ria yesterday. On Haida Gwaii."

"The local RCMP up there?"

"Yup. She agreed to return to Wynter Island voluntarily, so they put her on a floatplane first thing this morning. She should be arriving at the Water Aerodrome at Coho Bay Marina any minute. Lesley is up there waiting to get her."

"Okay, thanks for letting me know."

"No, that's not it. She specifically asked for you to be here when we question her."

"Me?" I said in surprise. "Why me?"

"I'm not a hundred percent sure, but I think it has something to do with her wanting you to hear her side of the story. I'm guessing because of your relationship with Daniel."

"Are Bob and Doreen okay with this?"

"Her parents haven't been told anything about it, other than that they can see Ria after we finish questioning her. Can you come? Billy's here, so leave Jupiter at the cottage."

"Okay. I'll be there in five minutes."

The five minutes turned into twenty as I made up a treat for Jupiter to gnaw on while I was gone. Why did Ria really want to see me? I wondered as I scooped peanut butter into the Kong. Just because Daniel had been my ex? Or was there something else? Did she realize that I, too, needed to be convinced of her innocence so she could be removed from the suspect list?

Ria was already seated in the interview room when I walked into the station. Billy ran to the station door to greet me. With his squat-legged run, he resembled a four-legged scuttling football. He stopped at my feet, pink tongue sticking out, all snuffly and happy. I gave him a quick pat on the head.

"Hello, everyone," I said as I joined them in the interview room. "I'm getting bored with this room, you know. I've been in here way more than I expected to be when I moved to Wynter Island."

"Do we need to repaint it for you?" Stewart asked dryly.

"No, but some new furniture might be a good idea. And please tell me you've got something to eat other than those maple cream cookies."

Lesley brandished a new bag of cookies. "We do. Chocolate digestives."

"Good."

I chose one and gestured the sleeve toward Ria, who shook her head.

"Okay, Kate's here now, so we might as well get started." Stewart pointed to the corner of the ceiling. "You need to know, Ria, that everything you say in this room is being recorded by that camera. Okay?"

Ria silently nodded her head in agreement.

"Can you say that out loud, please, as well as your name? It makes it clearer on the recording."

"My name is Ria Corker. Yes, I know I'm being recorded. I'm okay with that."

"The date today is May 5th. Sergeant McLeod and Constable Akiyama are present in the room as well as Kate Zoe Thomas, a suspect in this case. Ria, you do not need to say anything, but it may harm your defense if you do not mention when questioned something which you later relay in court. Anything you do say may be given in evidence. You told the RCMP on Haida Gwaii that you didn't want to speak with legal counsel," Lesley continued.

"Yes," Ria stated firmly. "I don't need a lawyer. I just need to tell everyone the truth."

"Okay," Lesley said and leaned forward, "what is the truth, Ria?"

"The truth is that I did see Daniel Apollinar on the ferry that Thursday morning, but I didn't kill him."

One of Stewart's eyebrows angled upward. "Then why did you lie about it? I asked you explicitly if you had seen the man in the photograph. You said no. Not even any hesitation. Just a flat-out no."

"I didn't want to get involved."

"'That's called obstruction of justice, Ria," Stewart informed her, his voice hardening with irritation.

A tear tipped over the corner of one eye and trickled down her freckled cheek. "I didn't realize it was that big of a deal."

Lesley blinked. "Murder? You didn't think murder was that big of a deal?"

"No, no, you don't understand." She placed her tightly clasped hands on the table, the heavy silver charm bracelet rattling against the wood surface. "I meant my contact with him was not that big of a deal."

"You don't get to decide that," Stewart explained, "And I don't believe that's the reason why you didn't tell us anything."

Ria's lower lip jutted out, and she gripped her hands even tighter together. "It wasn't important. No!" She raised one hand to stop Lesley from repeating herself. "What I'm saying is that I didn't have anything important to tell you about Daniel and his murder. I understand I should have told you that I talked to him on the ferry. I know it was wrong. But just because I made one mistake, that doesn't make me guilty of murder."

I took another bite of my cookie and considered her remark. A mistake doesn't make you a murderer, but lying to the police doesn't make you look innocent, either.

"Well, it certainly doesn't make a great impression," Stewart continued. "And it doesn't help us with our investigation."

"I know. Okay! I know!" Ria placed her face in her hands, the silver bracelet jangling against her cheek. "I just didn't want to look stupid."

Stewart peered down to see if he could make eye contact with her between her spread fingers. It looked to me like he was playing a game of peek-a-boo with a child. "Look stupid, how?"

"Stupid because I kept his lighter. On purpose."

"I don't understand," said Lesley.

Ria dropped her hands from her face, white indents appearing on her forehead where her nails had dug in like divots. "He was a cute guy. Someone new. Wynter Island is not the easiest place to find romance, you know. I've dated every available bachelor on the island."

"Not me."

"Alright, Stewart, every available bachelor on the island under the age of thirty-five and out of high school."

"Okay, I get it. The pickings are slim in the romance department on the island. So, you thought he was cute."

I smiled, remembering Daniel's crooked smile. *Yes, he was definitely cute. Was.*

"I saw him go out on the deck to have a smoke. I went out the other door and wandered over to where he was standing. I asked him if I could borrow his lighter."

"Which is what we saw on the video," Lesley said.

"Yeah. I tried to start a conversation, asked him why he was coming to Wynter Island. Tried to figure out if he was single."

"What did he say?" I asked.

"Not much. Said he was going to Wynter Island to talk to an old friend. And that he was staying at Kurt and Harald's B&B. I couldn't get much more than that out of him."

"So, then what?" Stewart asked.

"I slipped his lighter into my purse. He didn't notice. He finished his cigarette, said goodbye, and went back inside."

Lesley leaned closer to study her face. "Why did you keep his lighter?"

Her cheeks blushed a vivid red. "This is embarrassing." She glanced over at me before continuing. "I wanted an excuse to meet him again, okay? I had to work in Victoria on Friday, so I planned to go to the B&B on Saturday to return the lighter. Say he'd dropped it on the ferry, and I picked it up for him. See if maybe he wanted a tour of the island and to get a drink at the pub."

"But then you found out that the body of a man matching his description had been found in Steeltun Bay," I finished for her.

"Yeah. Mom and Dad were talking about it when I came down for breakfast on Saturday morning. They said the police thought foul play may have been involved."

"And rather than come to the station to tell us about seeing him—" Stewart continued.

"I panicked and wrapped up the lighter in a scarf and hid it in my bedroom drawer," she finished.

"Which is where I found it," Lesley said. "And when we came to talk to you?"

"I lied.  I didn't know anything about Daniel's murder, and I was embarrassed to admit I'd stolen his lighter in an attempt to see him again."

"The cover-up is always worse than the crime," I muttered to myself.

"What was that, Kate?" Stewart asked.

"Nothing, nothing. So, what happened yesterday morning?"

Ria sighed. "I was at work when I got the first call. Caller ID said Wynter Island RCMP, so I decided to let it go to voice mail. I listened to the message and realized you had figured out that I had lied to you about seeing Daniel. I panicked.  A crew was going to record a program on Haida Gwaii, so I asked if I could tag along. They were surprised, but said I was welcome to come. I turned off my phone and headed to the Inner Harbor to get on the floatplane."

"And what did you think was going to happen, Ria?" Stewart asked. "Did you think we wouldn't find you?"

"I wasn't thinking clearly.  I had lied to you guys about meeting Daniel, and I had something that belonged to him in my room! I needed time to think."

"And so, you got twenty-four hours and a night in the Haida Gwaii jail. Hope it was worth it for you," Stewart said.

"Why did you want me to be here today, Ria?" I asked. "I've got to admit, Stewart's call came as a surprise. I certainly wasn't expecting you to want to talk to me."

Ria looked over at me, her lower lip trembling again. "Because I wanted you to know that I didn't kill Daniel. And I wanted you to hear it from me. Do you believe me?"

I examined her moonlike face, swollen with tears, her nose red and dripping. She looked like the most inept murderer ever. Or was that her plan all along?

"What about the restaurant, Ria?"

Ria, startled, searched my face for a moment. For what? Clues as to how much I actually knew?

"What are you talking about, Kate?" Stewart asked in irritation. "And which restaurant are you talking about?"

I kept my eyes trained on Ria's face, ignoring Stewart's questions. "Did you sleep with him, Ria? Is that why you kept the lighter?"

"I, I don't know what you're talking about," Ria stuttered, looking plaintively to Stewart and Lesley for support.

"Did you think it was going to be something special when it was only a one-night stand?" I continued, my anger making each word louder and more forceful than the one before. "Did you want more? And you couldn't bear that it ended up being just wham, bam, thank you, ma'am?"

"Stewart, what is she talking about?" Ria wiped her eyes with a tissue, doing her best to appear shocked by my questions.

But was she really shocked? Was Ria perhaps far cleverer than she appeared? And was this how she was going to try and wriggle out of this? By playing the lonely, foolish young woman?

I explained to Stewart, "Sam Hanks told me that Ria worked as a waitress at the Lind during the summers."

"Yes, so? That was years ago when I was in college."

"I know. Years ago when Daniel used to sail through these islands. When he might have moored here on Wynter Island."

Lesley and Stewart swiveled back to Ria. She had balled the tissue up into her clenched fist and rested it on the tabletop.

"Is that true, Ria?"

"What? That I worked in the hotel restaurant while I was in college? You know that's true, Stewart. Do I remember some guy who was there years ago? Of course not."

"Yeah, well, what if it was more than just taking his order?" I tried to make eye contact with her, but she kept her gaze doggedly fixed on the tabletop. "What if it was something that left you feeling hurt and angry? Perhaps angry enough to make you do something when you spotted him again on the ferry?"

"Stewart, Lesley, are you going to arrest me?" Ria took a deep breath and raised her eyes to look at them. "'Cause I've told you everything I know. You've got to either arrest me and let me call a lawyer or let me go."

Stewart glanced from Ria to me, silently assessing the situation. "Do you have any concrete evidence to support any of this, Kate?"

Still attempting to get Ria to turn and look at me, I shook my head. "No. Not evidence. Just suspicions."

"Okay, then. Ria, you are free to go. I will call your father to come and get you. Even though you haven't been charged with anything, stay on the island. That includes no work trips to Victoria. Call your boss and tell her you need to take time off for emotional stress. We can get Dr. Lee to write up something for you. I want everyone to stay put until we can figure this out. Kate, follow me."

We stepped out into the office.  Billy, his tongue hanging out of his smooshed face, ran up to greet Stewart.

"How long have you known about this?" Stewart's voice teetered on the edge of anger. "You know it's a criminal offense to withhold information from the police during an investigation, right?"

"What information, Stewart? I don't have any information. All I have are suspicions and random guesses."

Stewart glared at me. "Well, these suspicions and random guesses seem to be entangling you more and more in this investigation. And when someone keeps on popping up like a bad penny? What do they say? If it walks like a duck and quacks like a duck, it's a...."

"Giraffe."

"Very funny. Go home. Stay out of this investigation. The last thing I need right now is to stumble over another body."

# Chapter Twenty-One

"You managed to find the house, alright.  Come on in." Michael opened the heavy walnut door wider to allow Jupiter and me to come inside.

"You've got a beautiful home," I said as I shrugged off my jacket and followed Michael into the living room of the airy, wood-beamed house. The West Coast Contemporary style, with its open concept and large windows, fitted perfectly in this forest setting.  "I'm guessing you're okay with my sidekick coming in?"

I gestured to Jupiter, who was following me slowly into the house, nose on the ground, apparently unhappy with the smell.

"Yeah, I'm fine with dogs in the house. We had a gorgeous springer spaniel, Buck, but he passed last year."

"I'm sorry. That's hard."

He gestured me toward the sofa, a cream leather minimalist style angled opposite two matching chairs. "It was. It was especially hard for Nate. You know, it's never easy the first time you lose something you love."

No, it wasn't. It was never easy to lose someone that you loved. Was it only two weeks ago that I found Daniel's body floating in Steeltun Bay?

"No, it isn't." I busied myself with moving some cushions on the sofa to cover my sudden tears.

"Can I get you some coffee? Maybe water?"

I settled myself down on the sofa with Jupiter beside my feet. "Water would be nice, thank you."

"Sure." He headed towards the kitchen.

I looked around the room.  An assortment of birch built-in shelves wrapped around one end of the room, leading up to a simple slate-tiled fireplace.  A large floor-to-ceiling window overlooked the forest, the flickering sunlight bouncing off the leaves and into the room.

Michael returned from the kitchen with a chilled bottle.

"It's a lovely house, Michael. It's interesting how that big picture window frames the forest, rather than the front yard."

"Yes, we wanted it to feel like we were up in a treehouse." He handed me the bottle and sat down in a chair across from me.

He wore tortoiseshell glasses today. I'd never seen him in glasses before, but they suited him. Gave him a more academic, intellectual air. His cologne, that mixture of seawater and fresh greens, wafted over to me.

"Are Anna and Nate here?"

"No. We've got a bit of quiet time to go over what's been happening."

I tried to rein in my thoughts. *Quiet time. Alone in the house. Just the two of us.* I shook my head and tried to refocus.

"And there's a lot that's been happening, Michael."

"Okay, hit me."

"Well, first off, did you know that Stuart and Lesley were able to figure out where Daniel's body entered the ocean?"

"Where was that?"

I paused. "The Sydney Cliffs."

Michael's head snapped up in surprise. "The Sydney Cliffs? But how did he end up there? He left the ferry on foot. And, by the way, does anyone know yet why he didn't bring a car with him?"

"Stewart says a Toyota Corolla was towed from the long-term parking lot at the Tsawwassen ferry terminal. It was an airport rental that was in Daniel's name."

He pursed his lips in confusion.  "He had a car but left it at the ferry terminal? Why?"

"They don't know. The assumption is that he arrived without a reservation and found there were no car spaces left. So he parked the car in long-term parking and walked on as a passenger."

"Which would explain why the only footage they have is of him hiking up the hill past the Lind hotel. He must have thought he could walk to Kurt and Harald's B&B."

"Or hitch a ride. But Stewart says he couldn't have gotten very far. There is too much traffic along Rte. 97 for him to have gone unnoticed for long."

His expression turned serious. "And that's where we lose him. After he hit the top of the hill in Harrow Village, he was picked up by someone."

"Yes," I said. "And that someone got him up to the top of the Sydney Cliffs."

"And killed him there."

"Probably. Remember those pulled-out clumps of moss we saw on our hike? I think they may have been ripped out during a fight between Daniel and the killer."

"But how did he get up there? The entire site was closed. The parking lot was even blocked off with a sawhorse and a closed sign."

I shrugged, helpless to find an explanation. "I don't know." I hesitated as a memory popped into my mind. "But the cliffs weren't closed on Thursday."

"What do you mean?"

"I saw Gwen moving the sign when Shea and I drove by."

"That's ridiculous. The cliffs weren't opened again until the following Monday."

"Are you sure?"

"Well, I should be. I'm the one who makes the decision whether the site is safe enough to reopen."

"Then what was Gwen doing there with the sign?"

"I've no idea."

"Is it possible that she might be involved in this, Michael?"

He paused, weighing the options, and then shook his head firmly. "No. I've known Gwen Wynter for years, and I know she's not capable of murder. You're just overthinking things. Perhaps the sign got knocked over by the wind, and she was just putting it back up? That actually happens quite a lot."

I thought back to that afternoon. The dirt road and the solitary figure of Gwen dragging something down the middle of it. "That's what Shea said when I told her."

"See? No great conspiracy."

"But if Gwen was there, Michael …."

"If Gwen Wynter is our murderer, then I'm Paul McCartney's long-lost love child. No."

"Okay," I hesitated, "if you're sure."

"Yes, I'm sure. Anything else?"

I leaned forward to take a sip of water and pat Jupiter's side. "Is what happened with Nate common around here?  I mean, for kids to ferry themselves out to isolated spots so they can drink or do drugs?"

"Or have sex? Yeah, it happens. I used to think that Nate would be smart enough to avoid that, but obviously, I can't say that anymore." He grimaced and took a sip of his coffee. "He's a teenager. Teens want their freedom. Living on a small island where everyone knows everyone else's business doesn't afford them much of that. Boredom is a big problem as well. On both Wynter and the other islands."

"At least they've got the Internet."

He nodded. "Yes. Not terribly fast Internet, but it's better than nothing."

"Well, it's certainly safer for him to grow up here than in the city."

"In some ways.  Crime on the islands is minimal.  Mainly drunk and disorderly charges. There is the occasional domestic violence charge, but that's about it. The only one I've heard of was between Shelley and Greg's dad years ago. But there is a drug problem."

"Drug problem? That sounds ominous."

"Well, the physical border between the US and Canada has been strengthened over the past few years to protect against smuggling, both drugs, and humans." He gestured in the direction of the Pacific. "But the water border? That's pretty porous."

"Are you saying there is drug smuggling here? On Wynter Island?"

"Here and all of the Gulf Islands."

"But most of the population consists of retired senior citizens.  Is the Garden Club running a meth lab that I don't know about?"

"He grinned. "No. Our problem is with the drug cartels. The ones from Mexico and Central America. They like to take advantage of all the secret coves and beaches on the islands here, just like the rumrunners did during Prohibition. It's a breeze for them to motor in from the States and dump drugs on an isolated beach or islet. Or rendezvous with a small Canadian boat out in the channel."

"How clever. Police on the islands wouldn't be able to spot them."

"Not unless they were brightly lit or the police had a tip."

"Have Stewart and Lesley been able to catch anyone?"

"Nothing big. I know there was some gossip going around about Dougie dealing weed for a few years, but he was never caught. Greg, however, was."

"What did he do?"

"Got into drugs in high school and moved quickly to the hard stuff. He had a criminal record by the time he was nineteen: possession with intent to sell. Cocaine and meth, I think. It was enough to put him over the top, and he had to spend ten months in prison."

"He seems like such a sweet kid."

"He is. Some people just get dealt a bum hand of cards. Shelley stood by him through everything, though. Paid his legal fees. Took the ferry over to visit him at the Correctional Center on Vancouver Island once a week. Never gave up hope."

"Is he doing better?"

"I think so. I haven't heard any rumors that he or Dougie are selling again. Not that there aren't others to take their place." He shrugged. "What's this I hear about Ria?"

"Another long story. She says she met Daniel on the ferry and stole his lighter so that she would have an excuse to stop by his B&B and see him again."

"But things went awry."

"Yes. When she heard about the murder, she realized that the lighter tied her to it. She panicked and ran away to Haida Gwaii."

"But she's back on the island now, isn't she?"

"Yes. Stewart gave her a warning but didn't charge her with anything … yet."

"Yet? Do you think she's guilty?'

I took a long sip from my bottle of water. "I don't know. I just feel there is something off about her story."

"I find it hard to believe that Ria Corker would kill anyone."

"Well," I turned to look out the window, "someone on this island did."

A car pulled into the driveway, its tires crunching over the gravel. Footsteps sounded on the front porch, and Anna stepped in, carrying several large recycled bags filled with groceries.

"Oh, hi, Kate," she said, her voice muffled by the keys gripped between her teeth.

"Hi, Anna."

Michael jumped to his feet and went over to help her. "Here, let me take one of those for you."

He untangled one of the heavy bags from Anna's hands and carried it into the kitchen before placing it down on the granite island. Anna removed the keys from her teeth and wiped a bit of saliva off her lip.

"Thanks, sweetheart. Too many groceries and too few hands to carry them," she laughed.

"Do you need my help with anything?" I followed them into the kitchen.

"No, you two can get back to business."

After a quick peck on the cheek, Michael returned to the living room.

"It's okay. I can help you put stuff away," I inserted quickly.

I needed a few minutes alone with her to try and find out what had happened at the police station. Something had upset her, I was positive about that, and the only thing I knew for sure was that it didn't have anything to do with Nate and their boat. Could it possibly have something to do with Daniel?

"I'm just here bringing Michael up to date on the murder investigation," I said.

"Oh, have they had a break in the case?"

"No. We're just catching up, really."

I handed her a package of eggs from the top of one bag. She placed them inside the fridge and quickly followed them with a few litres of milk and some fresh vegetables.

"Oh, Eccles cakes!" I pulled out a bakery box, pausing to look at the sugar-encrusted Welsh pastries. "I haven't had one of these in years!"

"Nate loves them," she smiled. "You can put them on the counter. "

I placed the box down and considered what I was going to say. Asking personal questions that were none of my business was something I'd gotten used to as a journalist. Uncomfortable, but necessary. It was always best to just get it over with.

"How did things go with Stewart at the marina the other day?"

Anna paused, one hand holding the fridge door open, the other gripping a plastic bag of oranges. She turned her head to look up at me. Her smile had dipped downward, her eyes suddenly shifting from warmth to ice.

"Why do you ask, Kate?"

Although the words were placid enough, her tone made it clear she didn't want to discuss this.

*Well, that touched a nerve.*

"Oh, you know, just asking questions."

"Why?"

"Because that's what I do. I'm a journalist. We ask a lot of questions."

She straightened up so that we were now face to face. "Am I being investigated, Kate?" Her words were quiet but intense. She was close enough that I could smell the sweet scent of her powdery perfume wafting over to me.

Rather than answer her question, I asked another of my own. "You seemed quite upset when Stewart mentioned that he would be going out to check on your boat. Was everything ok? "

She squinted angrily, her fragile skin creasing into fan-like wrinkles around her eyes. "No, everything was not ok. I had just found out that my son stole our motorboat and, while operating it without a license, managed to hit a dead body. I think that's enough to upset anyone, don't you?"

"What's going on in there?" Michael's voice called from the living room. "You're taking forever, Kate."

"It's nothing," Anna replied coolly, turning from me to place the oranges in the fridge and snick the door shut. "Kate was just saying good-bye. She's got somewhere she needs to go."

I had pushed as far as was possible for one day. I nodded at her match point and smiled, but she did not return it. I turned around to find Jupiter hovering behind me. He followed me back into the living room as I grabbed my coat and bag.

"Yes, that's right. Jupiter and I must hit the road, I'm afraid."

Michael stood up and walked me to the front door. "Thanks for coming, Kate."

I tried not to glance toward Anna in the kitchen. "I've got to keep my lawyer up to date on everything, don't I?"

In the half-light of the open doorway, a five 'o clock shadow was beginning to show along the side of one cheek and his chin. What would his kiss feel like? I wondered. Would the stubble rub against my face, causing my skin to flush angrily? Or would it be just another sensation to add to the taste of his lips and the touch of his skin?

"Kate?"

"Sorry, Michael. Thanks for having me and Jupiter over. We'll talk soon."

I purposely did not look back as we walked down the steps, jumped into the station truck, and drove away.

# Chapter Twenty-Two

The narrow road to Coho Bay ribboned out in front of me, bisecting large chunks of green pasture. I had never driven to this part of the island before. It held, so I had been told, the Tsetsuwatil pub & grill, a cafe, a marina and, most notably for me, the veterinarian.

"Guess what time it is, Jupiter?"

Jupiter looked over from his position in the passenger seat of the truck.

"It's vaccination time! YAY!" I imitated the sound of a crowd roaring. "You have no idea what I'm saying, do you, Jupe? Which is just as well because I'm guessing you're not going to be happy when you finally figure out where we're going."

Jupiter stared at me in silence for a few moments before returning to the window.

I slowed down as the road straightened out and headed to a dead-end in the parking lot. The small shopping center was nestled right alongside the edge of the bay. The pub hung out over the marina, offering a beautiful view of the ocean.

"Here we are, Jupe. Prepare yourself."

I climbed out of the car and went round to open the passenger door. Jupiter sat gloomily in his seat, not budging.

"Yes, I know it's a leash, Jupiter. I know you don't like it. But the vet has to have some way of controlling you while he's examining you."

A silent death stare from my dog.

"Okay, well, you can sulk all you want, but we have an appointment to get to."

I clipped the leash to his collar and firmly "helped" him out of the car. The office was on the second story, accessed by a wooden staircase on the side of the building.

"Here we go."

Looking like a mother trying to drag an errant toddler into a pediatrician's office, I slowly backed my way up the stairs, pulling Jupiter behind me.

"There you go, Jupe. Almost there."

I pushed open the door at the top of the stairs with my butt and dragged him into a small waiting area.

"I'll be out in a minute," a male voice called from behind a closed door. Within a minute, Ben walked out, drying his hands on a paper towel.

In bright daylight, he was more handsome than I remembered. Of course, the only other time I had seen him had been in the throbbing lights of Steeltun Bay. Tall, slender but not skinny, he had a short dark beard and mustache enfolding an oval face with a chiseled profile. His most dramatic style statement was his long dark mahogany-colored hair that he had braided down his back. His profile looked like a rather fetching show horse.

"It's nice to get a chance to meet you again, Kate, when you're not in the middle of some crisis." He smiled, his cheeks pushing upwards. "It's usually better to try and meet in less trying circumstances."

"I agree," I said with a smile, liking the warmth and humor in his voice, as well as his smile, which was wide enough to keep nothing hidden. But was that really the case? It felt like everyone on this island had something to hide.

"I've brought a reluctant pup to see you."

Ben crouched down and reached a hand out toward Jupiter, whose expression clearly said, *You've got to be kidding me*. Ben withdrew his hand.

"Well, Jupiter, it's not like we haven't met before." He glanced up at me and then back to Jupiter. "I come out to Shea's farm once a month to check on her animals. And that used to include you, Jupiter. Until this nice lady decided to adopt you."

Nice lady. It wasn't much of a compliment, but I'd take it.

"I think he's angry because I insisted on putting a leash on him." I waggled the red woven leash Shea had given me.

Ben straightened up and gestured me through into the small examining room. "Ahh, I see Jupiter. I'm not the problem. Her tool of oppression has dented your masculinity."

The examining room had at one point been a small office. An array of small cactuses perched along the windowsill, as well as a framed photo of a beautiful sunset in the mountains.

With no warning, Ben reached down, grabbed Jupiter around the legs as if he were a bale of hay, and deposited him on the examining table.

"There you go, Pup. I got you up here before you even had a chance to protest."

A little woof came from the other side of the examining room door, followed by a paw scratching at the door.

"Luce, you're fine. Go to your crate." He turned back to me. "That's Lucy, my King Charles Cavalier spaniel. She comes to work with me every day but usually stays in the admin office so that she doesn't spook any pets. Must be getting bored or needs a walk."

Lucy. Where had I heard that name before? I searched backwards in my memory. Yes! Ben had been on that list. The one that had listed all the islanders without an alibi for the time of Daniel's death. He had been out walking Lucy.

"Penny for your thoughts."

I started. "Sorry. I was thinking about your dog."

"Lucy?" He reached behind him to pull a syringe from a steel bowl. He rubbed Jupiter's shoulder with an alcohol wipe and quickly administered the shot. "See, buddy. That wasn't so bad, was it?"

Jupiter, who was still processing this sudden attack upon his flesh, gave Ben a lethal dose of side-eye.

"Why did you think about Lucy?"

"Stewart mentioned her the other day."

Ben laughed. "Stewart is talking to you about Lucy?"

"Yes," I hesitated and then decided to go for it. "We were discussing where people were on the day of Daniel's murder."

He deposited Jupiter on the floor and shifted his attention to tidying up his equipment. "You mean checking alibis?"

"Yes, that's right."

The back of his oxford shirt rose and fell as he cleared away the syringes and swabs. He finally turned back to look at me, his face as placidly innocent as a babe in arms.

"Stewart told you that I took Lucy out for a walk on Crimson Bay. By the way, do you know why they call it Crimson Bay?"

I shook my head no, determined to avoid getting sidetracked from my line of questioning.

"It's because there was a brickworks there in the forties or fifties. The factory building is long gone, but all of the leftover bricks were dumped in the bay. Over time, they've been worn down by the tide into small brick-red stones. At certain times of the day, the light hitting the stones in the water tints the bay a crimson color."

"Very interesting, but we were talking about your walk with Lucy?"

Ben turned his head to one side and examined me with a smile. "You are quite the sleuth, aren't you?" He dumped the gauze into the trash bin. "Yes, what Stewart told you is correct. I didn't have any patients that afternoon, so I took Lucy down to Crimson Bay. We had a nice long walk along the beach. Walked all the way up to the Salish Winds Resort. The weather was beautiful. A bit cool, but what else can you expect from British Columbia in the spring?'

"And nobody saw you?"

"No, nobody saw me. Nada. Niente. No one." He opened the examining room door to see a brown and white dappled spaniel sitting patiently on the other side. "Lucy, what are you doing here? I told you to go to your crate."

Sad spaniel eyes examined him balefully for a moment before she got up and walked over and stood silently by the front door.

"Oh, you need to go potty. Hold on." He grabbed a leash that was hanging on the wall. "Kate, Jupiter seems to be in great shape. We just have to keep on top of his shots and his flea/tick and heartworm treatments. I'll walk you to your car since Lucy has to go outside anyway."

"But what about the bill?" I found the haste with which he shuttled us out the front door unusual. Did Lucy really have to go potty that badly?

"I'll send you the bill. Don't worry. I know where you live," he laughed.

We quickly dashed down the stairs, Jupiter as desperate to get away from Ben as Lucy was to find a spot of grass.

"Well, thanks, Ben. I appreciate your being able to see Jupiter."

"This is Wynter Island." He stood patiently while Lucy relieved herself. "No one here is run off their feet. Everyone has some free time on their hands. By the way," Now that Lucy had finished, he walked back to where I was standing. Jupiter, watching his approach, began to pull firmly in the opposite direction. "Are you still looking for volunteers at CWYN?"

"Oh yeah. We've always got room for more volunteers. In fact, I could use some help at the next Fish Bingo broadcast if you're interested. Nate is grounded for the next few weeks."

"When is that? Thursday night?"

"Yup, Thursday night at eight o'clock. I need crew to be there at seven to help me get things set up."

"Well, count me in!" Ben said.

An elderly woman pulled into the lot beside us. A sizeable cat carrier had been secured by the shoulder harness on the back seat of her Mercedes.

"I'm sorry, Kate, but it looks like duty calls. Hi, Miss Moore. I'll see you upstairs." He turned and ran back up the stairs with Lucy behind him, pausing halfway up to wave good-bye.

"See you on Thursday!" I called out to his retreating back. "That wasn't so bad, was it, Jupe?" I said as we climbed back into the station truck.

Jupiter, his feelings hurt, turned his back to me and refused to comment.

# Chapter Twenty-Three

"It's a what?"

"A hawk."

"Where did Harald find an injured hawk?" I asked as Shea drove us at her usual breakneck speed towards the Legion. She had stopped by the cottage first thing to ask for my assistance with a rescue.

"Like so many of our lost and injured creatures, they congregate near the Legion's dumpster looking for scraps."

"So now the Legion has become the main stop on your underground railroad of animal rescues?"

She smiled. "I guess. I mean, it's lucky that Kurt and Harald are good guys, especially Harald. He's got a soft spot for all creatures."

"How did the two of them meet? Was it here on the island?"

"Oh no." Shea took the left turn, skidding her tires over the loose gravel. "They met online on one of those gay matchmaking sites. Harald was still living in Copenhagen then."

"But didn't the birthmark … I know this sounds shallow, but didn't it put Kurt off a bit?"

She smiled at the memory. "He didn't know. Harald photoshopped the pictures he emailed to him and insisted on communicating only by phone and text. No skype for him. Too clinical, he said. Not romantic enough."

"But, surely, it had to come out at some time."

"Yes." Shea braked at a stop sign for a nanosecond. "Kurt finally flew over to Copenhagen and went to meet him at a cafe. He spotted Harald hiding behind a menu at another table, trying to summon up the courage to tell him the truth."

"Oh my God! What happened?"

"He walked over to Harald's table, sat down, and waved for a waiter. 'I've been traveling for the past fifteen hours," Shea mimicked his deep bass voice, "and I don't know about you, but I need some food.' The birthmark wasn't as big a deal for Kurt as Harald thought it would be. They got married on the island last year."

"Okay, I haven't heard that love story before."

Shea turned into the Legion parking lot, swinging the Highlander around to the back of the building. I could see Harald crouched down by an object lying on the ground.

"Oh goodness," Shea sighed. "This looks worse than I thought it was going to be."

We pulled to a stop and jumped out of the SUV. Shea grabbed me by the arm and halted me in my tracks. "Let me go first. You follow quietly. The last thing we need to do is startle the bird, so he panics and injures himself even more."

"Okay."

We slowly walked up to where Harald was crouched down. He looked up, obvious distress in his eyes.

"Harald," Shea asked quietly. "Is he still alive?"

"Yes, but he's not looking good."

We crept close enough that I could see the smallish bird of prey resting on the tarmac. His eyes were open, his chest heaving with desperate pants.

"Kate," Shea asked softly, "go back to the Highlander and bring me the cardboard box with a towel and work gloves in it, ok?"

I dashed back to retrieve the items. When I returned, she and Harald were deep in conversation.

"Dougie can't take it over to the wildlife rehabilitator in Victoria?"

Harald shook his head no. "No, he had to go over to Vancouver for some reason. Took his big landscaping truck."

"Damn it," Shea muttered. "How about Greg?"

"I think he went with Dougie. They had some kind of business they needed to take care of in the city."

"For Christ's sake, the two of them bum around this island all the time. When I actually need them to do something, they are off gallivanting. I thought they were finished with those trips."

"Trips where?" I asked.

"Dougie had some job he was working at in Vancouver for a few years. He needed to go over a few times a month with his landscaping truck. Contract tree work, I think."

"You can't look after the bird yourself?"

She shook her head. "No, birds need particular care. He needs an experienced wildlife rehabilitator who works with birds of prey. I know a great one in Victoria. I've worked with her before. It's just I have other things planned for today." She sat back on her heels, staring down at the wounded bird. "I guess it's just you and me, Mr. Hawk."

"Do you need me to come with you?" I asked.

"No, no, he's docile enough, poor thing. It's not going to take two of us to control him. Harald, could you give Kate a ride back to her cottage?" She glanced quickly at her watch. "If I get a move on, I should be able to make the next ferry to Victoria."

"Sure. No problem."

It didn't take long for her to gently cover the hawk with a towel, and using her heavy work gloves, transfer him to the safety of the deep cardboard box.

"Okay, I'm off, guys. Thanks for the help. I'll text you as soon as I know anything." And she and the hawk sped off down Rte. 97.

"Here, Kate. You get into the van." Harald pointed to the white panel van with the Legion's name written across it. "It's unlocked. I'm going to grab the keys and tell Kurt where I'm going."

As I opened the van door, a waft of European men's cologne mixed with a hoppy wash of Carlsberg floated out at me. Within a few minutes, Harald jumped in.

"You live near Shea, right?" he asked as he revved the engine and headed out onto the road.

"Yes, Anna and Michael's rental cottage, the one that's a short walk from

Steeltun Bay.'

Steeltun Bay. I couldn't say the words without seeing the bay lit by flashing red lights, hearing the sound of feet splashing through the icy water.

"I'm sorry about your boyfriend," Harald said, his Danish accent thickening with his discomfort. "I haven't had a chance yet to extend my, well, our, condolences."

"Thank you," I said, looking out the passenger window.

I knew he was just being kind, as Shelley had been, but the last thing I needed was to be dragged back to memories of that evening. The only way to keep myself from falling over an emotional cliff was to focus on the future. Finding Daniel's killer and getting the station up and running were the only things I could deal with right now. Memories, grief, pain could all be dealt with on some nebulous future date.

Scrabbling for a way to change the subject, I suddenly remembered Shea's story. "Shea told me about you and Kurt. The two of you have a very romantic love story."

Harald's face split into a wide grin. "Yes, it is, isn't it? I'm lucky to have found Kurt."

"You are. This is your first marriage, right?"

Harald hesitated, and for a moment, the smile slipped from his face. "Yes, of course."

"For both of you?"

"Yes.

"Well then, you're soulmates." Daniel's face washed in front of me once again. "I found my soulmate. I found my one true love. I found my one and only forever and always." I recited. "A friend of mine read that out for her wedding vows."

"Do you believe that? That there is only one true love for each of us?"

"Oh, I don't know. I hope not. It's just something people say. Unfortunately for my friend, it wasn't true. Her marriage only lasted a couple of years. But you did find your one true love with Kurt."

There was another hesitation before Harald spoke again. "If you don't mind me asking, where did you meet Daniel?"

I got the distinct feeling it was now Harald who was changing the subject. "We met in Afghanistan. Kabul. I was working for PBS as a news producer. Daniel was a reporter for AP."

"Did you like it over there?"

I paused and considered the contradiction that was Afghanistan: an underdeveloped country trying to survive in a technologically advanced world. What stuck with me the most was the closeness of the people, the unbreakable bonds of family, of tribe.

"In many ways, Afghanistan was much more beautiful than I had expected. You think of a war-torn country, and you just imagine it as a colorless hell. But it really wasn't. Have you traveled in the Middle East?"

"Afghanistan? No. I visited Dubai once."

"Dubai is quite nice. Daniel and I used to go there when we had a few days off work. Just to get out of Kabul. What a culture shock that was! Going from donkey transportation to Ferraris."

"Yes, I can believe it."

I spotted a piece of paper stapled to a tree trunk. It was the poster advertising the upcoming discussion about local orca populations.

"I see that Anna is hosting a talk with your local member of parliament."

"Not member of parliament, that's Ottawa. Member of the Legislative Assembly is our provincial representative."

'Your MLA then. Discussing the diminishing orca population."

"Yes. Anna posted one of those up in the bar at the Legion."

I remembered the fury in Anna's eyes when I asked her about Stewart's visit to the marina. Was it possible that Harald knew something about that?

"She's really involved in politics, isn't she?"

Harald swerved onto the dirt road that led to Steeltun Bay. "Yes, the Green Party. She works a few days a week at their provincial office in Victoria."

"I heard that she may be considering a run for office herself."

Harald shot a quick glance over at my face. "Really? But everyone likes our present MLA."

"Yes, but there's a rumor she may be retiring."

"Oh, I see." His brow furrowed in concern.

That was odd.  Why would he be concerned about Anna running for election? "You don't want Anna to run for office?"

"No, of course not. I think she'd do a great job. It's just…." He didn't finish his thought, subsiding into a worried silence before trying again. "She has a life here on the island with Michael and Nathan. It would be a shame for her to," he paused again, "lose that."

"Why would she have to lose that?  Wouldn't she just commute from Wynter Island? And even if she couldn't, politicians often have to live away from home. She wouldn't be leaving Wynter Island permanently."

"Yes, of course."

"What is it, Harald?"

He looked like he was forcing his facial muscles into a pleasant smile. "Nothing. Nothing at all."

"It doesn't look like nothing. Do you know something about Anna?"

"It's bad business to gossip about your customers, Kate."

"What is there to gossip about?"

"I know how tricky you journalists can be."  He laughed to soften the rebuke. "One of my cousins in Norway is a journalist. Look, Jupiter is in the front window. He's been waiting for you to come home." Harald stopped the van in front of my cottage, relieved to finish our conversation. "I wish we could have a dog, but Kurt has allergies."

"Yes, I remember," I replied and stepped out of the van. "Thanks for the drive home, Harald."

And with a wave, he was gone.

I stood for a moment watching the Legion van disappear back down the dirt road.  Harald knew something, that was for sure.  Something about Anna. But did it have anything to do with Daniel?

Jupiter banged a paw against the glass window.

"Okay, okay, Jupiter. Calm down. I'm coming."

# Chapter Twenty-Four

"All right, here you go." The young woman wearing a T-shirt emblazoned with the words Tsetsuwatil Pub and Grill placed the sizable plate of food down in front of me. "One Coho Bay burger with extra pickle and fries and a pint of Dark Matter ale from Hoyne Brewing Company in Victoria."

"Thanks." I picked up the dripping glass and took a long sip. It was cold and smooth, richly dark with chocolate undertones and a nice alcohol kick at the end. "I needed this."

It had been a long couple of weeks. It felt like only yesterday I put my furniture in storage in Boston and packed my bags for this trip. Just yesterday that I had excitedly clambered up into the seaplane at the Vancouver International Airport for the final leg of my adventure.

"How's it cuttin', Kate?" a voice thick with t's and d's said from beside me.

Dougie stood beside the table in clean jeans and a dark green fleece jacket, his balding pate covered with a Blue Jays baseball cap. Since most of his work on the island was with trees, he was usually covered in a sticky residue of sap and needles. Perhaps he had been doing something other than landscape work this morning?

"I got this, Dougie. I know the correct answer." I placed my pint glass down on its coaster and prepared myself. "Like a knife."

"Good!" Dougie laughed, a loud and purely joyful sound.

"I had a look at some Newfoundland language sites online. I wanted to be prepared for your next volunteering session. Have a seat."

"Don't mind if I do." He pulled out one of the dark wooden captain's chairs placed around the round table. It, too, reeked of marine kitsch, as did the painted signs on the walls of the pub: The pessimist complains about the wind; the optimist expects it to change; the realist adjusts the sails.

*God save us from themed restaurants.*

"How are you doing? Do you want something to drink?" I waved at the waitress.

"That's not necessary. But if she's coming anyway, I'll have a Labatts Blue." Dougie took off his jacket and settled into his chair.

"Hi. Sorry to bother you, but could we have another drink?" I asked the waitress. "A Labatts Blue. Do you want something to eat, Dougie?"

He hesitated, a bit thrown by this question. "Well, I don't want to be a nuisance."

"It's fine, Dougie. Order whatever you want."

"Hmmm," He gazed longingly at my plate. "That looks good to me. I'll have what she's having. Thank you," he said when the waitress took the order away to the kitchen. "I should be buying a drink for you, not the other way around."

"Why?" I picked up my burger and took a bite.

"Well, you look like you've been hauled through a knothole backward."

I stopped in mid-chew. "I don't know what that means, but it doesn't sound very good."

The waitress delivered Dougie's beer, and he took a long sip before answering. "Well, what can you expect? You've been to hell and back since you came here."

I paused to think about his comment. It wasn't the most flattering thing ever said about me, but yes, there was no doubt I had been to hell and back since arriving on Wynter Island.

"How are you holding up, Kate? Really?"

I finished chewing and put the burger down on my plate. "As best I can, Dougie."

"I heard about Ria off and running away to Haida Gwaii." He leaned forward conspiratorially over the table. "Honest to God, I don't know why she came back here after college. If it'd been me, I'd a hit the road for Toronto or somewhere."

I shrugged. "I don't know. Maybe she's really close to her parents?"

"Well, Doreen's a sweetheart, but Bob? I know he loves her, but she's grown now. He's gotta let her live her own life."

"He doesn't? Even now that she's an adult?"

He shook his head. "I don't think so. Well, I mean, look at all the fuss he's made about her not getting the job at the station."

I nodded and took another bite of my burger.

"And that's not the first time. He's been doing this stuff for her entire life. I remember hearing about something that happened years ago with some guy."

"What happened?"

"I'm not sure, but I think she was having a bit of a romance with some journalist who was here writing a story."

"You mean about Oceanica?"

"Yeah, that's right. Anyway, she was in his room at the Lind Hotel," he waggled his eyebrows seductively, "when Bob stormed into the lobby looking for her. He was as angry as a cornered possum."

"What happened?"

"Well, Doreen eventually brought the two of them downstairs. People thought Bob was going to murder the guy."

"She was hardly a child."

He took a long sip of his beer. "No, but I think part of it was that the guy was quite a few years older than her."

"How old?"

He shrugged. "I dunno. I wasn't here then. Maybe like ten years older or so?"

I did some quick math in my head. If Ria was 19, that would have made Daniel about 29. Ten years older than Ria and a good five years before I met him.

Bloody hell! Could it be Daniel? Was it really possible that Daniel was the journalist who'd been writing a story about the Oceanica thefts? And ended up romancing Ria while he was here?

"I don't suppose you heard what he looked like?"

"No, although I'm sure someone remembers."

"So, the moral of this story, Dougie, if there is one, is that I shouldn't make Bob Corker angry?"

He wobbled his head from side to side. "Yeah, I know. It's hardly rocket science, is it?"

"And I think it's a bit too late for that now. He's already pissed at me for getting the job at CWYN."

"Yeah, I know. At least there's not much he can do about that. Not that he isn't trying his best."

I thought back to the ruined video shoot and the Facebook posts. "What do you mean?"

"I heard he's got a petition going around the island. Trying to turn up the heat on Gwen to get you fired."

I sighed. "He's certainly giving it his all, isn't he? Poor Gwen. She's had nothing but trouble since I came here. Perhaps she should have hired Ria for the job, after all."

"You don't mean that."

I swallowed the last bite of my burger and wiped my mouth with a napkin. "Yes, I do mean it. If I hadn't come here, perhaps Daniel would still be alive."

He leaned over the table toward me, looking straight into my eyes. "Ours is not to reason why. Ours is but to do or die. My mum used to like to quote Shakespeare to me."

"That was Tennyson, Dougie, not Shakespeare, but I get your point."

"We can't understand why things happen. All we can do is keep on going."

"That's true." I placed my dirty napkin down on the tabletop. "Very true."

"Where's your pup?"

"He's back at the cottage with a frozen Kong filled with peanut butter. He'll be fine for a couple of hours. I needed to have a break and come out and have a real meal that didn't include a dried cheese product."

He wiped his mouth and leaned back in his chair. "That was delicious, Kate. Thanks."

"Don't worry about it."

"Nah, you don't worry about it.  Everything will work out in the end. Okay? I promise."

I patted his hand on the table. "From your mouth to God's ears, Dougie. Your mouth to God's ears."

* * *

The truck bounced and thudded over the rutted drive up to Gwen's farmhouse on Wynter Mountain. Due to the rainstorm the previous evening, the view was significantly different than my first trip.  Rather than the previous wide-open expanse of ocean, I could only catch glimpses of the sea in between the waves of mist that still clung to the mountain's peak.

*Does Gwen ever get lonely up here?*

She didn't even have a dog to keep her company or offer any kind of protection.  Although, I guess, there wasn't much she needed protection from, other than perhaps the occasional mountain lion.

I pulled in beside Gwen's old Ford 150 and turned off the ignition.  I could see tracks in the dirt. Gwen must have had another visitor up on the mountain this morning. A boyfriend? No, Gwen wasn't the boyfriend type. Girlfriend? Nah, she wasn't the girlfriend type, either. She was the loner type. The aging hermit type. Gwen, alone up here on her family mountain with her fruit and veg. Why, then, had she been at the Sydney Cliffs on the day Daniel was murdered?

My mind kept circling back to that image: Gwen holding the closed sign on the road in front of the Sydney Cliffs. Had she been replacing a windblown sign? Perhaps. Or could she have been tidying up the scene after murdering Daniel? Also possible.

*I'll have to ask her about it today.*

I stepped out of the truck, my sneakers sinking into the wet soil.

"Boy, she really got hit by that rainstorm last night," I muttered to myself and started to walk around to the front porch stairs. "Go to the side door," I repeated to myself in a sing-songy rhyme. "No one uses the front unless they're being married or buried."

160

I stopped for a moment to look around at the old fruit orchard. Should I really offer my resignation? What if she accepted it? I would miss this place, along with Gwen and my merry band of volunteers. I would miss Shea and Michael most of all.

Michael. How had that happened? My feelings for him were like an unexpected fever, impossible to control or escape. How could my heart be so full of grief at the loss of Daniel and yet still zing with the sharp, true tone of a bell in his presence? My yearning for him was tangible, like a separate entity. It was unimportant that he was unattainable and not the slightest bit interested in me. I could not stop myself.

Rather than stopping at the front door, I went around the porch to the humbler kitchen door. There, on the doormat, sat a dozen eggs in a beaten-up cardboard egg carton tied shut with an elastic band.

"Are these from Vera?" I muttered aloud and bent over to pick them up.

As I raised my right hand to knock, an instinct, a skill that had lain dormant for over a year, kicked in.

I stopped and brought my hand back from the door, carefully examining the egg carton. What was going on? Something was off. I hefted the box slowly in my left hand. The weight was wrong. It didn't feel like it was full of eggs. Was there a faint aroma of almonds? I moved a few fingers underneath the cardboard to see if I could feel any eggs inside. An oozing slickness slid across the tip of my index finger. Slowly, slowly, I raised the egg carton above my head, looking for the telltale oil stain.

They were there, tiny shimmering oil droplets soaked into the cardboard bottom of one egg holder.

My heart stopped. It was an IED.

As I flung the carton with all my might away from the farmhouse, the mountain became silent. It was as if all the birds and creatures were holding their collective breath, waiting for what they knew was coming.

*Jupiter! Who will look after Jupiter?*

I flung myself face-down on the porch and covered my head with both arms as the quiet world around me exploded.

# Chapter Twenty-Five

"Here. Drink this."

Gwen handed me a small sherry glass filled to the rim with brandy. I took it down in a single gulp, feeling the bite of the alcohol against the back of my throat as its warmth traveled through me.

"Are you sure you don't want the doctor to have a look at you?" Stewart asked.

"Yes. Other than some scratches from where I hit the porch, I'm fine."

"Fine. She says she's fine." Gwen stood up from the antique chair she had been sitting on and walked toward the front parlor window to look out at the volunteer firefighters in her front yard. "She picks up a bomb and throws"—Gwen turned to look back at us, her expression slightly crazed—"throws it away, and then says she's fine."

"Well, I am, Gwen." I paused to do another mental checklist of my body, as I had done on the front porch, making sure there were no broken bones or missing limbs. "I learned how to handle IEDs in Afghanistan. I'm fine. You can stop fussing."

"Do you know how serious this is?"

I placed my empty glass down on a side table. "Oh, I know how serious it is, Gwen. You opened up the front parlor," I gestured toward the doorway, "and the front door. Someone had to have been near death for you to do that."

Gwen's lips trembled up into a half-smile. "You're well enough to be making jokes, so that's a blessing."

"It's a blessing no one was seriously hurt," Stewart said from his position seated awkwardly on an elderly buttoned ottoman.

"What's Lesley doing?" I asked.

"She's out there with the fire chief, making sure there are no hot spots left. Can you imagine what might have happened if we hadn't had a rainstorm last night? It's been dry for the past few weeks. Those trees would have gone up like tinder."

I sighed. "Gwen still lost a few, though. And that old fruit shed."

"Cleared it nicely for a new fruit stand. Didn't even need to pay anyone to come and tear it down for me."

Stewart glanced over at Gwen. "I'm glad you're taking this with a glass-half-full perspective, Gwen, but we can't forget that bomb was not supposed to go off in your old fruit shed. It was meant to go off in your hands, in your kitchen, as soon as you removed the elastic band and tried to open the egg carton. Most likely would have burned the entire house down."

Gwen sat back down into a chair, deflated. "Who would want to do this to me? It doesn't make any sense."

"No, it doesn't, and that's the problem here," Stewart continued on. "None of this makes any sense. Not Daniel's death, and now this attempted attack on you, Gwen. Why? We must be missing something important. Are you sure it was an IED, Kate?"

"Yes, absolutely. They are the bomb of choice for every nutjob member of the Taliban in Afghanistan. Easy to make, easy to find the materials, minimal training needed to build one. You'd hear of someone blowing themselves up by accident every few weeks. Most were bigger, you know, roadside bombs or car bombs, but there were package bombs too. If you spent any time there, you learned to spot the signs."

"Okay, you picked up what you thought were the eggs from the doormat."

"An old egg carton. I assumed they had been left by Vera."

"Was there anything that might give us a hint as to where it came from?" Stewart asked.

"Nothing."

"You picked it up and realized it was too light for a full egg carton?"

"Yes. And it felt.... off. And there was a faint smell of marzipan. It's hard to explain, but you learn to have a kind of sixth sense about things that are suspicious."

"And this sixth sense warned you it could be a bomb? Even here on Wynter Island?"

"Yes. I don't think I initially thought that. I just instinctively checked."

"And that's when you saw the oil spot."

I nodded. "I knew it was a bomb and most likely pressure-activated. I couldn't take the chance it might go off if I tried to move it somewhere."

"So you," Stewart paused to shake his head as if he still didn't quite believe it, "threw it."

"Yes, as hard as I possibly could, and threw myself down on the ground and covered my head."

Stewart stared out the window at the shattered debris of the old fruit shed. "Not a bad throw. You must have thrown that thing thirty feet."

"LA Dodgers, here I come." I hesitated. "Stewart, could someone have targeted Gwen because they were angry with her for hiring me?"

"I honestly don't know. Did the IED look professional to you?"

I paused and thought back over the details: no obvious signs other than the weight, smell, and the small stain of oil, no wires protruding clumsily from the side.

"I can't say for sure, but my guess is it was made by someone who knew what they were doing."

"Like someone in the military?"

"Stewart," Gwen gasped, "you can't believe that Bob did this!"

"I don't know what I believe right now, Gwen. A month ago, I wouldn't have believed you if you'd told me I'd be sitting here talking to you about a bomb! A murder and now this. I have to examine every possibility."

"Bob didn't do this," Gwen said firmly. "I've known him for years. He's an asshole some of the time, but he's not a murderer."

"Well, he's pretty angry," I reminded them. "He feels I stole Ria's job and that my presence here led to her ending up in the Haida Gwaii jail. And it's not like Bob doesn't have a history of losing his temper, big time."

"Well, so do a lot of people," Gwen huffed.

"Yeah, but Dougie told me over lunch today about another incident. Bob went nuts on some guy who got caught with Ria at the hotel."

"Yes, but that was years ago. It was a journalist or something."

"Yes, he was writing a news story on the thefts at Oceanica. Would you recognize him, Gwen, if you saw him again?"

Stewart narrowed his gaze. "What are you getting at, Kate?"

I held up my hand. "Just wait a second, Stewart. Would you remember him, Gwen?"

Gwen shrugged indecisively. "Maybe. I don't know. Why?"

I pulled my phone from my pocket, luckily undamaged by the blast. First, the ocean, and now a bomb blast. It certainly took a licking and kept on ticking.

I opened my photos and found an older one of Daniel in Seattle. I held the picture up in front of Gwen. "Could this be him?"

Gwen peered at the photo. "Yes, I think so. What is this about, Kate?"

I sat back in my chair, trying to rapidly put the random puzzle pieces together in my head. "That's a photo of Daniel."

Gwen gasped.

"Daniel, your ex-boyfriend?" Stewart asked urgently.

"Yes," I nodded, "my Daniel. He worked as a journalist in Seattle before he was transferred to Kabul. If Daniel was the journalist who did the story on Oceanica, he must have spent a fair bit of time here on Wynter Island. He stayed at the Lind Hotel and must have spoken with several of the locals. There could be any number of people who had some kind of connection to him. And that's not even including this blow-up between him and Bob about Ria."

"But why didn't any of them come forward?" Gwen asked. "I mean, not the killer. But all the other people on the island who knew him?"

"Because," Stewart spoke up before I could, "there was no photograph of Daniel in the newspaper. He was a name, a name they most likely didn't remember."

"Perhaps some, but not all," I said. "I think Ria remembered, Stewart. And also, perhaps, Bob. Which means that at least one member of that family has been lying to you. Again."

Lesley stomped, exhausted, into the room.

"Kate, how are you doing?" She sat down with a thud in an embossed oak chair with a needlepoint seat.

"Fine, thanks, Lesley. Did you find anything?"

"Only rubble. This kind of stuff is way beyond my pay grade. I mean, I wasn't trained to handle this stuff. Hunting out of season? Yes. Blowing people up? No. We're going to need to have the big boys come in."

"Big boys?" I asked.

"Yeah, the Crime Scene Investigation Unit as well as the Explosives Unit from RCMP headquarters in Surrey. Have they called yet, Stewart?"

"Yeah. They're coming over on the first ferry tomorrow with all their equipment. Singh is the investigator, I believe."

"So, what do you want me to do?"

Stewart stood up and walked to the front door to survey the explosion site outside. "We should wrap it up for now. Get everything taped off, get all the people out of here, and close the driveway off at the road. Make sure no one else comes up here until they arrive tomorrow. And we sit tight until we can pass all this information along to them. I'm going to hold off on speaking to Ria and Bob until the Investigations Unit gets here."

"Am I included in those people who have to get out of here?" Gwen asked.

"Yeah, I'm afraid so." Stewart turned to Lesley. "Is it safe out there now?"

"Yeah. The chief has gone over the whole site. No hot spots. It's safe for us to go."

"Can't I stay here tonight, Stewart?"

Stewart shook his head. "Fraid not, Gwen. Lesley and I will have to see everybody off the property and cordon it off until the explosives unit gets here tomorrow."

"She can come and stay with me," I offered.

"That's not a good idea," Lesley said. "I'd feel more comfortable with you under my roof, Gwen, after a murder attempt. Shea and Michael are on their way, so perhaps Michael can see you get safely home, Kate. And Shea can take Gwen back to the farm."

Two cars crunched to a stop beside the house.

"Holy shit!" Shea's voice shouted from outside. Footsteps clunked up the porch steps. Shea stopped dramatically at the open front door. "Your old fruit shed is gone! And Gwen, you opened the front door!"

Michael was right behind her. I tried not to look at him but couldn't stop myself from glancing at his face. My heart contracted at the fear and worry I saw there. Was it possible that he actually cared about me?

*Yes, but only as a client, as a fellow island resident. Someone in need of his help. That's all. Nothing more.*

"Yup," Gwen said. "and three of my old macs. Those were nice apple trees, too."

"Kate!" Michael finally spotted me and hurried over. "Are you okay?"

Shea was right behind him, her arms enfolding me in a bear hug. "I'm so glad you're fine," she whispered in my ear before releasing me. "I couldn't believe it when Lesley called to tell me a bomb had gone off. At Gwen's. And you were the one who threw it."

"Thirty feet, Stewart says. I'm thinking of a second career in professional baseball," I laughed, a sad little sound. "But I'm okay."

"What were you doing up here anyway?" Shea asked. "Gwen didn't know you were coming, did she?"

I shook my head no. "I had lunch with Dougie at the Tsetsuwatil pub. We were talking about all the crap that's been going on. So I decided to stop and have a talk about it with Gwen."

"The only person who knew you were coming here this afternoon was Dougie?" Shea asked.

"Yes, I guess so."

"And I was fast asleep on the kitchen sofa, oblivious to everything that was going on," Gwen paused. "Amidst all this craziness, I know one thing for sure."

"What's that?" Michael asked.

"I doubt I'm going to sleep that soundly tonight."

# Chapter Twenty-Six

"Morning, Kate," Stewart said from the front porch of Gwen's farmhouse as I hiked up the hill toward him.

I had parked my truck halfway down the mountain as non-police vehicles were no longer allowed up at Gwen's.

"Hi, Stewart. They've started right into it, haven't they?"

The front of Gwen's farmhouse had been sealed with crime scene tape, and two individuals in protective white paper jumpsuits were combing through the area that had once been the old fruit shed. A third officer was busily filming the scene with a small video camera.

Stewart lifted the crime scene tape, allowing me to pass underneath and walk up the stairs to the farmhouse.

"Yeah. Got here bright and early on the first ferry out of Tsawwassen. C'mon inside. Everybody is waiting in there for you."

"Still using the front door?" I asked.

"Yup. Apparently, we are still in the middle of an emergency situation. Gwen and Lesley are with the investigator in the front parlor."

I turned the front doorknob, not surprised to find it was a bit squeaky and stiff from lack of use, and walked in.

Gwen, Lesley, and a man dressed in full RCMP uniform were seated on the dusty furniture. He stood as I entered and strode over to me with his hand extended.

"Good morning. You must be Kate Zoë Thomas. I am Staff Sergeant Ian Singh, Investigator for the RCMP E Division based out of Surrey."

I smiled and shook his hand. He was around my age, tall and trim in his navy trousers with their yellow pipped lines and his white shirt with the epaulets on the shoulders. His skin was a rich maple color, almost teak-like, his thick black hair brushed off his face into a short, military-style haircut.

*Sikh, most likely. Very nice looking.* I gave myself a mental smack. *For Christ's sake, am I now checking out every man under the age of fifty? What the hell is the matter with me?*

"Nice to meet you, Staff Sergeant. Yes, I'm Kate." I nodded to the other two women sitting on the red velvet divan. "Morning, Gwen, Lesley."

Gwen patted the seat of the needlepoint-covered chair beside her. "Sit down. How are you doing?"

"Tired. A bit overwhelmed."

Gwen maternally patted me on the thigh. "You look a bit rough this morning. I didn't have a great sleep either." Gwen chuckled. "Oskar, Shea's new rescue cat, decided he needed to spend all of last night sleeping on the top of my head."

"Would you like any coffee or tea, Kate? Is it all right if I call you Kate?" asked Staff Sergeant Singh.

"Oh yes, no need to be formal here on Wynter Island. Hey, I'm beginning to sound like a local!"

"Yes, you are. You're putting down roots, and we're lucky to have you," said Gwen.

"Coffee would be nice. Where is it, Gwen? In the kitchen?"

"No, on the dining room table. I picked up pastries from Annie's Bakery this morning, so help yourself to one of those, too."

I busied myself with fixing my coffee and grabbed a cherry Danish before returning to the parlor.

"I'm going to guess, Staff Sergeant, that you would like me to go over everything."

"Yes, please." He smiled, his teeth bright and white against his skin. "Sergeant McLeod and Constable Akiyama filled me in a bit yesterday and again this morning, but it's always good to hear it in your own words."

"Okay." I took a bite of danish and chewed it meditatively for a few moments. "I drove up to talk to Gwen at about two yesterday afternoon."

"Did she know you were coming? Did anyone know you were coming?"

"Well, no, Gwen didn't know I was coming. I did mention it to Dougie, though."

"Who?"

"Dougie Whitstone. He's one of the volunteers at CWYN, the community TV station that I run."

"And where did you see him?"

"At the Tsetsuwatil pub. At Coho Bay. I went in for some lunch, and he happened to stop by my table. I asked him if he wanted have some lunch with me."

"So the lunch was unplanned."

"Ahh, yes. Does it matter?"

Staff Sergeant Singh smiled and shrugged. "Who knows what matters right now. It's important to get all the details right first, though. Dougie knew you were coming to the house?"

"Yes. I ran a few errands and then drove up here to Gwen's."

"And was there a particular reason why you were coming to talk to her?"

I paused. "I was coming to talk to her about whether I should think about resigning."

"Resign?" Gwen asked, shocked.

"I wanted to talk to you about considering it, that's all. Calm down."

Staff Sergeant Singh paused, his pen hovering over his notebook. "Well, resigning your job is a pretty big deal. Did Dougie know that was why you were coming?"

"Not exactly. He knows that I've had a difficult time on the island, and that this has affected people other than myself, such as Gwen."

"Has there been bad blood on Wynter Island?"

"Yes, toward me, not Gwen. If they hate me, wouldn't they just bomb my cottage instead? Why bomb Gwen's house?"

"Or not bomb anyone at all," Staff Sergeant Singh murmured. "So, did you notice anything unusual on the drive up here?"

I answered automatically. "No, looked pretty much the way it always does." I stopped. "I did notice there were some fresh tracks in the mud when I parked."

"Where was that?"

"Beside the greenhouses."

"I'll go out and have a look," Lesley said.

"Great. Thank you, Constable Akiyama. You noticed some fresh tracks, and then what? The egg carton? Anything distinctive about the egg carton? Brand? Color?"

I shook my head. "No. I don't think so. I just assumed they were from Vera."

"Vera?" Staff Sergeant Singh questioned.

"Vera is a close friend of mine," Gwen answered. "She lives here on the island. Keeps hens and uses people's old egg cartons to put her eggs in."

Staff Sergeant Singh scribbled some more notes before looking up again. "I'll need to speak to her. I'm sure Constable Akiyama can give me her address." He flipped to a new page. "So, Kate, what did you do next?"

"Well, I picked the carton up."

"And?"

"I had this weird feeling about it."

"What kind of a weird feeling?"

"I'm guessing you know I worked in Afghanistan as a tv news segment producer. I learned to keep an eye out for signs of anything suspicious."

"But there's suspicious in Kabul, and there's suspicious on a small island off the coast of British Columbia."

I sighed. "I know, but that's what I felt. I knew the weight was wrong, there was an odd smell, and then I felt the oil underneath. Since IEDs are pressure-sensitive, I couldn't take the risk of putting it back down. So I threw it."

"You threw it?"

"Yes, away from the house. I had no idea where it was going to land. I just threw myself down on the ground, covered my head with my hands, and hoped for the best."

*And thought about Jupiter. My last thought had been about Jupiter.*

"And that's when it exploded?"

"Yes. It took out Gwen's old fruit shed and a few apple trees."

"And Gwen, is that when you woke up?"

Gwen sat forward. "Yes. I was having an after-lunch nap and was awoken by this incredible noise. It's hard to put into words what it sounded like. It sounded like—like the end of the world. I ran for the kitchen door, pulled it open, and saw Kate lying on the porch, covered in dust and debris."

"And ?"

"I rushed over to see if she was alright. She told me to call the police and tell them that an IED had gone off."

"Which is what you did?"

"Yes."

"That's about it," I finished up. "I don't know anything more."

Staff Sergeant Singh closed his notebook and leaned back in his chair, his white dress shirt stretching across his torso. "So, Wynter Island is usually a peaceful, law-abiding place, right? The occasional fender bender and DUI. But for some reason, all that changed a few weeks ago. First, a murder occurs on the island. I believe the first on Wynter for almost eighty years?"

"Yes," Gwen nodded.

"And we have you"—he gestured to me—"a young woman who stumbles over the body of her ex-boyfriend, whom she believed was still alive and well in New York."

"I know, it sounds crazy."

"Well, murder usually is. Crazy, I mean. And yesterday, the woman who owns CWYN, the station where you work, was bombed. One murder and one attempted murder in under three weeks. In a place where nothing ever happens. All linked in some way to just one person."

"Well, when you put it like that..." I said.

"After I got the call yesterday afternoon, I did some research on Mr. Daniel Apollinar. I learned some interesting facts about your ex-boyfriend." He turned to look directly at me, his unflinching eyes telegraphing the importance of what he was about to say. "Did you know he was involved with the drug trade?"

His question sucked the air out of my lungs. I gasped once, twice, and then reached for my coffee to moisten my throat. "I don't know what you're talking about," I whispered.

Staff Sergeant Singh leaned toward me. "Your ex-boyfriend flew in on Delta flight 544 from New York via Toronto approximately three weeks ago. He picked up a rental car at the airport, a Toyota Corolla, and headed into the city."

"The city? You mean Vancouver?"

"Yes."

"I thought he drove directly to Tsawwassen so he could catch the ferry to come and see me?"

Staff Sergeant Singh nodded his head slowly. "He did, but not until the next day. The car rental company allowed Vancouver City Police to access his car's GPS record. They were able to track him driving directly from the airport to a building on Vancouver's Lower East Side."

"I have a feeling this is going to be very bad."

"That building is believed to be the home base for one of the largest drug operations in Western Canada."

The silence in the room matched the shock in my mind. Just nothingness. I took another gulp of coffee and nodded for him to continue.

"We, obviously, don't know what happened in the building, but a source told us he met with Don Chang."

"Who is that?"

"The head of one of the largest Chinese gangs, The Red Lions."

"A Chinese gang?"

"Yes, one of the triads that moved their drug-selling empire from Hong Kong to Vancouver after the Chinese takeover."

"But why would he go there? That doesn't make any sense!"

"Vancouver police reached out to the DEA in the States and asked about him. Apparently, he had shown up on their radar as well."

"What?" The room began to spin, eddying faster and faster around me. Gwen grabbed my hand and gripped it tightly.

"He had popped up in some locations where there was known drug activity. And I don't mean partaking in it. I mean the smuggling and selling of massive amounts of opium."

"Heroin," I whispered. "Afghanistan."

"Yes," Staff Sergeant Singh nodded. "The DEA did not have much, a few sightings, but considering his job afforded him the luxury of traveling in and out of Afghanistan, they put a watch on him."

"I don't understand what any of this means," I whispered.

"Neither do we, but it looks like he was involved with some pretty dangerous individuals."

"Which means what?"

"That his murder and this attempted murder may be the work of organized crime."

"Attempted murder?" Gwen repeated shakily.

"Yes, from the size of the crater and the amount of damage done, that bomb was meant to kill whoever opened it. More than likely, it was also made by someone with both experience and access to certain materials. We'll know more when we can look over the evidence the officers are collecting outside."

"I—I think I'm going to be sick."

I covered my mouth with both hands and ran to the bathroom, where I threw up all of the coffee and cherry Danish into Gwen's antique toilet.

# Chapter Twenty-Seven

I shakily splashed cold water on my face and rubbed it dry with a hand towel. I kept going long after my face was dry. Maybe if I rubbed long enough, I thought, I could somehow wipe away the previous five minutes of my life.

This was crazy. Daniel involved in drug dealing? My Daniel, who loved British New Wave music and Chicago-style popcorn? Who loved the movie 'The Shawshank Redemption' so much he could recite lines from it by heart? Daniel a drug dealer? It was madness, absolute madness.

A knock came on the bathroom door. "Kate? Are you alright?"

"I'll be out in a minute."

I placed the hand towel back on the rail and stared at my reflection in the mirror. I looked horrible: eyes bloodshot, skin angrily pink from the excessive towel drying. A woman in utter and complete shock.

I opened the bathroom door to Gwen, who was waiting with an enveloping hug.

"Do you want some ginger ale?"

"No, thanks." I shook my head. "I'm feeling better now. Let's get back to the RCMP officer."

Lesley had rejoined us while I was in the bathroom.

"Sorry, everyone. I think that was just a bit too much information for my system to take."

Staff Sergeant Singh stood up. "If you're not feeling well, Kate, we can talk at another time."

I walked over to my chair and sat down in it heavily. "No, let's get it over with now. Did you see anything, Lesley?"

"No. Any tracks that were there were obliterated by the other vehicles and footprints yesterday. Nothing to go on, I'm afraid."

I turned to Staff Sergeant Singh. "So, do you think Daniel's connection with these people might have had something to do with his death?"

Staff Sergeant Singh waggled his hand back and forth. "Perhaps. We don't know. If Don Chang was involved in his murder, why didn't he just kill Daniel when he stopped by his office? Or have someone take him from there to an isolated location where his body would never be found? Why was he murdered on Wynter Island? It doesn't make any sense. There has to be a local angle to this somewhere."

"We've already gone through most of the possible suspects on Wynter Island," Lesley said. "Kate, as the ex-girlfriend, was obviously a prime suspect, but why would she murder Daniel and build a bomb to kill Gwen only to then save her from the blast?"

"Machiavellian creativity?" I murmured.

Staff Sergeant Singh smiled. "That would be an incredibly complicated plan, and murders are usually only that complicated in books and movies. Who else?"

"Well, a teen confessed."

"To the murder?"

"Yes, he hit Daniel's dead body with a boat he had"—Lesley wiggled her fingers in air quotes—"'borrowed.'" She briefly explained what had happened with Nate.

"Okay. It wasn't the drunk teenager. Who's next?"

"Ria Corker talked to Daniel on the ferry and then 'borrowed' his lighter as an excuse to see him again."

"Another example of borrowing?" He, too, had flicked his fingers in the air.

"Yes."

"There's a lot of that going around here. What's her story?" Staff Sergeant Singh asked.

"She got caught stealing Daniel's lighter on the ferry and then lying about it and got herself into quite a mess. There's also," Lesley hesitated briefly, "her father."

"The women's father? How does he come into this?"

"His name is Bob Corker. Early sixties, known on the island for his bad temper and being overprotective of his only child."

"Having a bad temper doesn't make you a suspect for murder," Detective Sergeant Singh said.

"No, but having a history as an explosives expert in the Canadian military does. Especially when a murder was attempted with an IED."

Staff Sergeant Singh scrunched up his lips in thought. "Okay, I guess I'm going to have to talk to both of the Corkers. I should speak with this Vera, as well. Anyone else?"

"The only other suspect is Harald."

"Harald?" Gwen repeated in surprise. "I didn't know Harald was a suspect?"

"Yes," Lesley nodded. "He was the only person on the island who knew the time and date that Daniel was arriving. He's the one who accepted Daniel's room reservation. He also has no one to corroborate his whereabouts on Thursday."

"Have you done any investigating into Harald yet?" Staff Sergeant Singh asked.

"No, he is at the bottom of our suspect list. I was going to start digging through his cell phone records and social media accounts yesterday afternoon, but then all of this happened."

Staff Sergeant Singh stood up, stretching his arms so high above his head that his white shirt began to ride up. "Why don't you go ahead with that, Constable Akiyama. Let me know if you learn anything. I'm going to go out and check with the forensics team and see if Sergeant McLeod and I can make a few visits this afternoon."

* * *

I pulled the station truck over to the side of the road and put it into park. It

177

had been an exhausting day. First, the interview with Staff Sergeant Singh and then the realization that Daniel had this whole other side, other life, I knew nothing about. This was followed by an afternoon at the station planning Fish Bingo episode two amid the noise and mess of demo work. I couldn't bear the thought of another Kraft Dinner or cup of ramen, so I stopped at Vera's to get some fresh eggs for dinner.

I stepped out of the truck, Jupiter rushing to follow me out the open driver's-side door.

"No, Jupe. I'm just going to be a minute. You stay put."

I walked over to the red cooler and lifted the white lid. It was empty, obviously too late in the day to get fresh eggs. I turned around to head back to my truck when a shout came from the yellow house.

"Helloooooo!"

Vera stood on the porch of her cottage, vigorously waving one hand for me to come in. She wore a burnt orange sweatshirt and skirt set with a pair of mud-encrusted boots on her feet.

"Okay, Vera, give me a minute."

I climbed into the truck and turned down the driveway before pulling to a stop at the house. Vera walked over to lean in the driver's side window.

"Are you looking for eggs?" she asked. Her words were tinged with a hint of germanic briskness.

"Yes. Something light and easy to make for dinner. Next time I'm going to need to pick them up earlier in the day."

"Ptsh, come here." She beckoned me out of the truck with one hand. "I'm sure I can find you a few eggs for your supper."

I climbed out with Jupiter by my side. "That's kind of you, Vera."

"Ahh, it's nothing. I feel bad we haven't really gotten to know each other before now. Well, there was that morning at the General Store and we did meet briefly at the Legion on the night of—"

"The night I found Daniel's body."

"Yes." She was headed toward her chicken coop, with me following behind her. Suddenly she stopped in her tracks to turn and examine me. "You don't look so good. Are you sleeping? Eating?" Her eyes traveled from the top of my head to the tip of my toes. She didn't wait for an answer. "No, you're not. You need some chamomile tea and lavender essential oil. Also, ginseng or royal jelly might be good to give you a bit of energy, but I'm afraid I don't have either of those right now."

Vera opened the chicken wire gate to the henhouse and gestured me inside. She put her hand up to stop Jupiter. "You may be a good dog, but a chicken coop is no place for a creature with fangs like yours."

Her henhouse was an exact copy of her farmhouse, with multiple levels and a bright yellow exterior.

"Do you usually prescribe for people from your henhouse?" I asked while Vera rooted around for some eggs.

"Ahh, here is one!" She produced a warm, green-tinged egg. "That's from one of my Araucanas. Beautifully colored eggs." She delved back into the straw again. "I prescribe wherever I happen to be. Did you know that I used to be the pharmacist on the island?" She handed me another warm egg.

"Yes, I did."

A third egg was added to my hands. "Is three enough for your dinner, or do you want four?"

"Three is more than enough, Vera. Thank you."

"Eh, gut." Vera brushed the loose straw off her hands and made little *chooking* noises to her chickens. "Good night, ladies. I won't bother you again this evening. Now, come, I will show you my other animals."

Vera led me to a small barn, painted yellow to match both the henhouse and her cottage.

"Crackers!" I exclaimed.

"You know Crackers?"

"Yes, I do. I met him when I was out with Gwen one day."

Vera leaned over the wood fencing of the stall, looking at the two geese inside. "Yes, you are a naughty goose, aren't you, Crackers?"

Crackers examined her with his beady black eyes and went HOOONNKK.

"And this is Guinevere, his mate." Vera gestured toward a cream-colored goose with brown feathering around her wings and neck. "Guinevere is a good goose. Yes, a very good goose. She doesn't escape and go all over the island, getting into trouble."

Crackers opened his beak and let out another long HHOOOONNNKKK.

"Shush Crackers. You always have to try and have the last word. Now, this is Pork Chop." Vera led me to the next stall in which a sizable pot-bellied pig rested. "Pork Chop used to be a good boy until Crackers got ahold of him." The pig raised his head at the sound of Vera's voice and then went right back to sleep. "Crackers taught you a lot of naughty tricks to play on Vera, didn't he? The two of you escaping out of the paddock so you could go on adventures together."

"Did you get him from Shea?"

"Yes." Vera gestured toward Jupiter. He sat in the middle of the stable corridor, looking at both the geese and the pig with an expression of disgust. "Shea is good about sharing her animals. I see she has gotten to you, as well. It's nice to know Jupiter has a forever home."

"Yes, it is." I smiled down at my silver-gray pup, and he swished his tail back and forth.

"Now, let me get you a carton for those eggs, or you will crack them on the way home." Vera reached up to a rickety wood shelf that was packed with used egg cartons.

"Did you hear about Gwen?"

Vera stopped, her hand hovering in midair. "Yes, I did. Stewart came by with a man from Vancouver this afternoon."

"Staff Sergeant Singh. He's from the RCMP headquarters in Surrey."

"Yes." Vera grabbed a carton and pulled it down. "He said he thought it might have been one of my cartons that was used for the bomb." Her anguished gaze turned to me. "I would never do anything to hurt Gwen. She is like a sister to me."

I took the proffered egg carton and carefully placed my three eggs inside. "I don't believe they think you had anything to do with the bomb, Vera. More that you may have unknowingly sold eggs to the bomb maker."

"Bombmaker. On Wynter Island. I can't believe it. It makes no sense at all. I know every single person who buys eggs from me, every one, and none of them could have ever done something so horrible."

"Well, someone did. And someone killed Daniel."

Vera shook her head back and forth. "I don't understand what's going on. And I don't know what I can do to help the police. All of the egg cartons I use are secondhand. I don't know who gets what. Most of the time, people stop at the end of the drive, put their money in the box, take their eggs, drop off their boxes, and then leave. I never see anything."

"Did Staff Sergeant Singh ask you about what you were doing on the afternoon Daniel was killed?"

"Yes. He wanted to know if I'd seen anything or been seen by anyone. I can't remember everyone who drove by. I was busy working in my herb garden."

"You don't remember anyone?"

"Well, I noticed that Shea got eggs, and Ben and Dougie. Shelley Douglass stopped and got some on her way home from the ferry. She got out of her truck to say hi, so she can vouch for the fact that I was here. But that leaves two or three boxes that were sold without me seeing anyone. But I don't see how that helps anything."

I got into the truck. "C'mon, Jupiter. Up you go." I turned to Vera. "That's the problem, Vera. We have all of these little details, but can't seem to connect them into one single conclusion."

Vera rubbed her forehead, leaving tiny traces of dirt above her eyebrows. "Well, someone better figure it out sooner rather than later, or I'm afraid someone else on Wynter Island may die."

# Chapter Twenty-Eight

I placed the golden bingo cage on the restaurant table and turned the handle. The empty wire sphere spun around as the air whirred through its spokes.

"Hi, Kate," Ben said as he walked into the restaurant in a pair of cargo shorts and a T-shirt that read *We Do Things Higher in Colorado*. "A few minutes late, but I made it. What do you want me to do?"

"Could you bring in the remaining stand light, Ben? It's in the back of the truck. That will leave Dougie free to get the camera set up."

"Sure," he said and headed back out the door.

He soon returned with the light with a white filter attached to a black metal stand. "Where do you want me to put this, Kate? I don't know how to put it together."

"Over there." I pointed to the far left. "We'll use it as a fill. I'll show you how to set it up."

"It's so nice to see you volunteering for CWYN, Ben," Doreen said as she brought in a tray of cakes and a pot of coffee from the kitchen. Bob, apparently still smarting from his previous failed attempt at sabotage, was nowhere to be seen. "And you, too, Dougie."

"Well," Ben said as he plunked down the lighting stand, "Kate convinced me to give it a try."

"I think what he meant to say is that he kindly volunteered." I walked over to Ben. "Now, these two pieces go together like so, Ben. Then we place the filter on and angle it to give a nice fill light on the table."

"Is there anything left for me to do?" Dougie asked.

Lights, camera, bingo supplies, laptop, cell phone: I counted everything off on my fingertips. It looked like everything. "No, I think that's it. Except for our hosts for this evening. I wondered if you might like to help me tonight?"

Dougie had taken a seat off to the side and picked up a plate of cake. He stopped in mid-forkful to look up at me. "No, thanks, Kate. I prefer to stay behind the camera."

"Well, Ben, that leaves just you and me. Nothing like a trial by fire on your first day of volunteering."

"Okay," he said hesitantly, "as long as I don't have to do anything complicated."

I went over to the table and put two chairs behind it. "You sit here and spin the bingo cage. Pull out each ball, and hand it to me. I will be next to you, nattering away to the audience and reading out the bingo numbers."

"Okay, sounds easy enough."

"I can do the camera!" Doreen called out from her seat. She put down a plate of black forest cake and stood up.

I fixed her with a gimlet eye. "Doreen, you can push the record button when I tell you to. But don't touch anything else or walk into the shot to advertise the hotel."

Doreen nodded and walked over to the camera. I pulled out my laptop and readied the livestream to start.

"Three, two, one, and go!" Doreen pushed the record button, and I smiled into the camera. "Good evening, Wynter Island. If it's Thursday, that means it's Fish Bingo Night!" I gestured to Ben sitting beside me. "This evening, my helper is going to be Ben Navaerez, Wynter Island's favorite veterinarian. Thank you for coming tonight, Ben."

Ben stared blankly at the camera for a second before turning to me. "Thank you for having me, Kate. Should I start to spin the bingo cage now?"

"Not yet, Ben. First, we have to go over the rules. The grand prize for the winner of our first bingo game of the evening is a seven-kilo salmon, freshly caught this morning in the waters off Wynter Island. Our second prize is a fifty-dollar gift certificate from Linden Fields, the new family restaurant in downtown Harrow. Our final prize of the evening is for those of you with a sweet tooth. Wynter Island Chocolates has created a gift basket for us, filled with delicious treats!" I beamed at the camera. "Doesn't that sound nice, Ben?"

He nodded a little too vigorously. "Yes, yes, it does."

"We have some new rules for our game this evening. There have been some concerns about the winner of our last grand prize being an individual on the CWYN payroll. To be fair, we have decided that anyone receiving funds from the station or volunteering for it will be ineligible to win any of the prizes on Fish Bingo. You can still play. You just can't win. Everyone else, if you have a winning bingo, be sure to text a photo of yourself with your winning card to the number at the bottom of your screen. Let's get going! It's Fish Bingo time!"

Ben turned the handle, and the gold cage began to whir in a blur of colored balls. It came to a stop, and Ben reached in to grab a ball. "Here's our first one of the evening, Kate."

"Thank you, Ben. It is G as in golf, 27. G-27. And then I, as in icicle, 15. I-15."

Ben spun the cage again, ready to grab the next ball, when I heard my ringtone play on my cellphone.

"It's too early for a winner." I reached for my cell. "Remember, folks, we need a photo from the winner, not a phone call. Hello, CWYN Fish Bingo."

"This is unfair. If I win the damn fish without cheatin', I should be able to take home the prize!"

"Phil," I barked into the phone and then quickly lowered my voice, "now is not the time to discuss this. I already explained in my email what the new rules are for the game."

"I don't care 'bout no damn email. I care about justice!"

"Not now, Phil," I said and hung up the call. "Let's get back to the game, Ben."

"Here's the next ball, Kate."

I took the ball and held it up for the camera to see. "This is N-14, N as in Norman, 14. And you've already got the next ball ready for me, Ben. It says

O-32, is O as in orange, 32. O-32."

My cell phone began chirping. I picked it up and hurriedly opened the messaging app. "It looks like we may have another quick win at Bingo, folks."

I pulled up the message. It was a photo of Phil in the same dreary living room he had been in previously. However, this time he held a piece of paper that read "UNFAIR LABOR PRACTICES AT CWYN!" A half-filled bottle of Molson's Canadian sat on the coffee table beside him.

I quickly closed the app and slammed the phone back down on the table. "Let's get back to the game. The next ball is B seven, B as in boy, seven. Hopefully, all of you out there are starting to fill up your bingo cards!

My phone chirped. "Maybe we have a winner! Let's see!"

I pulled open the app, only to see a photo of Phil, sitting on the same filthy couch, holding another piece of paper up to the camera. It read, "PROTEST UNFAIR LABOR PRACTICES AT CWYN! BOYCOTT FISH BINGO! RISE UP AGAINST THE MAN!"

I closed the app and leaned toward the camera. "No winner yet, so would whoever is texting me *please stop*, so the actual winner can get through. Thank you." My phone began to play again. I grabbed it and pushed the answer call button. "Phil, I've had about enough of this. If you don't stop bothering me while I'm doing this show, I will never buy another salmon from you for as long as I live!"

Silence on the other end of the line. An older man's voice finally spoke. "Umm, this isn't Phil. I'm calling because I have a bingo. You know, on the Fish Bingo."

I sighed deeply. "I'm sorry about that. Thank you for calling, but you need to text me a photo of your winning card. That way, I can verify you are the winner." He hung up, and a photo flashed onto my phone screen. "Well, folks, it looks like we have a winner for our grand prize this evening. Now we can move on to the second-prize round!"

* * *

"So, Ben, how was your first night volunteering for CWYN?" I asked as we collected up the last bits of equipment.

"It was unusual." Ben moved the table back to its original place. "Do you usually get threatening calls and text messages during Fish Bingo?"

I smiled. "Apparently, on Wynter Island, that is the only kind of phone call I get. Although this is only my second time, so God knows what's going to happen next week."

Ben came over and stood beside me. "Well, I'm free next Thursday if you need another co-host."

"Kate, Ben, I'm going to head home if you're all packed up," Dougie called from the front door.

"Great. Thanks for your help, Dougie," I replied.

Doreen was scuttling around the dining room, sweeping up any loose crumbs from the refreshments she'd brought in.

"And thanks again for letting us use the restaurant, Doreen. It's very generous of you."

"Well, we open next weekend, so I'm afraid you're going to have to find somewhere else to hold it next Thursday."

"Oh, that's right! I forgot that Victoria Day is coming up. I'm so used to the Memorial Day weekend in the States that I forgot about the Canadian one."

"Well, you'll remember soon enough when all the tourists start arriving next Friday." Doreen glanced out the window. "That is if the weather holds, and we don't get another dump of rain."

"Do you have plans, Kate?" Ben asked.

"Plans? Plans for what?"

"The holiday weekend."

"Next weekend?"

"Yes."

"No, I don't think so, Ben. I haven't really thought that far ahead."

"Oh, okay," Ben answered, his breath catching awkwardly on the last word.

"Oh, for God's sake, Kate." Doreen put the broom up against the wall and picked up the full dustpan. "He's trying to ask you out!"

"Thanks, Doreen, but I can tell her that by myself." Ben turned back to me with one eyebrow rakishly raised.

I hesitated, looking from Ben's expectant face to Doreen's. Things were moving too fast. Afghanistan, Daniel, murder, Michael, bomb, and now this. Thoughts whizzed around my head like a tiny toy plane circling overhead. Did I want to go on a date with Ben? Not really. My heart drew me toward Michael, but that was an impossibility. So what then? Should I just sit alone in my cottage with Jupiter and a pint of Ben & Jerry's Mint Chocolate Chunk? Or go crazy and have dinner with an attractive single man?

"What did you have in mind, Ben?"

"Nothing fancy. I'm going to grill some seafood on my deck, maybe open a bottle of wine. It's nicer when you're not alone. Although I must admit, Lucy is excellent company."

I glanced over at Jupiter stretched out on the floor, snoring beside a half-chewed thigh bone. He was excellent company too, but was he enough? Didn't I deserve to find more happiness than that? Perhaps a real relationship with a living, breathing human? It wasn't going to be with Michael Rossino, that much I knew for sure. Even if his feelings towards me changed, that relationship would be a dead-end road littered with nothing but deception and heartache.

"Sure, Ben, that would be nice. When were you planning on having this?"

"Next Saturday, say seven p.m.? My home is around the corner from my practice. I can text you the address."

"I'd love to come." My phone chirped from my pocket. "I don't know who would be texting me. After all, Fish Bingo is over for the evening. It better not be Phil again." I pulled the phone out and glanced down at the screen. "Oh my God!!"

"What is it? What's happened?" Ben asked, moving quickly towards me.

"It's Harald," I gasped. "Shea just texted me to say he's been arrested for Daniel's murder."

# Chapter Twenty-Nine

The heavy wooden door of the Wynter Island Legion sat half open. Shea stuck her head in, glanced around, and gestured for me to follow her.

"I can see him. He's sitting over there."

We walked into the dark bar. No lights illuminated the room, only the early-morning sunlight breaking through the windows to send shafts of light bouncing over the empty chairs. The chemical scent of lemon Pledge and disinfectant filled the air.

"Kurt? It's Kate and me. We came to see how you're doing."

Initially, I could not even make him out. Seated at a table in the back of the bar, a bottle of something in front of him, he was merely an amorphous, motionless blob.

"Kurt?" Shea called again as we moved closer. "Are you okay?"

The dark blob slowly morphed into a human being. By the time we reached the table, I could make out an unshaven Kurt, his shirt and jeans crumpled, his eyes half-open. In front of him was a single highball glass and a half-drunk bottle of Crown Royal whiskey. Shea and I pulled out chairs opposite him and sat down.

Kurt raised his head to look at us. His eyes were swollen, bloodshot, and full of so much pain that it was hard for me to look at him.

"Kurt." Shea covered his hand with her own. He didn't even have the energy to shake it off. "What's going on? We heard about Harald."

Kurt said nothing and poured himself another two fingers of whiskey. "Harald is in jail. They arrested him last night. They're going to transfer him to Victoria sometime today."

"We know, Kurt. But why?"

He took a long sip from his glass before looking into Shea's eyes. "Because he killed Kate's ex-boyfriend." His gaze shifted to me. "I'm so sorry, Kate."

Time stopped. The dribble of Scotch trickled down the stubby neck of the bottle into the intricate crevices. The tiny dust motes floated through the shafts of the sun's rays. Harald had killed Daniel? Harald, the sweet man who fed stray animals? He had murdered Daniel? Whichever way I said it, it still didn't make any sense.

"What the hell are you talking about, Kurt?" Shea asked, her fingers clenching over Kurt's closed fist. "Harald didn't kill Daniel!"

Kurt slowly nodded his head up and down. "I didn't believe it either, but, but …" The words slipped out and then hung in the air between us.

"Start at the beginning, Kurt," I instructed.

He poured himself another drink. "It was Tuesday, no Wednesday. It was the day the RCMP team came from Vancouver to go over Gwen's house."

"Yeah, that was Wednesday," I agreed.

Kurt nodded. "Okay, so we got a call Wednesday afternoon, late, like around dinnertime. It was Stewart, asking Harald and me to come right down to the station. He said it was important. So we went. Didn't think much about it."

"Why did he ask you to go to the station?"

"Because Lesley wanted Harald to look at a photo she had found on his Facebook feed."

I nodded. "Yes, I remember Staff Sergeant Singh mentioning something about having her look into Harald's social media accounts."

"Yeah, him, the East Indian guy. He was there."

"I met him Wednesday morning at Gwen's."

"Well, we were in that little room they use to talk to people."

"I know it well."

"And Lesley pulls up a photo on Harald's Facebook account from years ago."

"Okay," said Shea. "A photo of what?"

"It was a photo of Harald and Nicholas, his Norwegian cousin, sitting at an outdoor café with some guy in Dubai."

"What was Harald doing in Dubai?"

"Nicholas and Harald have always been close. You know, the same age, spent summer vacations visiting each other, that kind of thing. Nicholas works for *Dagbladet*, the biggest newspaper in Oslo."

"I've heard of it," I said. "He's a journalist."

"Photojournalist."

"Okay, still nothing too shocking," Shea pointed out.

"I didn't think so either." A sad smile at Shea and me. "Until Lesley asked about the man who was sitting with them at their table."

"Who was he?" I asked, the dread sitting like lead in my stomach.

Kurt shook his head sadly. "Daniel Apollinar."

"What?!" Shea exclaimed.

Kurt nodded. "Yes, it was. Daniel Apollinar. Apparently, he knew Nicholas from Afghanistan and noticed him on the street in Dubai. He stopped and said hi."

Shea turned to me. "Do you know this Nicholas guy?"

"No." I shook my head firmly. "But that doesn't mean anything. I knew a lot of people, not necessarily by name. You see the same faces showing up at the same places. It's like spotting an I Heart Canada T-shirt when you're backpacking in Europe. You may not know the other person, but you're bonded by both being Canadians in a strange country."

"So, Harald said he had no idea who it was. Couldn't even remember the guy's name. He had only put the photo up on Facebook because it was a nice pic of him and Nicholas in Dubai."

"What was he doing in Dubai?" I asked.

"Nicholas invited him to fly out and join him for a few days of R&R. I guess a lot of journalists go there for a break."

I nodded. "Yes, they do. Not the safest country for Harald, though. They have a horrible record on LGBTQ rights."

"Well, I guess Harald didn't do anything that would have flagged him as gay. He told me about the trip. They went to the souk, rode camels, went off-roading in the desert: you know, all the tourist stuff. He had a good time. Never mentioned Daniel to me, but he told Lesley it was a passing meeting. Daniel was Nicholas' friend, not his."

"Okay, seems fair enough," Shea said.

"That's what I thought, too. Boy, was I stupid." Kurt chuckled bitterly.

"That was it?" I asked. "No more questions?"

"Yeah. She got all of Nicholas' contact info from Harald. Lesley told us they would call the Oslo police to set up a Skype session so she could interview him in Norway. We went back home. I thought the whole thing was over."

"But it wasn't," I said.

Kurt shook his head and picked up the bottle to refill his glass. "No. Yesterday evening, Lesley, Stewart, and the other guy,"

"Staff Sergeant Singh."

"Yeah, they all showed up at the house with a search warrant."

"Why?" Shea asked, confused.

"Because Lesley had done a lengthy interview via Skype with Nicholas that morning. The Oslo police had brought him into the station so she could question him."

"And he confirmed what Harald had said, I'm guessing," I added.

"Yes, he did. Confirmed everything. Confirmed he had invited Harald on the trip, that it was a chance meeting with Daniel, and that Daniel was his acquaintance, not Harald's."

"I'm not getting this," Shea said, drawing out her words.

"Neither did I. I told them they had no justification to search our house. Nicholas had confirmed that everything Harald said was true. He hadn't lied to the RCMP. The only way they were going to search our house was over my dead body."

"But," I mused, "how did they get a search warrant?"

Shea turned to me. "Can't they just ask for one?"

"No, they have to have at least prima facie evidence."

"What's that?"

"It's when the police have some basic facts they can present to a judge to suggest that someone may be guilty of a crime."

"Is that enough?"

"No, they need to have multiple pieces of prima facie evidence to prove probable cause. Probable cause is what allows the judge to grant them a search warrant. It's like one thing may be a coincidence, but two or more starts to look suspicious."

"Okay, what prima facie evidence did they have?"

I ticked them off on my fingers. "They had the evidence of Harald having met Daniel from the Facebook photo."

"Which Nicholas proved had nothing to do with Harald."

"Shea, just because someone says something, it doesn't mean it's true."

"Well, that's cynical," she sniffed.

"They had the photo. The only other thing I can think of is the fact that Harald was the only one on the island who knew Daniel was coming on the ferry that day."

"How did he know?" Shea asked.

"Because Daniel had booked a room online for three nights, starting the day he arrived here."

"Did he, Kurt?" she asked.

He shrugged his shoulders. "I don't know. Harald handles all of the B&B stuff. He had to know something because he knew there was a booking for one person for that evening."

"It doesn't sound like there was enough evidence to show probable cause to a judge," I said. "They must have found something else. What was it, Kurt?"

He drained his glass for the second time and rested it carefully on his beer mat. "What happened, Kate, is that they discovered that Daniel knew something about Harald that he didn't want me to find out."

"What the hell was that?"

Kurt's gaze followed the final traces of whiskey as they pooled at the bottom of his glass. "The reason Nicholas had invited Harald to go on the trip in the first place was because Harald was feeling quite depressed. Which makes sense, I suppose. After all, he had just gotten divorced from his first husband."

# Chapter Thirty

"What the hell!" Silence greeted Shea's outburst. "I'm sorry, Kurt, but what the hell!!"

He smiled, a sad shadow of his real smile. "I felt pretty much the same way when I heard it."

"I take it you didn't know Harald had been married before?" I asked.

"No." He shook his head. "You can add it to the list of other things he kept from me: his birthmark, his marriage, his divorce…."

"All right, we know Harald has never been a great one for confrontation, Kurt. But that doesn't make him a murderer," Shea said. "Did he say why he never told you anything?"

"Yes, he was afraid that it might scare me off. Because it had been such a whirlwind marriage: married within two months, divorced at six months."

"Well, I can understand that," I said. "We all have things in our past we'd prefer to keep secret from our partners. But someone had to know."

"Yes, his mom knew, as did his aunts, uncles, and cousins. He swore them all to secrecy because he didn't want to lose me. Must have felt like I was a 'good catch,'" Kurt muttered.

"Or someone he'd fallen deeply in love with," Shea added dryly. "Alright, I know it was a shock hearing about Harald's first marriage, but what does this have to do with the police investigation?"

Kurt stood and swayed from side to side like a palm tree in a hurricane. He quickly sat back down. "Shea, could you bring over some pretzels from the bar? I haven't eaten anything since lunch yesterday."

"Sure, no problem." She walked over to the bar and brought back a couple of small bowls of pretzels. "Okay, so what does any of this have to do with Daniel's murder investigation?"

Kurt took a handful of pretzels and noisily crunched them in his mouth before taking a swig of Crown Royal to wash them down. "It means they now have a motive for murder. Harald had met Daniel. Harald was the only one on the island who knew Daniel was coming. Harald had no alibi for Thursday afternoon. And most importantly, Daniel knew about his first marriage because Nicholas had mentioned it that afternoon in Dubai. So Harald had a reason to stop Daniel from arriving at the B&B and telling me the truth."

"That's a bit of a leap," I said. "Daniel most likely would never remember either Harald or the fact he had just gotten a divorce. I mean, I guess it's a motive, but it's pretty flimsy."

"Well, that's not all of it."

"There's more?"

Kurt nodded.

"Okay, hold that thought," Shea said as she stood up and grabbed her bag. "All three of us need some food and caffeine. Especially you, Kurt. I'll make a quick run to Annie's Bakery and be back in ten minutes. Don't go anywhere."

"Oh, I'm not going anywhere. I can't even stand up."

* * *

Fifteen minutes later, Shea returned with a brown paper bag full of donuts and a tray with three large coffees in it.

"I didn't know what you take in your coffee, Kurt," Shea said, "so I brought along some sugar and a few creamers."

She dumped the food onto the table.

"Okay, Kurt," Shea said and took a sip of her coffee, "you said there's more to the story."

"Yup." He put his donut down and chased it with a gulp of whiskey, which got him the evil eye from Shea. "You see, it's all gone too far now."

"What's gone too far?" Shea asked, biting into her chocolate cruller.

"It's no longer about him and me. There's more at stake here than whether I can forgive him for lying to me."

Shea shrugged her shoulders. "I don't understand. Why?"

"I do," I said. "It's the paperwork, isn't it, Kurt?"

He nodded.

"You see," I explained to Shea, "the cover-up is often worse than the crime. I can't believe how many times I have said that in the past few weeks."

"I'm still not getting it."

"Harald created a lie that he had never been married. He got all his family to agree to not tell Kurt the truth, but those kinds of things never stop there."

"It only becomes a bigger ball of shit rolling down the hillside," Kurt added.

"Yeah. So, Kurt and Harald decided to get married. But you can't just read a Walt Whitman poem under the trees and poof, you're married. You have to get a marriage certificate. You have to fill out government paperwork and—"

"Harald lied on those, too," she finished for me.

"Yes, he did," Kurt said and took a drink from his Styrofoam cup of coffee. "And not only on the marriage paperwork. On all of his immigration paperwork, too. Couldn't take the risk of me seeing him write down the truth, so he fudged it."

"Which means what?"

"It means"—I swallowed my last bite of donut and reached into the bag for a second—"Harald is now looking at a criminal charge for perjury."

"It's worse than a criminal charge. He may be deported from the country because he lied to Canada Customs and Immigration. And more than that, I don't even know if our marriage is still considered valid. He may not be my husband. He may never have been my husband."

Kurt put his head into his hands and began to quietly sob. Shea leaned over to place one hand against his damp cheek.

"Let's not jump directly to worst-case scenarios, Kurt. So that's why they arrested him for Daniel's murder?"

"It isn't Daniel's murder anymore, Shea." Kurt wiped the tears from his cheeks with the back of one hand. "There's also the bombing at Gwen's house."

"What? They think Harald bombed Gwen's house?" I asked in surprise.

Harald, the bombmaker, was even less believable than Harald, the murderer.

"They believe the two crimes are connected. That's why they needed to search the house. Not only for any evidence of Daniel's DNA but also for any bomb-making materials."

"And they found something," I stated slowly, the explanation unraveling before me. "Which is why they had enough evidence to arrest him."

Kurt nodded.

"What?" Shea asked. "What did they find?"

"I don't know. The police found a bunch of stuff in the basement. Lesley bagged it all up and took it away with her. It was some household cleaning stuff and some batteries and wires. And, of course, there were Vera's egg cartons."

"Well," Shea snorted. "If having Vera's old egg cartons in your house is grounds for arrest, I think most of Wynter Island is going to jail."

"It's not the egg cartons," I reminded her. "It's the whole picture. Remember, probable cause. One thing is explainable. Several things start to look suspicious. But why?"

"Why what? Why would he kill Daniel? Kurt already explained that."

"No." I picked up my coffee and took a long, meditative sip. "Why would he bomb Gwen's house? Even if he killed Daniel, there is no reason for him to want to harm Gwen. That makes no sense at all."

A sharp knock came from the front door. I looked over my shoulder to see Michael and Ben standing in the open doorway.

"Sorry for barging in," Michael said as they made their way into the dark bar. "I met Ben at Kurt's house. He had the same idea I did: that it might be a good idea to check in on Kurt after what happened last night."

"We thought we'd try the Legion after we got no response at the house," Ben said. "Hi Kate, Shea. Didn't think I'd be seeing you again so soon, Kate."

To distract myself from looking at Michael's face, I smiled in Ben's direction. "Wynter Island is a pretty small place, Ben."

"How are you doing, Kurt?" Michael walked over to where Kurt was sitting at the table. He held the nearly empty whiskey bottle up to the light. "Not much of this baby left. Please tell me it wasn't full when you started it."

"A little bit was gone," Kurt said.

"At least you're getting some coffee and food into you. That's a good start." Michael said. "How about Ben and I take you home, Kurt? I think you could use a shower, some clean clothes, and some sleep."

"Harald. They're taking Harald to Victoria today," he slurred urgently. "I need to go and see him before he goes."

Michael gestured for Ben to come over, and they each put one arm under Kurt's. They lifted him slowly, as if he were a dead tree they were carefully maneuvering out of a yard.

"Nobody is going to see Harald today, Kurt. Okay? You can see him when they allow visiting hours at the jail in Victoria. Maybe another day this week. Right now, you need to go home and sober up."

I watched as they hauled Kurt out of the Legion. There they were: the first two men I had even thought of since breaking up with Daniel. The first was not only very much married, but utterly oblivious to my feelings. The second was obviously attracted to me, but I felt nothing for him but friendship.

*Just my bloody luck.*

# Chapter Thirty-One

"Hey, where's Jupiter?" Stewart wanted to know as I walked into the quiet RCMP station.

I stopped briefly to pet the overexcited French bulldog, who ran up to meet me at the door. "He's with Shea for the next couple of days. What happens to Billy if you have an emergency? You don't take him along in the patrol car, do you?"

Stewart grinned. "I love that. Put your hands up and stay where you are. Don't mind the Frenchie that's madly licking your legs." He gathered together a few pieces of paper and placed them in a manila file folder. "Billy goes in the crate when I have to attend to things outside of the station. What's up?"

I pulled out the old wooden chair and sat down in front of Stewart's desk. I reached into my pocket to retrieve something and placed the item firmly, palm down, on the desk. "This is what's up."

Stewart leaned forward and picked it up. "Your passport? I'm not following."

"I'm going to Vancouver for a few days. Meeting an old workmate for dinner this evening, having a relaxing day in Stanley Park tomorrow. Now I know," I hurried to preempt Stewart from replying, "you said I couldn't leave the island."

"I'm glad you remember something I said."

"Yes, and I also remember what Staff Sergeant Singh said. And that was before you arrested Harald."

"What did he say?"

"That the RCMP no longer considers me a viable suspect. They feel that I wouldn't murder Daniel, bomb Gwen, and then suddenly change my mind and save her from the aforementioned bomb."

"That's if the killer and the bomber are the same people."

My mouth puckered in shock. "You don't think they are? But you've arrested Harald for both crimes."

"Yes, I know." Stewart examined the ceiling, his smile disappearing into the wilds of his auburn beard. "I can't wrap my head around the fact that Harald murdered someone. Harald is the guy you call when you want to have a chat or go for a drink and a laugh. He's the last person I would expect to plan a murder."

"Even to protect his marriage to Kurt?"

Stewart nodded. "Even to protect his marriage to Kurt. Look at the lengths he's gone to in the past to avoid dealing with difficult situations. Is that the kind of person who suddenly becomes a criminal mastermind?"

"You don't think he did it."

Stewart shook his head sadly. "I don't know. The evidence points to him, but I'm still not sure. We found materials for a bomb in his house, but it doesn't make sense that he would want to hurt Gwen. Why is she a threat?"

"Don't ask me. I don't understand it, either. But I need to catch the next ferry, so we need to get back to my request."

Stewart placed my passport into his desk drawer and snicked it shut. "Fine. Go. At least I know you can't run away to Cuba if I've got your passport."

I stood up, a wide grin spread across my face. "Cuba? Shea said you go to Rio de Janeiro if you want to escape extradition." I put my hand up and laughed. "Forget I said that. See you in a couple of days."

"Be careful!" Stewart called out after me. "Dangerous things have a bad habit of happening around you!"

* * *

The breeze blowing in off the ocean was strong enough that I needed to close the zipper on my windbreaker. The sun counteracted the cool breeze though, bathing my face in a lovely pre-summer warmth. I took another sip of my coffee and chased it with a bite of bran muffin. I couldn't have found a better place to sit: a white bulkhead at the prow of the ferry, wide enough that I could stretch my legs out in front of me like I was on a chaise lounge.

Living on-island was so different from the passing perspective of the ferries. Viewed from Active Pass, you only saw the waterfront properties, expensive homes hidden by long drives, or protective gates. From this vantage point, there was no poverty in the Gulf Islands, no tumbledown shacks, or old cars junked in the back of people's yards. From here, the islands consisted only of quaint cottages and cedar-hewn modern homes with long stairs cascading down to the water's edge. In this world, everyone had their own motorboat and a private dock where tanned children in brightly colored lifejackets lolled, trailing their toes in the ocean.

"Not many will go in the water, though," I murmured to myself.

The water here was freezing cold, even in the heat of summer. Boy, did I know that.

*Daniel.*

The dark blue ocean was fanning away from in front of me as the ferry chugged towards Tsawwassen. My fear of water was lessening, which was good. I had found the strength to run into the ocean that night, and I was sailing over the water right now with only a slight tremor of panic simmering in my stomach.

"Kate? Is that you?" a voice asked from beside me.

I glanced up to see Shelley standing there. "Oh, hi, Shelley. I didn't realize you were working today. Why don't you sit down? I'm just enjoying the view."

Shelley settled herself down beside me. "I guess I should take every opportunity I can to take a load off, shouldn't I?' She laughed and waved towards the black athletic band supporting her knee. "I've got a fifteen-minute break, so I thought I'd come out here and soak up a little Vitamin D."

"Me too." I closed my eyes briefly and let the heat of the sun warm my face. "Did you enjoy coming to watch Fish Bingo the other day?"

She laughed. "It was a hoot. I can see why Greg enjoys volunteering for you. I can't believe Fisherman Phil. He throws a fit if he wins. He throws a fit if he loses."

"It doesn't take much to make Fisherman Phil throw a fit."

"Well, he is definitely a character. We have a lot of characters on Wynter Island. They seem to get swept up onto our shores like bits of driftwood or empty beer bottles."

"And which is Fisherman Phil?"

"Empty beer bottles," Shelley said with a smile. "Definitely empty beer bottles. How are you settling in?"

I paused to look at the water ahead. We were coming out of Active Pass, and I could see the Georgia Strait and the city ahead of us. "Fine, I guess. Things have been so crazy, it's hard to know how I'm doing."

"Well, at least they've got someone under arrest. That should give you a little bit of peace."

"It would if I believed they had the right person."

Shelley glanced over at me, surprised. "You don't think Harald did it?"

"No, I don't, and neither does the RCMP."

"What?" she said, her brow furrowing in shock. "But Harald's been arrested. He's being held over in the Victoria jail, isn't he?"

"Yes, but it just doesn't feel right. Why would Harald want to hurt Gwen? It's crazy. Stewart thinks that maybe they've got the wrong person. That it may be someone else on the island."

"Wow, okay. That's surprising. Why did they arrest Harald then?"

"Because there was a fair amount of evidence against him and a lot of pressure to get someone behind bars. But I think they're hoping there will be some other break in the case."

Shelley paused to digest this information. "I don't know whether I should say this," she started and hesitated.

I put my paper cup of coffee down and turned my full attention to her. "Say what?"

"It's just that I don't want to get anyone in trouble," her voice trailed off.

"Shelley," I said with some urgency, "is it something about Harald? If it is, you've got to tell me."

She shook her head no. "No. See, that's the problem. It isn't about Harald. It's about someone else. I pushed it aside because I thought Stewart had caught the murderer. But if Stewart thinks it might be someone else who killed your boyfriend…."

"Shelley, what are you talking about?"

She took a deep breath. "Okay, I was on the same ferry as Daniel that day. Did you know that?"

"Yes, Stewart told me."

"I heard a couple arguing out on the deck as we neared Wynter."

"Who was it?'

"I don't know. I wasn't paying that much attention. People have arguments on the ferry all the time. I know it was a young man and woman, one of them with dark hair, the other with reddish hair."

"Reddish hair?" *Like Ria's?*

"Yes, I'm pretty sure."

"I didn't say anything to Stewart because it could have been anyone. And then, when Harald was arrested, I thought the case was closed."

"And you didn't recognize them?"

"I didn't have a chance to even get a good look at them really. Just heard them out there."

"Did you hear anything they said?"

"No. It seemed like the woman was angry with the man more than the other way around. That's all I can tell you."

Had it been Ria? Had she been angry with Daniel? Mad enough to hurt him? Perhaps even to kill him?

* * *

The sunny weather stayed with me for the drive from the ferry into downtown Vancouver. The city hadn't changed much since the last time I had been here. Just more of everything. More cars, more people, and many more buildings. As I crossed the Granville Street bridge, I could see that the towering condo buildings had continued to breed and expand throughout the downtown core. With the late afternoon sun simultaneously hitting their glass windows, the reflective light was almost blinding.

But it was still Vancouver. The blue mountains hung over top of downtown like protective deities. The teenage musicians busked in the street, most likely for drug money. And the citizens flooded the sidewalks, individualists who wore shorts in December and whose only response to the frequent rain showers was to pull up the hood on their jackets.

I pulled up in front of my hotel, grabbed my overnight bag, and handed my keys to the valet. As I pulled on a pair of black linen trousers and a loose white sweater, Shelley's words roiled around in my brain.

If Ria and Daniel had been arguing on the deck, that meant Ria had lied. To both me and the police. She hadn't just wandered up to a cute guy to ask him for a light. She had recognized him. Or maybe they still knew one another? Was it possible their little romance hadn't been snuffed out by Bob's dramatic scene at the Lind Hotel? Had it continued? Could Ria have been hiding an ongoing relationship with Daniel all along?

* * *

Guu Garden was tucked inconspicuously into a row of small shops across the street from the lushly landscaped Robson Square Courthouse. The walls were painted a muted green and hung with framed imitation woodblock prints. The atmosphere was West Coast modern: sleek lines, softwood tones, with small tables surrounded by 1960s-style white Danish chairs. The light was low and inviting. The best possible light to be seen in by a prospective partner. But I wasn't here to see a partner. I was here to see an old friend.

"Kate!" A petite blonde dressed in a business casual pair of navy slacks and cream top stood up from a nearby table and dashed over in her tottering heels to wrap me in a hug. "It's been a long time!"

I hugged her back. "Yes, it has been, Cindy Lou."

"Oh my God, not that damn nickname again!" she laughed, her small, sharp-chinned face tilting up toward me. She led me over to a seat at the table. "I haven't heard that since I left CBC Newsworld in Toronto!"

I settled myself down and picked up a menu, a teasing grin pulling at the side of my mouth. "You mean they've never seen 'How the Grinch Stole Christmas' in Vancouver?"

Cindy picked up her menu. "It's not that they haven't seen it; it's just they aren't as mean as my previous co-workers in Toronto."

"Oh, come on! It's too good a nickname! A woman named Cindy who marries someone with the last name Hu? It's too good to pass up."

"Well, maybe it has more to do with the fact that Hu is not an uncommon name here in Vancouver. Also, my co-workers haven't watched "The Grinch Who Stole Christmas" over and over again like someone I could mention. They haven't put my name together with the little girl from Whoville in the movie and come up with Cindy-Lou Who."

"Well, they just need to sharpen up then. What shall we have?"

"This is a nice izakaya place. You know, like Japanese tapas. Why don't we order some sake and tea and have them bring an assortment of different plates of stuff for us to try?"

I closed my menu and placed it back down on the table. "Sounds good to me."

Cindy beckoned a waiter over and told him our order.

As he walked away, she reached across to grab my hand. "How are you doing? Daniel's death must have been awful for you."

I paused. "Yes, it was awful. In fact, life for the past year has been pretty goddamn awful."

"I know. First Afghanistan, and then the breakup, and now Daniel. I can't believe he's gone. I thought telling you about the job on Wynter Island would make life easier for you, not harder. I'm sorry."

"There's nothing to be sorry for. Wynter Island is a beautiful place, and running the station there is going to be fun. I just need to find the answers to some questions I have, and then, hopefully, I can move on with my life."

"What questions?"

The waiter arrived with an assortment of small plates, ranging from sushi to lightly seared tuna and chicken *karaage*, crispy and delicious.

"This looks great." I helped myself to a few pieces and placed them on my plate. "I guess the main question I need answered is why Daniel flew all the way out to Wynter Island to see me in the first place."

"I thought that was obvious. He wanted to get you back."

I took a mouthful of tuna and chewed for a moment. "Yes, but what changed? He told his family he would be able to explain something to me that would make things better. Something new. What was it?"

"Do you have anything else to go on?"

"Yes." I hesitated. "You know the RCMP and the Vancouver City Police have been investigating his death?"

"Yes. Luckily, there hasn't been much press about it here."

"Well, part of that is thanks to you for not pushing the story in the newsroom. The RCMP on the island have also been trying to keep things quiet. The last thing the Wynter Island economy needs right now is a bad tourist season. An RCMP officer told me that Daniel was on the DEA's watch list."

"DEA? Do you mean Drug Enforcement Administration? In the States?"

I nodded. "Yes. He was tracked driving from the airport to an office on the Lower East Side. The police said he met with a Chinese gang leader, Don Chang. Does that name ring any bells?"

Cindy choked on her sip of sake, putting the china cup back down onto the table with a clatter. "Does that ring any bells? My God, it's like a four-alarm blaze, Kate!"

# Chapter Thirty-Two

"Well," Cindy paused, "where do I start? I mean, to put it simply, he is a bad guy."

"I figured that part out."

"No, I mean BAD GUY in capital letters. He heads the Red Lions. It's a gang, triad, whatever you want to call it, that was based in Hong Kong but transferred here before reunification. They trace their roots back to Mao and the Cultural Revolution."

"You sound like you know what you're talking about."

"Oh yeah, you can't be involved in the news biz in this city without being aware of who the Red Lions and Don Chang are. You get on Don Chang's bad side? You better make sure your estate is in order."

I gulped. "Okay, so the Red Lions started during the Cultural Revolution?"

"Yes." Cindy took a bite and chewed momentarily. "They were part of the Communist Red Guards. When Mao purged them from the People's Army, they were sent away to 're-education camps.' They decided to reeducate themselves right into a massive criminal drug network."

"Are they based in Vancouver?"

"Now, yes, but their roots are in China. That's where they control corrupt politicians. It is also where they control massive factories that produce fentanyl and then use their political influence to smuggle the drugs through customs and ship them here."

"Okay. Powerful people."

"Yeah, extremely. They cut the heroin with fentanyl here in the Fraser Valley and then sell it across Western Canada."

"So they don't have any connection with the heroin trade in Afghanistan?"

Cindy shook her head. "No. Most of the heroin we see here doesn't even come from Afghanistan."

"I thought Afghanistan supplied the entire world. They've got enough of it over there."

"That area, the Golden Crescent, ships mainly north to Central Asia and Russia or east through Turkey to the EU." Cindy slurped her drink. "It wouldn't make logistical sense for them to ship everywhere. Remember, these drug syndicates are running international businesses. Product A to Location B in the simplest and fastest way possible. You'd be hard-pressed to tell the difference these days between the CEO of a major company and a drug kingpin. Business is, after all, still business, whether it's widgets or heroin."

"Yeah, but then they use their sizable profits to fund wars."

"At least they do in Afghanistan and the Middle East. Other drug cartels don't have such lofty political ambitions."

I took a piece of *unagi*, the delicious soy-infused grilled eel. "The Red Lions wouldn't have anything to do with 'The Golden Crescent' drug trade, would they?"

"No. The heroin in B.C. comes almost exclusively from Mexico."

"Mexico?"

She nodded. "Some of it crosses the US southern border and makes its way overland here, but a lot of it comes into Canada by boat."

"Boat? You mean those massive container ships?"

"Yes, and a smaller amount via camouflaged speedboats. They often use the Gulf Islands as a place for drop-offs. It's easy for the Mexican drug cartels to drop some of their shipments there and not be spotted by anyone, particularly Canada Customs."

"Yeah, I heard about that." I sighed and poured out a thin stream of green tea for myself. "So, no connection at all between Don Chang and Afghanistan?"

Cindy shrugged her shoulders. "Sorry, but no. Are you sure they said Daniel met with Don Chang? I find it hard to believe Daniel just waltzed in and was allowed to talk to him."

My chopsticks hovered over a yummy piece of salmon sushi, the flesh rosy red against the sticky white rice. "They're sure."

"Well, he must have had some high-up connections because Don Chang doesn't meet with just anyone."

"What does the Chinese community think about the Red Lions?"

Cindy snorted. "They either hate them or are afraid of them, or both. The vast majority of Chinese Canadians want to work hard and make a better life for their children. The last thing they need is for the white community to start viewing them as drug smugglers or gangbangers. They already get enough flack for the increases in property values around here."

I laughed. "I was at your wedding, Cindy. I met your mother-in-law. I don't think I would ever call her a gangbanger."

"No, I don't think so. By the way, are you still talking to someone about what happened in Afghanistan?"

"No, I haven't had the time to try and hunt up a therapist on Wynter Island yet. If there is one. I may have to go to Victoria to see someone." I finished up the last piece of sushi and wiped my mouth with my napkin.

"Well, you need to find a therapist, Kate. ASAP. To be abducted, your interpreter murdered—"

"I know, Cindy," I cut her off. "I know how bad it was. At least Mark and I were lucky. We were saved by that US Army battalion driving by. That was a miracle."

Cindy wiped her mouth with her napkin, her brown eyes doubtful. "Was it truly a miracle? I heard a rumor they were tipped off."

"Tipped off?" I said, startled. "Who would have tipped them off? The only people who knew our location was the Taliban. They'd never snitch to the US military."

Cindy laid a handful of bills on the table, waving away my attempts to pick up the tab. "Perhaps. But I'm sure that's what I heard from one of our reporters."

We headed out to the sidewalk and shared a quick goodbye hug.

"Now that I'm living here, we've got to do this again sometime," I waved as I headed down Burrard Street to my hotel.

"Yes, as long as you don't tell anyone here in Vancouver that horrible nickname!"

# Chapter Thirty-Three

The ferry was mainly empty as I clambered up the heavy gauge metal marine steps to get to the observation deck. I had my choice of faux leather seats to sit in. I settled down in one with my purse dumped on the seat beside me. The large front window, which displayed stunning scenery during the day, was utterly black at night. The scarcity of light on the ocean and the islands meant there was only the occasional flicker from a waterfront home. The ferry cocooned me in its well-lit hub.

I contemplated my day and a half in Vancouver. It had been lovely to see Cindy, and hear about Chris and their two girls, but I hadn't learned much helpful information on Don Chang. He was a bad guy. I already knew that. He sold drugs. I already knew that, too. So what was the connection between Daniel and the Afghani drug trade? Between Daniel and Don Chang? Between Daniel and Gwen?

"What is the connection, Daniel?" I asked, half to myself, half to his celestial spirit. "What is it I'm not seeing?"

No answer came back to me from the silence.

And now there was Ria. Every clue I stumbled over seemed to be leading me right back to Ria.

I stood up in frustration and grabbed my bag. Time to get something to eat. Something fattening and delicious.

The café was situated behind the observation area. Its usually full checkout aisle was empty except for one elderly woman hunched over the counter, picking out the best piece of apple pie. I grabbed a plastic-wrapped Nanaimo bar and a cup of tea and headed to the register.

"Just these, please," I said and placed them down beside the cashier.

"That'll be five dollars."

"Shelley?"

Shelley paused in confusion for a moment and then smiled. "Hi, Kate. Boy, we keep running into each other, don't we?" She placed my bill in her register. "I'm going on break in a few minutes. Can I join you for a cup of coffee?"

"Sure," I replied. "I'm sitting in the observation lounge. Pretty hard to miss me. There are only three of us in there."

"Great. I'll see you in a couple."

* * *

I was only a couple of bites into my decadently sweet, creamy Nanaimo bar when Shelly sat down in the seat next to me. She placed her paper cup of coffee on the floor and unwrapped a chocolate chip muffin.

"This is my dinner. I hope you don't mind if I eat while we chat?"

"No, not at all."

"I'm glad we ran into each other again. I've been thinking about what I said to you the other day." She looked out into the darkness surrounding us and sighed. "I feel like such an idiot for not saying anything to anyone at the time. I mean, I might have been able to stop Harald from being arrested."

I took another bite of my Nanaimo bar. "Well, it's not your job to solve the case, so I wouldn't beat yourself up about it. That's Stewart and Lesley's job."

*And mine.*

"What do you think I should do?"

"I would go and tell Stewart exactly what you told me."

"Right away? Like tomorrow?"

I nodded. "Yes, first thing tomorrow. Get it all off your chest, and let the RCMP take it from there. Okay?"

Shelley chewed on her muffin for a moment. "Okay." She let out a big breath, and her shoulders relaxed. "Enough about the murder. Did you have a good time in Vancouver?"

"Yeah, I met up with an old friend I used to work with in Toronto."

"You must miss the big city, living out here on Wynter."

I thought about that for a moment. Did I miss Boston and New York? Yes, there were things I missed: movie theatres, drive-thru coffee, the anonymity of a big shopping mall. But I'd gained a lot from Wynter as well: Jupiter, friendship, peace. Or at least some semblance of peace. Perhaps an early attempt at peace.

"It was nice to visit, but it's good to come back to Wynter."

"Have you had any time to get out on the island yet? Get out into nature? That's the one thing we have in spades."

"I've done a bit of hiking up to the Sydney Cliffs."

"That's the best view on the island."

I glanced down at the black brace enclosing her left knee. "If you don't mind me asking, how can you hike with that?"

"Oh, this?" She patted the black-strapped object. "I only use this when I'm standing for my job. The rest of the time I use"—she paused and rephrased—"used my old walking stick. It got me up and down the mountainside quite nicely. Unfortunately, I left it out on the deck, and some tourist walked off with it. Saw him getting off the ferry in Vancouver with it, but, obviously, I wasn't able to run after him."

"That's too bad. Can't you get another one?"

"Yes, but that one was a birthday present from Greg. He carved beautiful vines into it and cut this little hooked piece of wood at the end." She demonstrated by bending over the tip of her pointer finger. "It was the perfect length for me to hook things open, like Vera's egg cooler, from my truck. It was a lifesaver. No jumping in and out of the truck to get mail and such. Greg says he'll make me a new one."

I popped the last mouthful of Nanaimo bar into my mouth. "It seems like you and Greg are pretty close."

"Yes." She smiled and nodded. "We are."

"No one else on the horizon?"

"No," she answered firmly. "My first marriage was pretty awful. When I shut the door on that one, I made sure to double-lock it while I was there. And that's okay. Greg and I have found a nice middle ground where we can live together without me being constantly in his business." She picked up her coffee and took a sip. "How about kayaking? Do you like water sports? I'm pretty sure Anna and Michael keep a kayak for guests at their cottage."

I shook my head. "No, I'm not fond of the water."

Shelley laughed and took another sip of her coffee. "And you came to live on an island? You gotta get over that, sweetheart."

"I know."

"Can you swim?"

"Barely. It's more that I panic and then everything just goes to hell."

"You're going to need to learn," she insisted, her brows drawing together in concern. "Sooner rather than later. It's important, very important, to be able to swim when you live out here."

"I'm sure I'll be fine," I said.

"Why don't you take some baby steps first? Get used to being out on a boat. A real boat"—She gestured to the lounge around us, smiling—"not a large, floating coffee shop."

"I don't know." The panic rose from my stomach to my throat, swelling and preparing to choke me. "I'm not ready for that yet."

"Maybe,"—She continued as if I hadn't said anything—"we might be able to come up with an exchange of services."

"A what?"

"Greg has been thinking about getting back into kayaking. Perhaps he could borrow your kayak for a few weeks and see if he wants to start saving up to buy his own."

"Oh, sure." I sighed in relief. "I don't have a problem with that."

"Great." She rubbed her hands together as if she had just bartered a deal with GM. "And Greg can do something for you in return. How about he takes you out on our boat? He could take things slowly, help you start to get used to the water."

"No, I don't think so."

My defiant tone made her smile. "Well, we're docked at Coho Bay Marina if you change your mind. Greg could motor down to Steeltun Bay to pick you up. Just let him know."

"Sure, maybe someday."

Shelley packed up the remains of her dinner and headed back to the café.

The lights of Wynter island began to glimmer in the darkness up ahead of me as the ferry swung around to enter Hope Bay. Was it possible? Possible that I might one day take her up on her offer?

I stood up and grabbed my bags to head down to the main deck.

"Not anytime soon," I muttered to myself.

# Chapter Thirty-Four

"Kate? Kate?"

Karina, the star of her eponymously named yoga show, was dressed in a pale pink spandex bodysuit with tights, like a menopausal wood nymph. She swayed back and forth on one of the grass paths in Vera's enclosed apothecary garden, apparently attuning her spirit with the earthly vibrations.

"She does talk a lot of nonsense," Dougie whispered to me as we positioned two cameras from different angles.

"Well, she's an 'energy teacher' as well as a yoga coach," I replied.

"Is that them crystals and stuff?"

"I'm not sure, Dougie. I think it involves astral traveling or something. You know, auras and such. It's what my father would call 'New Age shit.' "

"Exactly. I think I'd like your father," he said as he untangled the audio cables.

"I think he'd like you, too." I smiled. "He comes from a long line of plain-spoken Welsh folk. They love a beer, a chat, and a good community sing-along."

"Sounds good to me."

Bob walked over to us. He had adopted a more neutral manner with me: not nice enough to be considered friendly and not angry enough to warrant being kicked out of the station. "Kate, Karina needs to know where you want her to put her yoga mat."

"I think right in the middle of the main garden path will be fine."

I gestured toward Vera's apothecary garden. Just past it, I could see the

216

chicken coop and then Crackers, Guinevere, and Pork Chop watching us from the paddock. Jupiter dozed near them in the shade of the stable door.

"Right in the middle, Karina," Bob called out. "Yes, Kate says right there on the main path." Bob walked back over to help Karina resettle herself.

Vera wandered over to stand beside me. "You know, I do believe in this stuff," she said and paused, "but she is a bit too much."

I chuckled. "That's terrible coming from you, Vera. Look at all your herbs and potions, and salves. You're the epitome of Back to Nature living."

"Well, I was raised with that in Germany. You know, you use nature and the spirit to bring the body back into alignment and good health. But," she gestured toward where Karina was wobbling while doing the tree pose on her newly repositioned yoga mat, "I don't know what that is."

"That is," I made sure all my cables were flat on the ground and properly plugged into Vera's farmhouse, "a middle-aged woman who is dressed like a kindergarten ballet student."

Vera laughed and clapped her hands together in glee. "Exactly. All of that pink, and the tights and everything. All she needs is a tutu."

"Yes, but she is also the star of our show. And she insisted that we get some of her yoga shows recorded so they would be ready to roll as soon as the station was up and running. I'm afraid we just need to make the best of it."

"I understand." Vera zipped her lips shut. "Nothing more from me. But that's so funny, kindergarten ballet student. But enough laughing. You're right. We need to focus on our problems."

"Our problems?" I leaned back from the viewfinder to look at Vera's face. "Don't you mean our show?"

"No, our problems," Vera continued, her lips jutting out in a pugnacious frown. "Daniel's death, Gwen's attempted bombing: these are all our problems."

"Well, Stewart would say they're Harald's problems now."

"Pfft." Vera expelled the sound, something between a spit and a swear, from her mouth. "Harald didn't do anything, to either Daniel or Gwen. You know that."

I paused, replaying the conversation with Shelley over again in my mind.

Was Harald innocent? Was Ria the murderer? My gaze traveled to where Bob was attempting and failing to get a lapel mike attached to Kara's bodysuit. Was Bob her accomplice? Had he built the bomb for Ria out of a misguided desire to protect his only child?

Vera snorted. "They don't know Harald like we do. And we know Harald couldn't have done any of those horrible things."

I finished setting up my shot before turning back to Vera's worried face. "Then who did it, Vera?"

"I don't know! I wish I did. I wish I could remember things the way I used to!"

"Remember what?"

Vera threw her hands up in the air. "If I knew that, then I would have remembered it, wouldn't I? It's something at the back of my mind that keeps bothering me. Poking at me in the middle of the night to wake me up, or while I'm having breakfast, or in the bath."

"What does this thing that's bothering you say?"

Vera looked directly into my eyes, her own deadly serious. "I know something, and it has to do with my eggs."

"Eggs. Okay, well, Vera, I've got to get to work on our show."

"Fine, fine. There's got to be something I can do to jog my memory," she muttered to herself as she headed back to her cottage.

I gestured to Bob to move to the side. "Everyone, out of the way of the cameras. I'm going to count you in, Karina, and you can start with your first poses of the day. The sun salutations."

"But there's no music!" Karina shouted from where she was standing in mountain pose in the middle of the garden.

"I know," I said. "I already told you we will add in the music in post-production. Just pretend there is lovely music playing. Everyone, on the count of three. Three, two, one, and go!"

* * *

The road out to the Tsawout reserve was quiet, hardly another car to be seen. After the shoot, I had dropped Jupiter at home with a frozen Kong dog toy and returned to the truck. I needed quiet to think about everything, and the open road felt like the best place to find it.

Although I had pointed the truck north towards the part of the island designated as a provincial park, I found myself turning left at the fork towards the Oceanica salmon hatchery. I idled the truck by the locked front gates. It was difficult to see much, other than the warehouse they must use to package and then ship the salmon. From the road, there was a brief glint of water and a glimpse of the wooden pens.

*Is Phil the Oceanica salmon thief?*

But even if he was, would he really have murdered Daniel over it? A journalist who had initially covered the thefts so long ago? Did he really believe Daniel was returning to the island after all this time purely to 'out' him to the police? That was a stretch, to say the least.

I turned the truck around and bounced and shuddered my way down the rutted road toward Sam Hank's house. I pulled into the gravel drive, surprised to see Sam seated on the front step, a bottle of Molson's Canadian resting beside him.

"Hey, Kate. Wasn't expecting to see you today," he said as he gestured me from the truck.

Jojo ran to greet me, giddy at the arrival of someone new. "Hey, Jojo." I gave her neck a pat. "Hi, Sam. I didn't expect to be seeing you today, either."

He patted the concrete step beside him, and I sat down, pulling my jacket a little bit tighter around me as I did so.

"You were magically drawn to the reserve?" His smile broke across his face like a crack in a piece of seamed walnut: strong, stark, aged. "I didn't know I had that kind of power. Want a beer?"

I nodded my head. "Sure, what do you have?"

"Some Molson's, a Carlsberg, I think."

"I'll have the Carlsberg, thanks."

Sam retrieved the bottle from the fridge and returned with it to the stairs. "Here you go. So, what's up?"

"I went for a drive to think, to try and piece things together, and I ended up here."

"I can see that." Sam took a long sip from his bottle.

"It's so confusing, Sam. Just when I think I've figured out what happened to Daniel, my theories evaporate like smoke."

He nodded his head slowly. "Have you found out who the Truth Warrior is yet?"

"No. Facebook won't tell us anything, and I can't find anyone other than Will who has those kind of computer skills."

"There's got to be someone on the island. You just haven't found them yet."

"And I don't think I will."

"Don't be so hard on yourself. Remember, you saved Gwen's life. That's not an insignificant thing. And something I should thank you for."

"Why?"

"Well," He stared at an otter surfacing in the ocean. Its head popped up like a gopher from a hole, scanned the horizon, and then disappeared back beneath the water with a flip. "Gwen means a great deal to me."

"Is that because she is the matriarch of this island, or is that because of some *bow chicka bow wow* that I'm unaware of?"

Sam smiled. "Both, but primarily the latter."

"I had no idea."

"It was a long time ago, when we were kids. But thank you, anyway, Kate."

We slipped into a companionable silence as the sun slowly started to move towards the west.

"You know what's crazy, Sam?"

"What?"

"I thought for a while that Gwen might be the killer."

Sam put his bottle down and turned to me in surprise. "Are you serious?"

I nodded. "Yeah, I am. I saw her over at the Sydney Cliffs on the day Daniel was murdered. She was doing something with the closed sign. I thought she might have been trying to tidy up the murder scene."

Sam picked up his bottle and took a drink. "Oh no. She was replacing the sign."

"That's what Michael said. It got knocked over by the wind or something."

Sam shook his head. "No, that wasn't it."

"What was it?"

Another long sip. "Well, she stopped because she couldn't see the sign. Technically, there was nothing stopping anyone from climbing up the cliffs."

"Where was it?"

"Well, that was the weird thing. She thought it had been stolen, but she found it hidden behind a tree beside the road."

"Hidden?"

"Yeah, some stupid kid's prank. I don't know why they think that kind of stuff is funny."

I put my bottle of beer down on the cement step with a sudden, sharp smack, my eyes widening in shock. "I do."

"You do what? Have I had too much to drink?" He held his half-full bottle up to the sun. "This is still my first one."

"No, I know why it was hidden, Sam, and why Gwen's house was bombed!"

"Really? Maybe I should switch to Carlsberg, too!"

I scrabbled in my pocket for my phone. "It wasn't a prank, Sam. It was a ploy, a ploy to get Daniel up to the top of the cliffs."

"Okay, still not following you."

"No sign meant Daniel would willingly climb to the top of the Sydney Cliffs. But the sign had to be moved back before anyone realized it had gone, or a passerby might figure out someone had been up there illegally."

"Now I got you."

"And if Nate had not hit Daniel's body that night with his dad's boat, we wouldn't have known he was even thrown off the Sydney Cliffs in the first place!"

"But Gwen realized it had been hidden."

"Yes," I rapidly dialed. "C'mon, Gwen. Answer. Answer the damn phone! Gwen, this is Kate. Call me as soon as you get this message, okay? It's important."

I dialed another number. "Shea, you've gotta answer. C'mon, not you, too! Shea, it's Kate. Call me as soon as you get this. It's important."

I quickly typed out a text message. *Shea, I spoke with Sam. Gwen may be in danger and she's not answering her phone. Call me. K.*

I stood up in panic. "Gwen not only knew that the sign was hidden, she must have found it while the murderer was still there at Sydney Cliffs. If the murderer had already left, the sign would have been replaced at the road."

"Which is why Gwen's house was bombed! It wasn't because of you and the station. It was because she might have seen something or someone when she was fixing the sign!"

"Exactly. I've gotta go, Sam. I've got to talk to Stewart and Lesley. Damnit, I left Jupiter at home. I'll stop quickly and pick him up on the way. I'll call you."

I dashed to the truck and screeched out of the driveway and onto the street.

"Kate, be careful! Jojo, we've got to go and find Gwen!"

# Chapter Thirty-Five

The sun was drifting west, the sky fading from blue to yellow to a subtle peach hue along the horizon when I turned the truck into my driveway. I saw Greg waiting for me on the front step.

"Greg?" I climbed out of the truck, pausing to look for his car. It was nowhere to be seen. "This is a surprise."

"Yeah. Sorry, I should have called first. Mom said she talked with you on the ferry about me borrowing the kayak?"

"Oh yes, of course." I breathed a sigh of relief. How silly. I was seeing boogeymen everywhere. "You've come to get the kayak."

"Yes. I already have. I just wanted to check with you to make sure it's okay."

I stepped past Greg and unlocked the front door, allowing Jupiter to race out like a whirling dervish. I crouched to try and hold him still, but he insisted on zooming back and forth up the driveway a few times before he was willing to be petted.

"Of course, it is, Greg. I'm not sure how you'll get it home, though."

"I brought my mom's boat down to Steeltun Bay. I carried it down there. It's the easiest way to move it to the Coho Bay Marina."

"Oh, of course." I began to inch my way back up the steps with Jupiter. "I'm afraid I can't chat, Greg. I've got to go."

He leaped up two steps to block my path to the front door. The anxiety in the pit of my stomach returned like a swirling tornado. "Why don't you come for a boat ride with me? Mom said you were interested in seeing the island from the water. It looks like it's going to be a beautiful sunset tonight."

"Not today. I have something important I have to do."

"Don't be like that." He reached in the open front door to pull Jupiter's red leash off the hook where I kept it. "Look, you can bring Jupiter as well!"

"Greg," I started to say I never used the leash, but stopped myself. "You need to go. Now."

I stared directly into his blue eyes, leaving no doubt as to whether I meant what I said. Greg smiled sadly and shook his head.

"I was hoping you weren't going to be stubborn."

"Excuse me?"

He reached his right hand behind his back and pulled a small snub-nosed revolver from his waistband, and pointed it at my stomach. "This would have been so much easier, Kate, if you'd just come for a walk."

"What the hell is going on?"

Jupiter lifted his lip in a soft, menacing growl.

"I don't want to shoot your dog, but I will if I have to. C'mon, put his leash on and let's go for a walk." He took a few steps down the stairs and stopped for me. "I mean it, Kate. You either do what I say, or I shoot you both here. I really, really don't want to, but I will if you leave me no choice. We're too far down this road to stop now."

I stared at him in silence for a few moments, and then snicked the leash onto Jupiter's collar. Jupiter pulled away at the sound of the click, but I reined him back in. Time. I needed time. As much as I could possibly buy.

"Okay, we'll go for a walk. Just don't do anything stupid."

"That's better." He gestured me forward with the end of the revolver and pointed it toward Steeltun Bay.

Greg? Greg was the killer? My mind raced over this new detail while I tugged an irritated Jupiter beside me. It made no sense at all. Why? Why would he kill Daniel? My phone vibrated in my pocket. Did I dare try and grab at it? No, too dangerous.

"Why are we going to Steeltun Bay, Greg?"

He said nothing, waving me ahead with the gun. As we rounded the corner, I saw a red motorboat waiting there, the kayak resting beside it on the dock.

"I don't understand, Greg. Why are you doing this?"

He nudged me along toward the dock. "Because she needs my help."

*Who is she? And what kind of help does she need?*

As we walked to the dock, I spotted a figure moving around in the back of the boat. Was it Ria? Had Ria managed to hoodwink both her father and Greg into helping her kill Daniel, and now me?

"Ria!" I called out suddenly.

The shapeless figure moved from the back of the boat to the prow, its face sharpening into focus as it neared us.

"So you still think it was Ria, Kate?" Shelley leaned forward to grab my arm and pull me aboard the boat. I initially resisted, until Greg's gun poked me in the ribs. With a tug of the leash, a disgruntled Jupiter followed me into the boat. "I'm afraid not."

"It was you? You and Greg?"

She unhooked the boat's mooring rope and tossed it to Greg on the dock. "Not Greg," she answered sharply. "Just me."

She powered the boat into reverse and inched it away from the dock. Once clear, she switched off the reverse and chugged slowly into Steeltun Bay.

"It was kind of you, Kate, to offer to let Greg borrow the kayak. You're a kind person."

"You don't have to do this, Shelley."

She continued on as if I hadn't said anything. "It's always the kind ones, isn't it? You always get the shit end of the stick. I always thought I was kind. Or at least I tried to be. But that asshole of a husband, he beat it right out of me."

I glanced around the deck. It was empty, devoid of even a bottle of water, anything I might use as a weapon. My phone vibrated in my pocket again, but I didn't dare reach for it.

"It was before Stewart arrived. An older RCMP guy named Glenn. He was a nice guy. Tried to get me to report Bill. Press charges. Would call the doctor in the middle of the night to come and stitch up my forehead."

"Shelley!" My voice rose steadily in panic. I could feel Jupiter tensing beside my leg. "You killed Daniel. You won't get away with it! Someone will figure it out!"

"But I couldn't. I couldn't stand up to him. Until he hit Greg." She turned to look at me, her soulful eyes pleading for something. Was it absolution? Understanding? "I had to protect my son. I still have to protect my son."

"What the hell are you talking about!"

The other woman pulled the throttle back, so we were idling in the middle of the bay, abutting the open water. "I have to protect Greg, Kate. I'm sorry."

"You already said that, but I still don't understand. What is going on?"

"I have to finish this. All of this: Daniel, Gwen, you. Tie up all the loose ends so that Greg can be safe."

I turned to glance back at Greg on the dock. He was busy placing the empty kayak into the water.

"What is he doing?" I asked, all of the horrific possibilities of what might happen unreeling in front of me.

"He's making it look like this was an accident. They won't ever find your body. That was my big mistake with Daniel. He was dead when I pushed him over the cliff with my walking stick. He floated. You and your dog won't."

I checked to see if Greg was still aiming the gun at me. No, his attention was focused on pushing the kayak away from the dock. How much distance was there between us now? Maybe a hundred, a hundred and fifty feet. Would that be enough to throw off his aim?

I didn't know.

The water slapped against the side of the boat, playing a staccato counterpoint to my racing heartbeat: beat, beat, beat, slap. Beat, beat, beat, slap.

I gripped the side of the small motorboat and stifled the mixture of panic and rage that was trying to burst free from my mouth. *Stay calm. I've got to stay calm. That's the only way to survive this. Be calm.*

A warm body pressed against my leg, and I placed one hand down to rest on the silver-grey fur. I glanced up. Was this my opportunity?

Yes, it was. I took a deep breath.

*At least I'm not alone. I won't die alone.*

"You bitch!" I spat out and lunged towards Shelley. "You killed Daniel!"

I wasn't fast enough. Shelley held a stout stick ready and brought it up between her two hands to shove me back onto the deck.

Jupiter leaped up from the floor of the boat, growling. Before Shelley could hit him with the stick, he had jumped on her, his jaws snapping shut on the edge of her T-shirt.

"You stupid dog!" She screamed and threw Jupiter overboard, his teeth ripping open her T-shirt as he flew through the air.

A single gunshot sounded, and Jupiter splashed into the water. I couldn't hear the splash, or anything else either, as the crisp, sharp sound of the shot reverberated inside my skull. Shelley's mouth moved soundlessly, screaming something at me while blood ran across her stomach.

*Jupiter!*

I couldn't see him breaking the surface of the water. Had he been shot?

Before Shelley could even move to push me overboard, I turned and, without thinking, breathing, or even contemplating my imminent death, jumped over the side and into the freezing ocean.

# Chapter Thirty-Six

I was eight again. The waters of Georgian Bay closed over me like I had slipped soundlessly into a movie. I could just make out the blurry orb of the sun shining down on me through the lake's surface. I fought, kicking and splashing against the heaviness of the water that dragged me down. I could do it. Daddy would save me. Or Lizzie. Someone would save me. I kicked and took in a mouthful of water. It was salty, not fresh. I kicked again and used my hands to try and propel myself upwards.

The water was so cold. Why was it so cold in Lake Huron in the middle of July?

I broke the surface momentarily, hands splashing and scrabbling to keep my head above the water. This wasn't Ontario. This wasn't Lake Huron. This was the Pacific Ocean, and the woman who had murdered Daniel was motoring away into the sunset with her son.

I fought to keep my head above water, hoping for some sign of Jupiter. But I saw nothing. Desperate, I smacked at the water as if it was something permeable I could grab onto. I was alone. I momentarily stopped fighting and slipped below the surface again. It was so quiet here. The cold began fading, and a trickle of warmth spread up from my toes. That felt nice. But why was I getting warmer when the water was so cold?

And where was Jupiter?

Dead. Jupiter was dead. Shot by that asshole, Greg.

I fought to reach the surface again. Still no one and nothing in sight. Was this how it ended? After covering wars and being abducted in Afghanistan, I would just quietly drown in the Pacific Ocean?

I slipped below the surface again, my arms beginning to spasm through a combination of exhaustion and the cold. But warmth, that lovely warmth, was spreading through my body. It seeped across my stomach, enfolding me in its comfortable blanket.

Why was I warm? Was it the sun's corona breaking through the ocean's surface? Was that keeping me warm? But it was always warm on Georgian Bay in July. Was I on Georgian Bay? No. No. I needed to focus. I was in the Pacific, and the warmth meant only one thing: I was dying.

I gathered what remaining strength I had left and propelled myself out of the water. I still couldn't see anyone, but something brushed up against the back of my head. What was it? A seal? An otter? I tried to turn, but the exhaustion pulled me downward. I sank below the surface. As I relaxed my spasming limbs and allowed the ocean to swallow me whole, I saw a red rope float into my line of sight.

Red rope. It moved closer as I slipped deeper under the water. Close enough for me to see, it was attached to the body of a four-legged animal, paddling on the surface.

*Jupiter!*

With strength I had no idea I still possessed, I pushed myself up, hands clawing against the icy water, straining for the end of the red leash. I was almost there. Almost. I stretched out one hand and grabbed it, feeling the pull as Jupiter swam with all the strength in his body to pull my head above the water.

I broke the surface for one last time. Gasping, choking, coughing, sobbing, all at the same time.

∗ ∗ ∗

"Kate! Kate!"

I heard the shouts, but didn't know where they were coming from. I floated on my back, one hand holding the end of Jupiter's leash as he towed me to shore. My legs kicked with whatever strength I still had left to try and help propel us both across the water.

Splashing and more shouting. The voices were getting louder. Either the voices were coming to us, or Jupiter and I were nearing the shore. Another splash and what sounded like someone swimming. There was a loud thunk as voices shouted their encouragement. The sound changed from swimming to paddling. I heard the ferocious smack of the paddle entering the ocean at the beginning of the stroke. The kayak! Someone had got to the kayak!

Suddenly, my face slipped from sunshine to shadow as the bulk of the kayak pulled up behind me. Someone was blocking out the sun. Jupiter's body started to be pulled out of the water, the leash in my hand dragging me right behind him.

"Kate, Kate, are you all right?"

A man's voice. It didn't matter whose it was. It could be Bob for all I cared. I felt the thud of Jupiter's body being placed in the kayak vibrate down the leash as strong hands pulled me into the boat. The hands gripped underneath my armpits and tugged until I was lying half draped over the bow of the kayak, half of my body still in the water.

"Kate, I'm here. You're okay. Both you and Jupiter are okay."

*Michael!*

Michael's tanned face hovered above me as I pushed my stiffened lips into as much of a smile as I could manage. He leaned closer, examining my face for any injuries.

"I feel warm, Michael. I'm not supposed to feel warm, am I?"

"No, it's hypothermia setting in. It's not going to be easy, but let me try and get this kayak back to the shore. Can you hold on so I can paddle?"

"I think so."

"Well, you've got a death grip on Jupiter's leash. Let me transfer your hand to the side of the kayak, and hold on for all your worth."

He moved my hand from the leash to a plastic handle of some kind. I gripped on, maybe not for all I was worth, but at least for my last two bucks in change.

With a bobbing turn, Michael piloted the overweight kayak back toward the beach. I heard voices getting closer, and then the splashing of people rushing into the water.

"Michael, let me get the bow. Ben and Shea, come and help."

The momentum forward picked up pace as hands grabbed the front of the kayak and started to pull it shoreward. The splashing increased as the water became shallower, and legs began to appear beside me. A crunch announced the bottom of the kayak striking rock.

"Here, Kate, out you come. Shea, you get the dog."

I didn't know whose voice it was, but the strength and confidence in it made me feel loved and safe. I wrapped my hands around the warm neck and buried my face into the long gray ponytail. I looked up as Sam Hanks smiled down at me.

"Damn, girl, you know how to get yourself into trouble, don't you?"

"Sam."

"Shush now, let's get you on the beach. Shea called Ben. He's just arrived with all of his EMT stuff."

I shifted my gaze and saw Shea crying and holding a wet and exhausted Jupiter. Ben shook a silver foil sheet onto the pebbled beach.

"Okay, we're going to get you wrapped up in this," he said. "It will help bring up your body temperature. Stewart and Lesley are on their way. Shea, did they notify the Coast Guard for the ambulance boat?"

Shea shook her head, sniffling. "I don't know. Lesley didn't say. All she said was that she would handle everything and get Stewart down here."

Sam shifted me onto the foil sheet, and Ben wrapped it tightly around my body. I began to shiver, my limbs spasming inside their aluminum cocoon.

"You're all right, Kate. Your body is just going into shock. I wish I had something hot for you to drink, but let's try some good old-fashioned chocolate. Can you chew this?"

I nodded, and Ben placed a square of chocolate on my tongue. It melted into an amalgam of flavors and textures, the sugar burning its way into my system.

"More?"

I opened my mouth. Ben placed another square inside.

"You keep eating the chocolate, okay?"

I nodded again and looked past Shea to see someone else kneeling beside me on the beach.

"Vera?" I started out, but was quickly shushed.

"Shhh, do what you're told and eat your chocolate." Vera pushed her silver hair away from her face, perhaps also rubbing away a tear at the same time.

"But what are you—"

"Did you not hear me? You be quiet. I will do the talking."

"How—"

"Goodness, Kate, do you listen to anyone?" Sam asked.

Shea leaned over me. "Vera and Sam are right. Be quiet and eat your chocolate. Vera will tell you what happened."

"Me?" Vera said, "Why do I have to—"

"Vera," Sam cut in, "tell the story."

"You know something? You are getting pushy in your old age, Sam Hanks." Vera moved closer to me on the beach. "Sam called me in a panic. He said neither of you could get ahold of Gwen. He wanted to know if she was with me."

"But she wasn't," Sam replied.

"No, she wasn't. She's in Victoria today doing some shopping and catching a movie. She's not due back until the last ferry tonight. I asked Sam what all the fuss was about, and he said you'd had some kind of breakthrough on the murder."

I nodded slowly. It was hard to do, wrapped in foil and positioned on the rocky beach. The sun was dipping closer to the horizon, painting the sky a pink and peach watercolor.

"Well, while I was on the phone with Sam, Shea came through on that caller-waiting thing."

Shea cut in. "I had gotten your text and called you, but you weren't answering. I tried Gwen, and she wasn't answering either. I was getting concerned."

"That's when she called me," Vera continued. "To see if I knew what was going on. After all, you did your yoga shoot at my house this morning."

"I'm getting confused," I whispered.

Ben offered another square of chocolate. "Eat this."

I opened my mouth, and he placed it on my tongue. A sweet Holy Communion.

"Anyway, I said Sam was on the other line, because there was some news about the murder. Shea said the only news she'd heard was that Shelley's walking stick had been found. It washed ashore on a beach near Hope Bay. And that's when," Vera paused theatrically, "I remembered what was bothering me about the eggs."

"The eggs? Weren't we talking about Shelley's walking stick?" Michael asked.

"We were."

"Well, which is it then: the walking stick or the eggs?"

Vera's brows drew together in irritation. "It's both, Michael. Perhaps you should just listen to what I am trying to say." She turned back to me. "Shelley always stayed in her truck to pick up her eggs. Because of her bad leg. Always. She used that little hook on the end of her walking stick to open up the cooler. Except for the day Daniel died. On that day, she got out of her truck and walked over to pick up her eggs."

"There's no law that states that getting out of your truck to pick up eggs makes you a murderer," Ben said.

"Yes, but it was the niggling difference that bothered me. It was that something unusual, out of character, that I couldn't explain. And it all cascaded down from there. Not only had she stopped using the stick to get her eggs, but I realized I hadn't seen Shelley with her walking stick since the Thursday Daniel disappeared. And that was after seeing her with that bloody thing every day for the last three years."

"But it was stolen on the ferry by some tourist from Vancouver," Ben said.

"That's what Shelley told us, but then Shea said it had been found on a beach here on Wynter. Why would she lie to us about a tourist stealing her walking stick? It made no sense. But what if something had happened to the stick on the day that Daniel was murdered, something that led to it floating in the waters off Wynter Island before it washed up on our shores? I told Shea to meet me at your cottage," Vera said. "and I went back on the other line and told Sam to do the same thing."

"And when we got to your cottage, your truck was there, but not the kayak," Shea said. "Also, your front door was wide open, and Jupiter was gone."

I glanced up at Shea. "The leash?" I whispered.

"Yes, I noticed that was gone, too. Jupiter hated when you put him on a leash. I called Michael and told him it looked like you might have gone down to Steeltun Bay to kayak, but you weren't answering your phone. He immediately said something was wrong. You'd never go into the water voluntarily." She turned to Vera. "I told Vera what Michael had said, and she, well, she…."

"I told her I believed Shelley may have killed Daniel and was possibly trying to kill you in Steeltun Bay."

# Chapter Thirty-Seven

"Okay, let's go back a bit, Vera. You said it all started with the eggs." Stewart, his notebook open in front of him, gazed down at his boots, which were getting rapidly soaked by the incoming tide. The portable radio on Stewart's hip crackled. "Stewart? Lesley here."

"Stewart, I've got her. Peaceful, no attempt to evade custody. She is in need of medical assistance. I will call Dr. Lee and have him meet us at the station."

"Is it serious?"

"No, but she does need to be looked at. She has some pretty nasty lacerations across her stomach. Apparently, they came from Jupiter. I'm pretty sure he's had his shots."

"Okay, you handle that. I'm getting things tied up here at the site. I called Saltspring detachment. They are sending some officers over to help us."

"One more thing, Stewart. She confessed to everything. Murder of Daniel, attempted murder of Gwen and Kate. Says Greg had no knowledge of any of it."

"She's lying, Stewart," I said from my position on a stretcher on the Coast Guard rescue boat. I was still tightly wrapped in the space-age tin foil blanket, with several heavy woolen ones added on top of it. The shivering had finally stopped, as had the fogginess that had permeated my brain. "She's trying to protect Greg."

"Lesley, once I'm done here, I'll head out to look for Greg. They are about ready to leave in the zodiac for the Saanich Community hospital. They're going to have an ambulance waiting for her at the docks in Sidney."

"Okay. I will wait for you to get back to the station before we try and get a statement from her."

"Sounds good." Stewart clicked off the radio and returned it to his hip. "Alright, Vera, where were we?'

Shea piped up from where she was holding Jupiter beside my stretcher. "I called Vera because I was worried about Kate and Gwen. I told her Shelley's walking stick had been found on the beach."

"That was all I needed to hear, Stewart," Vera said dramatically. "It all came back to me."

Stewart shuffled his feet. His boots were now totally soaked. "About the eggs, you mean."

"Yes. Shelley stopped using her walking stick on the same day Daniel was pushed off the Sydney Cliffs. She said it had been stolen by tourists. Why, then, did it wash up near Hope Bay?"

"That's a bit of a stretch, Vera," Stewart muttered as he made notes.

"Well, I prefer to think of it as brilliant deductive reasoning."

Stewart paused, appeared for a moment like he was going to say something, and then thought better of it and returned to his notes.

"So, Sam and I agreed to meet Shea at Kate's cottage. When we got there, she, Jupiter, and the kayak were gone. Shea called Michael to see if he knew whether she'd gone kayaking on Steeltun Bay."

"And I knew as soon as I heard that," Michael said, "that something was terribly wrong. Kate's scared to death of the water."

"Bad turn of phrase to use right now, Michael," I murmured as the EMTs positioned my stretcher into the belly of the zodiac.

One of the two Coast Guard officers piped up from his position knee-deep in the ocean, holding the amphibious zodiac steady on the beach, "Okay, we're chasing daylight right now. We've got to get a move on. Who is going with her to Sidney?"

I examined the faces surrounding the boat. Shea, holding a sodden Jupiter in her arms, Ben standing beside her, and Michael on the other side of the boat resting his hand on my blanket.

I couldn't touch him, but I blew a kiss toward Jupiter. "Jupe, you stay here with Shea and Ben. They can check you out and make sure you're okay. I'll come back. Don't worry." I swiveled my head to the opposite side, too tired to fight the insistent desire to have him close to me. "Michael, would you come with me?"

He patted my shoulder in agreement. "Sure. I'll call Anna when we get to Sidney."

"Fine. Then everyone who is coming, get in the boat." The officer gestured to Michael to climb into the zodiac. "The rest of you, get out of the way, unless you want to get sprayed by the propeller."

Michael jumped in, seating himself on the edge of one pontoon beside me.

"Put this on." The officer threw him a lifejacket, and he quickly pulled his arms through and buckled it up.

"Okay, everyone ready? Kate? You okay?"

"Yeah."

"This is going to get noisy, so it may be hard for you to communicate with us. You also don't have any free hands to gesture with. If you're in pain, try and alert Michael, okay?"

Michael's face, his salt and pepper hair still wet with seawater, stared down at me with such caring and compassion. I started to tear up.

"What's this?" He wiped a tear away with his thumb. "Don't tell me you're going to start to fall apart now?" he gently teased.

"No," I whispered.

He bent down to speak in my ear as the other Coast Guard officer pushed the zodiac away from the shore and clambered aboard. "I know it must be hard, but it's finally over. You can take all the time you need now to grieve for Daniel."

The officer at the helm turned on the engine, and it began to thrum deeply, vibrating across the inflatable pontoons. He nudged the throttle, and we bounced forward on top of the waves. He looked back to make sure we were clear of the rocks and then pushed the throttle fully forward. The engine rose to a high-pitched scream. The wind and sea spray whipped by us, making it impossible to hear anything.

I gazed up at Michael's face, now in profile, as he looked west toward Vancouver Island.

Tears streamed down my face, and I couldn't brush them away. Who was I crying for? Daniel or Michael? Or perhaps both?

I really didn't know.

# Chapter Thirty-Eight

"Knock, knock. Are you ready for some visitors?"

Stewart and Staff Sergeant Singh filled the doorway to my hospital room.

I put down the magazine I had been reading. "Yes, come on in. I'm feeling fine. The doctors kept me here overnight as a precaution."

Stewart removed his peaked hat, and Staff Sergeant Singh proffered a small box of chocolates.

"I thought you might like something sweet."

"Thank you, that's kind of you." I placed it on the side table. "I wasn't expecting to see you today, Staff Sergeant Singh."

He smiled, his smooth teak-colored skin crinkling beneath his eyes. "Well, when Sergeant McLeod called me yesterday afternoon to tell me the latest news, I decided to take the ferry over this morning and join him when he came to see you. I have also been busy in my little corner of the universe, working away, trying to solve this puzzle. With the arrest of Shelley and Greg Douglass yesterday afternoon, it looks like we may finally have all the remaining pieces to this puzzle."

"Greg, too? You were able to find him?"

Stewart nodded. "Yes. He was hiding at Dougie's house. He broke down and told us everything."

"And filled in a lot of the blanks," Staff Sergeant Singh added.

I sat taller in the bed and readied the pillows behind my back. "Well, fill me in, because I can't make sense out of any of this."

Staff Sergeant Singh nodded his head for Stewart to start.

"Well, we believe all of this started about fourteen months ago in Afghanistan."

"That was when I was abducted."

"Yes. We're not sure of a lot of this, but I think our educated guesses are likely to pan out. We had a lot of help from the DEA and the US military, so we have a decent amount of information. Our guess is that when Daniel realized you had been kidnapped by the Taliban, he called a contact of his in Kabul, a Nazeer Sharif."

"That name doesn't ring a bell with me," I said.

"Nazeer Sharif is a senior member of the largest drug trafficking ring in Afghanistan."

I gasped. "Why on earth would Daniel go to him?"

"Because he knew Sharif was the only person who had enough leverage to get the Taliban to tell him where you had been taken."

"What?" I shook my head, even more confused.

"The Taliban and the drug traffickers in Afghanistan have a symbiotic relationship. The Taliban takes a tax from the farmers who grow the poppies, the labs that turn it into heroin, and the traffickers that use the Taliban's influence to smuggle the drugs out of the country."

"So the Taliban makes a lot of money to fund their holy wars, and the drug traffickers ship their product safely out of Afghanistan," Stewart said. "A win for everyone."

"We are not sure," Staff Sergeant Singh continued, "but we believe Daniel cut some kind of deal with Sharif. Sharif would use his contacts in the Taliban to find you, and Daniel would have to do something for him in return."

"Which is how the US military found us. Cindy was right. Someone did tip them off."

Staff Sergeant Singh nodded. "Yes. Unfortunately, they were too late to save your interpreter."

"Poor Aziz." I sighed, remembering the lone shape on the bank of the Kabul River. "What did they want Daniel to do for them? I can't believe he would have anything to do with selling heroin."

"Not heroin, but the proceeds from it."

"Money?"

"Yes. Drug trafficking is a massive global enterprise that creates immense profits, and —like any other business—they need to move that money around the world. Moving vast sums of money over international boundaries can be difficult if you don't want those dollars being traced."

"Daniel laundered money for the drug traffickers?"

Stewart nodded. "Yes, it is called bulk cash smuggling. And Daniel was the perfect transporter for Sharif."

"Why?"

"Well," Staff Sergeant Singh continued, "Daniel had no criminal record, a long history of traveling in and out of Afghanistan for legitimate business, and most importantly, access to the VIP lounge at Kabul International Airport."

"He used the VIP lounge as a comfy place to wait for his flights. It made things a lot easier. A lot of us used it."

"Then you'll know that travelers in the VIP lounge don't have to undergo main customs and security screenings. Nor do they have to have their money scanned by bulk cash counters, as the rest of travelers leaving Afghanistan do."

"Yes," I murmured. "I hadn't thought of that. Did he just have to do it once?"

"No. Once a criminal organization has its teeth into you, they're not going to just let you go," Staff Sergeant Singh replied. "That was Daniel's problem. He was too valuable for them to allow him to quit. The DEA says they have CCTV footage of him having contact with various drug operatives in the US, most likely delivering cash, up until a few months ago."

"Which is when I broke up with him."

"Yes."

"That means the woman in his apartment wasn't a lover! She was a courier picking up money!"

I covered my mouth in shock, the sudden pain in my gut making me want to wretch. He had been telling me the truth all along! And I hadn't listened to him. I punched at the blanket beside me in rage. If only I had listened to him, if only I had responded to his texts, if only….

Staff Sergeant Singh grabbed my fist and held it firmly in one hand. My breathing slowed, and he released my hand and rested it back down on the blanket.

"Most likely. The DEA believes it was around this time he attempted to terminate his working relationship with Sharif."

"But Sharif wouldn't let him go?" I asked, breathing deeply to try and calm myself.

"It's complicated. Our guess is that Daniel kicked up such a fuss that Sharif felt it was best to cut him loose as a cash courier."

"And so he was finished with it," I murmured, mainly to myself, "and was flying out to tell me the whole story. I get it now." I paused. "Then why was he killed?"

"Because a man like Sharif doesn't have the compassion to let people go, Kate," Stewart said. "Daniel was now a threat. He was no longer useful to Sharif, plus he had plenty of information about Sharif's network of drug dealers in the United States. He could use those names to buy himself immunity from prosecution or even relocation to the Witness Protection Program."

"So it was Sharif who killed him," I whispered.

"In the greater scheme of things, yes. But Sharif wanted to keep his hands clean, so he decided to call in a favor. He knew Daniel was going out to see you on Wynter Island."

"How did he know that?"

Stewart tipped his head to one side. "You think a man with his kind of money and power can't keep tabs on where someone is traveling?"

"Okay," I said, my brain working its way through the steps. "He knew Daniel was flying out to Vancouver, so he sent him on a final errand to see Don Chang."

"And Sharif called in a favor from Don Chang," Stewart added.

"Yes," replied Staff Sergeant Singh. "One Don Chang was only too happy to perform."

"Why?"

"Because he benefited in a number of different ways. He stayed in the good books of Sharif and, more importantly, some of Sharif's friends in the Mexican drug cartels."

"The other plus for Chang," Stewart continued, "was that he had the perfect person for the job: Greg Douglass."

"Greg? Not Shelley?"

Staff Sergeant Singh nodded his head in agreement. "Yes. Greg had been a small-time dealer for Chang before he did time in prison and decided to leave the business. This gave Chang an excuse to pull him back in. His location on Wynter Island made him quite useful to Chang and his associates in the drug world. In fact, we have our suspicions that he may have been transporting shipments of drugs that were dropped on the island back to Chang before he was arrested and sent to prison."

I thought of Dougie's landscaping truck going back and forth to the mainland. Hadn't Michael said there were rumors that Dougie was involved in the drug trade along with Greg?

"If Greg didn't kill Daniel," he continued, "Chang said he would put out a hit on him. If he did kill Daniel, Chang now had something he could hold over Greg's head to reel him back into the drug business."

"A win-win," I said sourly.

"Exactly," said Stewart. "But he misjudged Greg Douglass."

"How?"

"He never considered that Greg might refuse to kill Daniel."

"What? He refused to do it?"

"Yes, he refused to do it," said Staff Sergeant Singh. "He told Stewart and Lesley last night that he broke down and told his mom everything. He told her he couldn't kill anyone. Not in cold blood."

"But Shelley could," I said. "To protect her son, she would do anything."

"And she did. Don Chang, believing Greg was the killer, told him they had made sure Daniel couldn't get his car on the ferry and would have to go on foot. Shelley made sure he was on that boat. After all, she can hop on and off any ferry in the fleet as a B.C Ferries employee with no record. She spotted Daniel and called Greg. Greg stepped up to do his part in the plan."

"So Greg was involved?"

"Yes, but only as an accessory. His mother convinced him to let her kill Daniel. All he had to do was help with some small details."

"That's what he meant. She needs my help. What did Greg do?"

"He created a diversion," Stewart replied.

My mind ran back over the events of Thursday morning, finally stopping at the memory of the fire engine sirens howling across the island. "The fire!"

"Yes," Stewart said. "He started a small fire on the building site. This gave him the few minutes of extra cover he needed to dash over to the Sydney Cliffs on his way to the Lettucetown store to get the usual coffee and donuts for the construction crew."

"And at the Sydney Cliffs," Staff Sergeant Singh seamlessly continued, "he moved the sign out of the way so it would appear to Daniel that the park was open."

"And no islanders would show up to hike, because they knew it was supposed to be closed," I added.

"Yes, leaving Shelley free to stop her car and offer Daniel a lift to the B&B, use the fire trucks as an excuse to 'call' Harald, and then tell Daniel that the road to the B&B was blocked by fire trucks. They had to fill an hour or so of time, so she was going to show him the best views on the island."

"Which was the Sydney Cliffs."

"Yes. She was planning on pushing him over the edge, but he must have realized something was up, and they had a struggle. Unluckily for him, she picked up a piece of rock and—"

"Hit him on the head," I finished for him.

"She used her walking stick to roll his body off the ledge, but lost her grip on it at the last moment. It went over the edge with Daniel," explained Stewart. "She raced as quickly as she could back down the hillside to put back the sign, but...."

"But what?" I asked.

"As she was headed back down the path, she saw Gwen putting the sign back up at the road."

"Did Gwen see Shelley? Or her vehicle?"

"Not that we know of, but Shelley couldn't be sure. So Greg told Don Chang there might be a witness."

"So it was Don Chang who built the bomb. Or told one of his employees to build the bomb," I said.

"Greg went over on the ferry to Vancouver and met someone at a Starbucks in North Delta. He got the instructions for how to activate it and brought it and a small revolver back home to Shelley."

"So it was someone with experience and access to specialized materials who built the bomb. Not Harald pulling crap out of his basement."

Stewart's cheeks reddened slightly. "Harald was released first thing this morning," He glanced at his watch, "and will most likely be arriving back on Wynter with Kurt on the ten o'clock ferry. He's got other battles to face, but at least for now, he can go home."

"Thank God for that. Kurt was a mickey away from Alcoholics Anonymous," I muttered. "So Shelley killed Daniel and then attempted to murder Gwen. But why me?"

Stewart laughed. "Haven't you figured that out yet?"

Staff Sergeant Singh smiled, a slight chuckle escaping his lips. "You were 'gumming up the works,' so to speak."

"Huh?"

"Kate," Stewart leaned forward over the railings of the hospital bed, "they planned for you to take the fall for Daniel's death. It was dumb luck, from their perspective, that you found his body. They assumed he would never be found, and eventually, the police would follow his trail to Wynter Island. They would then arrest you, his angry ex-girlfriend, for his murder."

"That wasn't very nice," I said.

"Not nice!" Stewart hooted in laughter. "And it wasn't just that you found the body, but you also found the bomb, saving Gwen and thus taking your name off the suspect list."

"Their last resort," Staff Sergeant Singh continued, "was to try and fake your death. It would look suspicious, but they really felt they had no other way to go. Shelley thought you should appear to have kayaked off into the sunset with Jupiter and either had an accident or killed yourself out of guilt."

"She and Greg are now in custody," Stewart added. "I doubt it will go to trial. They have both confessed and will cut some sort of deal with the Crown Prosecutor."

"From our point of view," Staff Sergeant Singh said, "we may get some hard evidence the Vancouver police can use against Don Chang. That would be a nice fat fish for us to catch, let me tell you."

I gazed out the window at the lush green gardens surrounding the small, local hospital. I wasn't sure which direction I was facing, but wondered if Wynter might be visible between the row of birches blocking my view.

"What about Ria?"

"Ria never met Daniel. Well, I shouldn't say that. She might have served him at the restaurant during the summers she worked there, but there was no relationship between the two of them."

"But what about Bob finding them at the Lind Hotel?"

Staff Sergeant Singh shook his head firmly. "Another journalist came out to the island for the Oceanica story. It wasn't Daniel."

"But Gwen identified him from the photo!"

"Not exactly. She said similar," Stewart said. "The actual reporter was approximately the same age as Daniel, with short brown hair. And he was someone whom Gwen had only seen in passing almost seven years before."

"But I was so sure! What about the fight on the ferry between the couple who looked like Ria and Daniel?"

"Lies made up by Shelley."

"But Ria looked so guilty….."

Staff Sergeant Singh smiled. "That's why we hunt for facts, Kate. They're far more reliable than feelings."

"The Truth Warrior?"

"Greg," said Stewart. "He took a course in computer programming while in prison."

"And Anna's secret?"

Stewart examined his fingernails for a moment. "No, you don't need to know anything about that."

"But she was so upset about you going to the marina to check out their boat? She must have had something to hide."'

"You need to leave that alone, Kate. It has absolutely nothing to do with this case. She was not in any way," he paused, considering his words, "breaking the law. It's a personal issue between her and Michael."

Personal issue? I paused to consider this. What secret could Anna have that included the boat? And why did it involve the two of them? It suddenly hit me. Had Anna been using the boat for some secret liaison? Something that would have been captured on CCTV? Like boarding the boat with an illicit lover?

There was a commotion of voices and footsteps in the hallway, followed by a gaggle of people pushing into my room.

"Kate! How are you doing!"

Gwen rushed in, holding a balloon with Get Well Soon emblazoned across it. She bent down and wrapped her arms around me. She was followed by Ben, Vera, and Sam. Vera held a vase full of zinnias in her hands.

"Right out of the garden," she said and set them down beside Staff Sergeant Singh's box of chocolates.

Ben and Sam stopped by the side of the bed. Sam reached out a hand to hold mine for a moment.

"Hi, Sam." I smiled up at him and then turned to everyone else. "And Gwen, and Vera, and Ben. You guys didn't have to come! They're going to release me sometime this morning."

"Hi, Stewart," Gwen said and nodded at Staff Sergeant Singh. "And you, too, Staff Sergeant Singh. You gentlemen must have caught the first ferry to get here before us."

"Yes," Staff Sergeant Singh said and leaned forward with his hand extended. I took it and shook it soundly. "We had some important business we had to finish up with Ms. Thomas. But we should be going and give all of you a chance to visit."

"Yes," Stewart chimed in, replacing his RCMP hat. "I'll see you back on the island, Kate."

"Thanks to both of you," I said to all the smiling faces surrounding me.

"Thank you to all of you for coming. It makes me feel like, like …" I hesitated as tears started to blur my vision.

"Like you belong," Gwen finished for me and wiped away the tears with her thumb.

I couldn't say anything. I shakily nodded my head in agreement.

"Hey, did you guys start without us!" a male voice shouted from the hallway. Nate entered the room, stopping at the end of my bed. "You said you'd wait for us at the elevator."

"Yeah, talk about party poopers," Michael said, following him in holding a small vase of lilies of the valley.

His gaze met mine. My heart hesitated expectantly. Beat, pause, beat. I searched his eyes for something, anything, that might show he reciprocated the sudden, heated intensity of emotion I was feeling. But his eyes, their hazel depths partially obscured by his glasses, held nothing but kindness and sympathy. He handed me the vase of flowers.

"Mom, we're in here!" Nate shouted, the click of her heels echoing down the linoleum hallway.

Anna walked into the room and up to my bed. Her auburn bob lay beautifully smooth and shiny, a waft of Thierry Mugler's Angel following her into the room.

"How are you doing, Kate?" she asked in her soft Scottish brogue.

"Fine," I lied, and then wiped the remaining tears off my face. "Perfectly fine."

# Acknowledgements

There are many people to thank for their assistance with this book. Lourdes Venard was a great editor to help me with my first attempt at this genre. I also had excellent editorial assistance from John Payne and Jessie Crockett. A big thank you to Linda McHenry for all the time and energy she spent teaching me the ins and outs of Deep POV. Lisa Lieberman, Dale T. Phillips, and Sisters in Crime New England offered me a home for my questions and concerns about writing a mystery. For reading those first drafts, I must thank my husband, Stuart, and dear friend, Arlene Berg. It is rare to find people who love you, but are also willing to tell you uncomfortable truths. And as always, I must thank my two sons, to whom this book is dedicated. They, and our assorted pack of small furry creatures, always loved and supported me—as long as I made them dinner.

— *Summer 2022.*

# About the Author

Kim Herdman Shapiro worked as a journalist in Canada for many years, with experience in both print and broadcast journalism. Her book, *Gelato with the Pope*, highlights her time as a syndicated travel columnist in the Nineties.

In addition to her travel column, she has written feature articles for numerous publications, edited a monthly children's publication in British Columbia, and had her poetry published in *Do Whales Jump at Night?: A Canadian Anthology of Children's Poetry*. She won a Microsoft Network award for best website for *Footloose*, one of the first digital e-zines on the internet.

For the past eight years she has been working on her video project, *What the Hell is a Toque?* This chronicles her travels with her sons from Newfoundland to Vancouver Island and north to the Canadian Arctic.

Kim is also a board member of Sisters in Crime New England.

She lives in New Hampshire with her husband, two sons, and three dogs.

SOCIAL MEDIA HANDLES:
www.facebook.com/kim.h.shapiro.

@kimhshapiro - instagram
@kimhshap - twitter
@kim.h.shapiro - tiktok

AUTHOR WEBSITE:
  www.kimhshapiro.com

# Also by Kim Herdman Shapiro

*Gelato with the Pope: and other adventures of a travel writer in Europe*, Bamberry Cove Books